DANC ... XILE

AN EXILE NOVEL, VOLUME 3

K.J. JACKSON

First Edition: October 2021
ISBN: 978-1-940149-64-6

K.J. Jackson Books

Historical Romance:

Stone Devil Duke, *Hold Your Breath*
Unmasking the Marquess, *Hold Your Breath*
My Captain, My Earl, *Hold Your Breath*
Worth of a Duke, *Lords of Fate*
Earl of Destiny, *Lords of Fate*
Marquess of Fortune, *Lords of Fate*
Vow, *Lords of Action*
Promise, *Lords of Action*
Oath, *Lords of Action*
Of Valor & Vice, *Revelry's Tempest*
Of Sin & Sanctuary, *Revelry's Tempest*
Of Risk & Redemption, *Revelry's Tempest*
To Capture a Rogue, Logan's Legends, *Revelry's Tempest*
To Capture a Warrior, Logan's Legends, *Revelry's Tempest*
The Devil in the Duke, *Revelry's Tempest*
The Iron Earl, *Valor of Vinehill*
The Wolf Duke, *Valor of Vinehill*
The Steel Rogue, *Valor of Vinehill*
The Heart of an Earl, *Box of Draupnir*
The Blood of a Baron, *Box of Draupnir*
The Soul of a Rogue, *Box of Draupnir*
Exiled Duke, *Exile*
Wicked Exile, *Exile*
Dangerous Exile, *Exile*

Paranormal Romance:

Flame Moon
Triple Infinity, *Flame Moon #2*
Flux Flame, *Flame Moon #3*

Be sure to sign up for news of my next releases at

www.KJJackson.com

DEDICATION

– As Always,
For my favorite Ks

{ CHAPTER 1 }

It sat white.

Across the street, a gleaming wall of marble in the midst of wretched, dirty chaos.

The whole of London havoc. So many people. So many horses, carriages, carts, wagons. So many sounds. So many *smells.*

So many jarring collisions smacking into her broken arm.

So much pain.

But there sat the Alabaster. Or so it had to be. What else would be on this street, named for the very white mountain of stone it was? Five stories. White marble from street to sky. Each window lined with gauzy white curtains that only peeked at shadowed darkness within.

White on the outside. Shadows on the inside. What had she been expecting?

Her right fingers unclutched from holding her left arm in the only position that didn't aggravate the pain, and Ness reached out to touch the shoulder of a passing girl, maybe twelve, dirty and disheveled but easy enough to stop.

"Please—is that the Alabaster?" Her voice a whisper, she couldn't speak any louder. The last of solid air had left her lungs a day ago, leaving only tattered wisps of breath.

The girl's wide orbs of eyes looked to Ness's face, then at her left arm hanging unnaturally at her side. The girl's eyes went wider, the whites of them swallowing the top half of her face.

"It is, ma'am."

The girl hopped quick steps away from Ness. Not that a broken arm was contagious. A broken spirit, maybe.

This was it, then.

Her gaze found the white wall with its neatly symmetrical windows. There. A door. One door, painted black.

But odd. No one walked in front of the building.

Decrepit piles of brick buildings stood on either side of the structure, where people were gathered all along the street. Hawking wares. Carrying baskets. Dumping pots into the street. But if they were walking, every single person would venture to the edge of the white building, then step out into the street to move in a wide arc around the front of the place, then would veer back onto the walkway to continue onward. Almost as though a curse sat at that black door, taunting anyone that dared to step too close.

Ness attempted to focus on the street—wagons, horses, and carriages crisscrossed in front of her, going in and out of focus. Ten more steps was all she needed. Make it across.

There. Open space in front of her.

She darted forward, her feet tripping, stumbling in the muck of the street. Sliding, leaning forward. Forward with enough momentum to hit the door.

Agony seized the left side of her body as her left arm got between her and the hard wood.

Her right hand grasped onto the golden handle, the only thing that held her upright. With the side of her head, she banged on the door.

Nothing.

She tried the handle, tried to open the latch. It was frozen in place, immobile. She slammed into the door with her right shoulder, only to suddenly realize the door lacked hinges. It would never open. The whole of it—the door, the handle—it was nothing. A façade. An entry to nowhere.

Her grip on the handle loosened and she slid down, crumbling onto the wide front stone step, everything draining away.

Hope. Energy. Willpower.

Her eyes slid closed, her body too parched to even offer up tears.

"You can't be here, lass."

Her eyelids cracked open to find a large form drifting above her, swallowing what little light the London clouds allowed. Her hand went up, reaching for the handle of the door. The door that didn't open. With strength she thought long gone, she wedged her feet under her, pulling herself upward, her blurry gaze on the darkness that was a man above. "Blackstone. Talen Blackstone. I need to talk to him. Only him. Juliet sent me. Only him."

The last of the words left her tongue and every speck of determination that had gotten her this far abandoned her, leaving her to fall, slip downward, consumed by blackness that swallowed her whole.

Blackness in itself, a gift.

~ ~ ~

Standing at the front of his desk, his knuckles resting on the worn wood, Talen Blackstone stared at lines in a ledger with a decided frown stretching his face.

Expanding his empire into Hoppler's territory in the rookeries had been proving trickier than he'd imagined when the opportunity had been presented by Hoppler himself. An offer born of respect, as Hoppler was currently attempting to disentangle himself from the most sordid enterprises currently in his realm.

Talen had to make some hard choices about what ventures to keep, and what to set free into the world to fend for themselves. It was a risk. The businesses he cut loose could very well rise up under a new hungry cutthroat ready to set war upon him for territory.

He already knew what he wanted to set free. But the numbers didn't agree with his assessment.

His hand ran across his eyes, clearing the jumble of blurry numbers from his sight. The whole of it exhausting. Change was coming and he didn't care for change. Steady. Straightforward. That's what he liked. That's what he excelled at. Not grey areas. Not attempting to predict the future.

The door behind Talen opened without a knock and Talen shoved off from the desk, turning around. Only one person entered this room without knocking.

Declan moved into his office and at his side…*shit.*

Talen froze, his body and limbs suddenly cast in stone he couldn't break free from. A familiar terror raced through his bones—a terror that he worked damn hard to never have to feel in his life.

"Tal." Declan closed the door behind him.

Talen didn't look to him, couldn't shift his eyes off the pitiful being that Declan had just ushered into the room.

If a portal to hell had opened, snatched this woman from the earth, sank her into the depths of torture, then spit her back up atop the dirt, she would have fared better than she currently did.

The devil had nothing on the hell that already existed in this land. Demons of men. And the destruction that one of those demons had obviously wrought upon this woman was almost too much to bear.

A face beaten to mush. Black, swollen skin on every part of her body that showed. Cuts, lines of dried blood snaking across every surface.

The petrification of his muscles eased and Talen puffed out a sigh, looking from the swaying woman in a dark cloak in front of him, to his best friend and partner. "Why are you bringing me this, Declan?"

Declan lifted a hand to the woman to prop her up before she fell over and the instant his fingers wrapped around her upper left arm, a squeak came from her bruised lips.

She jerked out of Declan's grasp and lost her balance, teetering, her slow feet not able to keep up with her momentum.

Talen's hand flung out, clasping around her right shoulder to force her back upright. Lots of cloth, little meat under his fingers. Easy to push.

His gaze landed on her face for the smallest second and he quickly looked back to Declan. "Why?"

His same height, Declan met his gaze, unruffled by the annoyance in Talen's voice. He shrugged. "She would only talk to you. She faded out, outside, and the only thing she spoke when I nudged her awake was your name."

"I didn't know that request would gain just anyone access into my office."

His office was sacred.

He could count on one hand the only people that had ever been allowed in this room. From his vantage in his office, he could see down onto the main room of his gaming hell, the Alabaster, from the windows that lined one wall. He looked down, a dark figure in the shadows, and it only magnified the mystery of his persona that he'd cultivated over the years. No one looked up. No one got into his office. He wasn't to be trifled with.

Declan didn't squirm under his glare. "Madame Juliet sent her."

That made him pause.

It made the woman pause as well, as her battered face turned to Declan. Talen assumed surprise was in her eyes, if he could see her eyes through the black, swollen skin that fully swallowed her left eye. But her right eye showed definite shock.

Her face turned back to him and the distorted line of her lips opened, the tiniest voice squeaking out. "Juliet Thomson. Hide me." She gasped a breath, her voice fading as if each word was taking her last shards of strength. "Selkie South Brothel."

With that, she crumpled downward. Not falling forward, backward, to the left or right. Straight down, her body disappearing into a pile within her dark cloak, the hood covering her face.

Dead? Possibly.

But not likely with his luck.

His body still, Talen took a measured breath, concentrating on the air going into his lungs. His look shifted to Declan and he pointed at the lump of her body on the floor. "You brought her in here. You get to bring her out."

Declan shook his head, his arms threading across his chest. "You can't be thinking the street, Tal. You see the state she's in."

His scowl sliced into his friend. "I'm not an ogre, Declan. I'm also not stupid. If Madame Juliet sent her, this is serious. Put her upstairs in the Blue Waters room."

Declan nodded, then moved to pick up the woman. He glanced over at Talen as he stood with the girl draped over his arms. "You're paying attention now?"

Talen looked to the tiny form swallowed in the cloak in Declan's hold. "Aye. I'm paying attention now."

{ CHAPTER 2 }

"She's awake."

With a nod to the gentlemen playing Faro in the private Peacock room, Talen moved past Declan to the door his partner had just entered with the news. There was a sizable amount on the table at the turn. A breeding stable of racing horses, land in Dorset, a mine in Cornwall. All going to the house if the cards flipped well.

None of that was more interesting than the woman that lay in a bed two floors above him.

Declan followed him out of the room and Talen looked over his shoulder to his friend once the door was closed. "Did she say anything?"

"Verity indicated that she wouldn't say anything. Only your name."

Talen heaved a sigh. Not that he expected anything less.

His long legs carrying him fast up the stairs, Talen entered the Blue Waters room without knocking.

Going directly to the side of the bed, he stared down at the mangled mess of the woman's face framed by disheveled dark brown hair—a face so bruised and battered and swollen it roiled his stomach to look at her.

Nevertheless, he had to at least look into her one eye he could see as he talked to her. Respect. Madame Juliet would demand it of him, and he owed her. Madame Juliet was the bawd at the Den of Diablo, the central gaming

house owned by Hoppler, his main rival and begrudging compatriot in rookery empire building. The last Talen had heard, Madame Juliet was headed north with a Scot, posing as his betrothed.

This lump on the bed was apparently a result of that ill-advised scheme.

Focusing on the oddly colored amber eye looking up at him, he pointed down at her arm closest to him. "Declan said you were seen getting off the Edinburgh mail coach. You rode in a mail coach all the way to London from Edinburgh with your arm like this?"

Her left arm lay atop the blue coverlet beside her body, the bottom half of her forearm grotesquely jutting the wrong way out from her elbow.

Her right hand clutched the top of the coverlet, pulling it up under her chin. Her voice still a squeak, her one eye didn't look away from him. "You are Talen Blackstone?"

He nodded.

Her good eye closed, her head tilting back into the pillow. "Why am I naked?"

"We took off your cloak after your body collapsed, dead to the world, and we saw your arm. We had to make certain there were not other bones askew."

She gave the slightest nod.

At least she didn't fight him on it or take offense. Not that she was in a position for either reaction.

Talen cleared his throat pointedly. "I repeat, you rode in a mail coach all the way to London from Edinburgh with your arm like this?"

"I—" Her breath left her and it took concentrated effort for her to suck in air and force words out. Her right eye opened to him. "I did. I had to."

She was lying. He'd seen her battered body. Bruises everywhere. The broken arm. The pain—every jolt of the coach would have been torture. Days of it. No woman could have suffered that and not gone mad.

He stared at her.

She stared back with her one open eye. In the middle of her unfocused look, her amber iris challenged him.

She blinked and her head shook slightly before her unfocused right eye veered off to the side, then snapped toward the ceiling searching again for him. "You are Blackstone?"

Talen stilled. She wasn't following the conversation. That wasn't good. "I am."

"Juliet." She gasped a breath. "Hide me. Selkie South Brothel. Hide me, please."

The door opened behind him and he looked over his shoulder. Declan had popped his head into the room. "She's here."

Talen nodded to him and returned his attention to the woman. "You are safe here. The bonesetter is ready. We have to reset your arm properly."

"I know." A whisper, so thin he almost didn't hear it.

"It will be painful."

"I know."

At least she knew what was coming. Better that than the shock of what was about to happen to her.

Talen reached into an inner pocket and pulled free a small vial, tugging the stopper from it. He set it to her bottom lip, but she didn't open her mouth, sudden fear in her one good eye.

"It's laudanum. I don't know that your heart would survive this without it."

Staring up at him, it took silent seconds before her lips slightly parted. He tilted the vial, the liquid dropping into her mouth.

"What's your name?"

Her mouth closed and her throat visibly flexed and constricted as she swallowed. Even that looked to hurt. "Ness."

He nodded to her as Declan came into the room with the bone setter, Mrs. Jenkins, in tow. A thick woman, her sturdy hands of steel had the strength of ten men for the limbs he'd seen her twist and set. There was none better in the area, in the whole of London, for that matter.

Mrs. Jenkins went directly to the side of the bed, wedging herself between Talen and the woman and she bent, her fingers skimming over Ness's arm. Ness didn't flinch away from Mrs. Jenkins's touch.

Mrs. Jenkins grunted as she bent further over, looking from all angles at Ness's wrecked arm. "Ye did this to her?" She didn't look back to Talen.

"No."

"Did you give her anything?"

"Laudanum."

She grunted again, then stood straight, her focus on Ness's face. "The laudanum will help, child, but the best we can hope for is that ye pass into darkness for a spell during the worst of it."

Ness's good eye closed and she gave a slight nod.

Mrs. Jenkins spun and pointed at Declan. "Ye hold her legs." She looked to Talen. "Ye get in the bed with her and hold her body back, Mr. Blackstone."

His eyebrows lifted. "You want me in bed with her?"

"I want her upright and a force holding her back against me pulling. This break isn't kind how it's started to fuse back together. It should have been reset days ago." She shook her head, obvious disgust on her face at his lack of calling for a bone setter sooner. "Either that laudanum was too much or she's in a fever. The child can't even hold her eyes open."

Talen didn't bother to correct Mrs. Jenkins on any of the assumptions she'd made. The woman would think what she did—she'd never be any different.

He moved to the opposite side of the bed to approach Ness from her right side and crawled onto the mattress. He lifted Ness's torso up as he slid into place behind her, positioning her between his legs. He wrapped one arm around her waist and the other across her upper chest, attempting to make sure the coverlet didn't shift too low for modesty's sake. He'd already seen Ness's entire body, but he didn't need Mrs. Jenkins thinking any worse of him, or she'd never come back to the Alabaster to set another bone.

Ness was slight, as though she'd been slim before this had happened to her, and then she hadn't eaten for days. Even more gaunt than he had noted when he had checked her body for injuries earlier.

And hot. Her skin boiling under his touch. He hadn't realized fever had taken her over.

Pushing the bottom of the coverlet aside, Declan found her legs at the base of the bed and locked his hands onto her ankles. Ness's eye had remained shut, her mouth silent, her body limp as the laudanum had already taken a hold of her.

Or not.

The second Mrs. Jenkins pulled Ness's upper left arm away from her torso, Ness went rabid—screaming, legs kicking, her body thrashing.

The pain brutal or a hallucination taking a hold of her, Talen wasn't sure.

Her right leg kicked, jutting up and out of Declan's hold and her knee cracked Declan in the right eye as he tried to retrieve it. It was enough to send him flailing back a step. "Bloody hell—"

"Ness—calm," Talen ordered into her ear. "We're fixing your arm so be still."

She froze, her body tense against him. But she stopped whipping about. Her head turned, her right ear pressing against his chest as she looked away from what was happening to her left arm.

Mrs. Jenkins was quick, wrenching and manipulating Ness's arm into position as she realigned the bone.

But with every twist, every yank Mrs. Jenkins made upon her arm, Ness's body flinched. He felt it in her muscles. But she didn't scream. Didn't kick. Didn't fight the pain.

Her chin merely curled down, taking every stitch of torture the grinding of marrow against marrow caused.

Talen had seen plenty of bones set in his day, some in the strongest of men. Men he'd had to punch out so they wouldn't hurt the bonesetter. None of them had ever taken this sort of pain with the stoic silence that this woman did.

Whereas he didn't truly believe her before—that she had ridden the entire way from Edinburgh to London in the mail coach with her arm like this—he believed her now.

She and pain were well acquainted.

That didn't stop her body from shaking, the agony overwhelming.

Of all of it, that struck him. How her body shook uncontrollably against him. A life in overt turbulence.

One last wedge of Ness's arm and Mrs. Jenkins looked up to him, satisfied. "I'll wrap it with a splint." She leaned over to dig through the satchel she'd dropped on the floor and pulled free a plank of wood and long strips of linen. "Ye need to have her leave it in place for weeks, a month, more if it still pains her. It cannot slip out of place."

Talen nodded. "We will keep it wrapped."

Mrs. Jenkins was quick to set the wooden splint along Ness's forearm and then wrap it with the linen to lock it into place.

She stood straight, her gaze resting on Ness's face that was turned away, quivering against his chest. Mrs. Jenkins pointed to Ness's head. "And have the apothecary get an ointment for her face to relieve the swelling, the poor pup."

"Thank you for the prompt work." Talen motioned his head toward Declan. "Declan will take care of you."

Mrs. Jenkins picked up her bag and followed Declan out of the room.

This was the moment when he needed to extract himself from Ness's body, but her shaking had yet to cease.

There was something inherently wrong about it, the thought of abandoning the tiny waif while she was still quivering.

One would think he was going soft, for how long he sat there, his arms wrapped around her body, trying to soothe the residual shocks of pain rolling through her.

But sit he did.

Until the trembling eased and her body relaxed against him, a deep laudanum-induced sleep taking her over.

Thank the saints.

He'd never stood for a woman sleeping against him, but in this case, he'd take it. Anything to ease the torture in her body.

He finally allowed himself to take a deep breath and he realized how uncharacteristic of him it was, caring at all if her pain eased. When had he started to care about the wretched souls?

Never.

Which told him he needed to get out of that room posthaste, as Ness had already wasted too much of his night.

Talen shifted her body gently away from his chest and pulled his left leg from the side of her, then laid her body back onto the bed.

Taking care to not disturb her left arm too much, he tucked the coverlet up and over her chest and atop her toes.

Poor pup indeed.

Madame Juliet better have a good reason for all of this nonsense.

{ CHAPTER 3 }

Talen entered the Blue Waters room two days later, determined to get answers where Madame Juliet had sent him none.

He'd been expecting a message, a note from Juliet, which he'd gotten—but it had been short and raised more questions than given answers. Namely, who exactly was this woman Juliet had sent to him?

Time to get the answers he needed from the most likely source.

He closed the door of the Blue Waters room with a loud snap and Ness stirred, her one good eye blinking hazily until she realized someone else was in the room with her.

She rolled onto her right side, trying to push herself to sitting, but her arms were heavy, her head bobbing in a slow circle, her focus out of her right eye blurry.

Good. She was still deep in the fog of the laudanum he'd had Declan carefully administer to her throughout the last two days. It'd been necessary. Necessary for her pain, aside from the fact that the last thing he'd needed was a caterwauling woman in pain a floor above the Midas Room—where the highest stakes were won and lost.

At her movement in the bed, his hand lifted. "No, Ness, do not sit up. It is too much for you."

She collapsed downward, sinking into the bed, gratitude in the exhale seeping past her lips that were now less swollen. Her right eye focused on him and the plump

bruise about her left eye had finally eased enough so he could see a sliver of that eye.

Her mouth parted, words croaking past her lips. "You are Talen Blackstone?"

How many times was he going to have to answer that question from her?

Talen veered, moving to the tea pot beside the bed. He poured a shallow cup for her, then moved to the bed, holding it to her lips. Drips of it snaked into her mouth until she pulled away.

Setting the cup on the bedside table, Talen moved to stand beside the bed, his fingers tapping on the light blue coverlet that hung over the edge of the mattress as he looked down at her. "Aye. I am Talen Blackstone and I have some questions for you."

Her right eye, still unfocused, drifted up the front of his body to land on his face. "What?"

"Who sent you?"

"Juliet. Juliet Thomson." The name was drawn out, her voice drifting from high to low. Damn the laudanum still in her brain.

He nodded. "I understand she went north with a Scotsman. You met her there?"

"I did."

"Why did she send you to me?"

"I need help."

"And she thought I would help you?"

For the slightest second, her right eye seemed to focus on him directly. "You're the only one that can protect me."

Doubtful.

Sending the slip of a chit like this deep into the heart of the rookeries was far more dangerous than the hundred other places Juliet could have sent her. But Juliet had sent Ness to him. Which meant that the danger lurking about the woman was significant.

Danger he wasn't sure he wanted to invite into his life at the moment.

He stifled a sigh. He already knew everything he was asking Ness. The letter from Juliet had told him this much, but it had been clearly written in haste.

Ness needs to be hidden, protected.
No one can know she's with you.
She is off-limits.

Details had been lacking. Especially on that last line. Did Juliet really think he couldn't keep his cock in his trousers? Especially when it came to a battered and bruised woman?

But Ness's story thus far matched what Juliet had written. Small favor. At least he wasn't dealing with a liar.

"Do you know who I am?"

"You're Talen Blackstone. You just told me that."

He shook his head. "No. Not my name. Do you know what I am, what I do here in London?"

She blinked. Then blinked again, slowly, like she was trying to make her mind work through the opium muddle that had taken over her brain. "Juliet said to mention the Selkie South Brothel."

"Aye."

Her look lifted to him. "So you deal in brothels?"

"No." He exhaled a sigh. "Not since the one I had burned to the ground."

Her right eye opened wide. "But, Juliet—no. She cannot be…I cannot believe it."

"Believe what?"

"Juliet couldn't have been from a brothel—she said she knew people—the wrong sort of people, but I never imagined. But then you and that other man called her 'Madame Juliet.' I remember that." Her head shook. "But no. Not Juliet."

Talen smirked. "She does know the wrong people. And she is exactly what you are afraid to think she is. But I can tell you this, Juliet is a lot of things, including a very good friend to you if she called in the Selkie South Brothel favor for you."

Her right hand lifted, heavy and slow, and she set her fingertips along her hairline at her temple. Her head shook slightly. "I am sorry. I cannot think…think quickly at the moment. Why can I not think?"

"You still have laudanum in your body."

"You gave me laudanum?"

"Aye."

"Why?"

"To ease the pain as the bone in your arm was reset."

Her head shifted on the pillow, her gaze going down to her left arm. "I…I didn't even notice. When did that happen?" Her right hand went down and her finger started to tug at the bandages.

"Two nights ago." He grabbed her hand and pulled it away from the bandages. "Don't move it. The bonesetter was specific."

Her hand jerked out from his hold as though he'd scalded her. Between that and how she'd recoiled from Declan's touch, it was clear she didn't react well to men.

But then she looked up at him, her peculiar amber eye settling on him with wariness. "Why do you owe Juliet?"

"She didn't tell you?"

Ness shook her head.

He took a step away from the bed. "Then it's not my place to tell you."

She nodded, more to herself than to him. "Whatever she did, it must have been enormous for you to take me on. I realize you want nothing to do with me."

She was astute, even with a half-addled mind and only one good eye.

"It was enormous. She saved numerous lives." He crossed his arms over his chest. "But that is long in the past and I'm more concerned about the present. Juliet said you need to be hidden. I want to know why."

Her mouth clamped closed and Ness turned her face away from him, burying her head deep into the pillow.

"No answer? Fine. Then I can presume it has everything to do with this? The broken bone, the cuts and bruises?" He motioned to the full of her beaten body. "But it would make it a hell of a lot easier if I knew who I was protecting you from. So, who did this to you?"

Her head shifted on the pillow and she looked up at him. "I cannot tell you."

Talen stifled a sigh. He wasn't about to argue with an opium-foxed woman. Especially one that didn't trust him. The questions would have to wait for later.

"Then you will rest more." His arms relaxed to his sides and he inclined his head to her. "Clear your head. And I will ask the questions when your mind is once again your own."

The brown and blue deep shading of her cheeks quivered and her mouth shifted into what he assumed was a smile. It was hard to tell for the bruises and the cut along the side of her mouth.

Talen turned and walked toward the door.

"Mr. Blackstone."

He paused, turning back to her.

"Thank you. Thank you for helping me." Her voice escaped in a whimper, a pitiful warble so soft, as though she'd never been shown the slightest kindness and couldn't quite believe she'd been allowed to stay there.

It shot through his chest at that moment—the cracking of her voice wrapping around something deep within him he couldn't quite identify. The jolt of it reared so strongly he almost didn't recognize it. But there it was.

A visceral need to protect this woman.

In his chest.

In his gut.

And he always trusted his gut. It had gotten him this far.

As much as he'd like to, he couldn't ignore it now.

Ness was his to protect, at least for the time being.

{ Chapter 4 }

Ness cracked her eyes and stilled.

Stilled, waiting for the pain that had consumed her body for days to shoot through her limbs, twisting her stomach into such a hard knot she never expected to stand straight again.

The pain didn't come.

Or at least, not as brutal as it had been. The pain in her left arm was now an ache that drifted between torment and an intense itch. The itch most likely because of the heavy bandages that wrapped her arm, keeping it immobile.

She flexed parts of her body, finding that all of her muscles that had been clenched so tightly during the last days held onto residual soreness, but the sharp burn in them was gone.

Her right hand escaped from under the coverlet and her fingers went gently to her face. Bruises along her cheek stung with the touch, but the swelling had gone down about her eyes and her lips.

Wait.

She could see out of her left eye again.

Her eyes opened wider, blinking. She could see properly again. See the coved ceiling above her with fat cherubs painted about the expanse. Whimsy sure to send fantasy into dreams.

Her look focused on one unusually round cherub, the dimples in his cheeks particularly mischievous. Cherubs?

Why were there cherubs, of all things, on the ceiling? She was in a gaming hell, wasn't she? Cherubs didn't belong in a gaming hell. Or had she been moved? Or maybe this wasn't a gaming hell at all. Maybe she had dreamed that.

Her fingers drifted away from her face and she looked around the room, trying to place herself.

Thoughts. Real thoughts in her head. Not demons and ghosts and torture and the disconcerting kaleidoscope of the world shifting about her.

The room seemed to be the same. There were two plush blue upholstered chairs by the healthy fire in the fireplace. Had she had a bath there? Snippets of her body being submerged in warm water flashed through her head.

Her hand went to her bare upper chest, her pinky landing on the ruffle of a chemise. Pushing herself upright in the bed, she shoved the coverlet toward her waist and looked downward. A silky white lace chemise draped over her body. She'd been naked at one point, she remembered that.

Someone had obviously dressed her. But dressed her in what? The lace of the chemise swooped down far along her breasts, her nipples almost visible through the open weave of the lace. The chemise had either belonged to someone much larger, or far less chaste than her own wardrobe allowed.

But her body was clean. The scabs of blood gone.

She made a note in her mind to thank the person that had ushered her through the ablutions.

Before she could take in more of the room, the door opened without preamble and a man walked into the room.

Instinct sent her right hand to grasp the coverlet and pull it up over her chest.

The man froze just as the door closed, his stare locked onto her. "You're awake."

She had to blink. Then blink again.

She squinted at him. Blinked. Squinted again.

No. Impossible.

Dead. He was dead. Been dead for thirteen years. Dead, but standing in front of her.

Her jaw dropped, breathless words drifting from her mouth. "Conner Burton. It's you."

The man's forehead wrinkled. "Who?"

"Conner. Your voice is different, raspy, older, but it's you. I would recognize your eyes anywhere." Her hand went over her mouth. "But no…it can't be you."

She leaned forward in the bed, scrutinizing his face. The cut of his jaw—strong and square, not as soft as it once was. His cheekbones stone slices—a life lived hard, reflected in his features. Dark blond hair with strands that dipped into brown. But it was his blue eyes that she remembered well—so light, the color of a wispy blue sky in the brightest part of the day.

This wasn't a ghost. This was a man. Not the boy she once knew, but the boy grown into a man. A man glaring at her. "But it is you."

The wrinkles creasing his brow unfurled and he shook his head, taking three steps toward the bed. "I'm no one you know, Ness."

"But you are. You're Conner Burton."

He stopped by the side of the bed, looking down at her with a harsh crinkle around his blue eyes that told her he thought she was fully mad. "I'm Talen Blackstone."

Her head snapped back. "No. No." She looked away from him to the window and then her gaze shot back to him. Had she gone mad? "You're Talen Blackstone? You're the one?"

He sighed, his brow re-wrinkling. "Must we go through this again? How many times are you going to ask me that question?"

Her gaze met his. "How many times have I asked you that?"

"Too many."

"It is you?"

"Aye."

"But it is not. You're not Talen Blackstone. You're Conner Burton."

"I'm not." His arms crossed over his torso as he scowled down at her. "I've never heard that name in my life."

She'd seen this man—whoever he was—just like this before. His arms wrapped across his massive chest, his blue eyes hard, impenetrable as they took her in. Standing there just as he was now. Had that been a day ago? Two?

She was losing her ever-blasted mind.

Or the alternative. Her gaze dropped to the coverlet, cringing at her own question. "Am I dead?"

"No."

Her neck craning, she looked up at him. He'd also looked at her like this years ago when she'd aggravated him.

A much smaller version of him, of course, but the same. Conner. It was *him*.

Impossible.

"Conner, what are you playing at? It's me—Ness—do I look so awful that you cannot see me through the bruises?"

His head angled to the side as his lips pursed. "Fine, I'll humor you. Just how do you think I know you?"

"How could you not remember? You were eleven. I was ten. I hated you."

"You hated me?" His mouth set into a hard line. "You're seeing crooked if you think I'm this Conner boy. At eleven I was on a Royal Navy ship in the war, swabbing decks. I'm an orphan set to sea at an early age. Nothing more. I'm not what you think you see."

"But how can that be? What about before that?" Her hand jabbed out to reach up and grab his forearm. "You're Conner. You were the first boy that I fancied myself in love with. You—"

"No, you just said you hated me." He jerked a step backward out of her reach. "Keep your story straight, Ness."

"I did. I did say I hated you." Her head bobbed up and down, her voice going manic. "But then I adored you. You were eleven and I was ten and we played in the fields in Cumberland every summer before that. I hated you because you tormented me and you were fast and I could never catch you until you slowed down for me. But then you slowed down for me. And I didn't hate you anymore. And you were sweet. And I thought the sun revolved around you. I always thought we would grow up and I would marry you."

His boot clomped onto the wooden floorboards as he stabbed another step backward, his head shaking with a snarl on his lip. "Shut your mouth. You don't know me and you are mad. Pure crazy."

Her mouth clamped shut, the sting of his words striking her to her core.

No. She couldn't be. Not now. Not mad.

Hell. What if she was? What if one of the punches into her face had addled her brain?

She sucked in a breath, trying to stop her voice, but words still flew from her mouth with her exhale. "But, you…you don't remember?"

His shoulders lifted, no recognition in his face. "No. I'm not this boy you think you see—Conner—I can tell you that."

"But…but how could you not…" She tugged the coverlet off her lap and swung her legs out of the bed, her toes touching the floor. He had to be Conner. He had to be. She was sure of it. How could he not remember her? She wasn't mad—she wasn't.

She stood, her balance wobbly. "But how do you not remember?"

He didn't move a muscle. "I don't know you, woman."

"You do."

His face broke at her last insistence, fury rising so quickly in him it set his eyes ablaze, the whole of him morphing into a seething bull. "This is what Madame Juliet sent to me?" His hand whipped out from the hold against his body to wave in front of her face. "A madwoman? This black and blue face?"

He took a threatening step toward her, leaning over her small frame. "Let me give you a word of advice, Ness. It would behoove you to know me for who I am and to quit this silly nonsense that has scattered your brain, for I am out of patience."

"Would it?" She glared up at him. What should have her scurrying back into the bed, didn't. He was Conner. She was sure of it. Conner would never hurt her. Never.

"Aye. It would. The man you came to for help is the man you should be talking to. Talen Blackstone." His upper lip lifted as he seethed in a breath. "Now, I came in for one thing, and I mean to get it."

"Which is?"

"To get an answer out of you. Who did this to you?"

That. He'd asked her that before. Fuzzy snippets of that demand from his lips floated through her head. But she couldn't chance it. Couldn't tell him what had happened. Gilroy's reach was too far, too evil. No one could know where she'd come from. Who had done this to her. Juliet had told her to keep that information to herself.

She shook her head. "I cannot tell you."

"You can and you will."

She didn't think it possible, but he leaned farther over her, making her spine crack as she arched backward to not be swallowed by him.

"Or you can vacate my establishment." His voice rumbled around her. "Vacate my area of London."

Her right hand flew up, pushing on his chest. "No—no—you cannot kick me out."

He grabbed her hand from his chest and flung it downward. "I can and I will."

Her head shook, fear as stark as blood on snow freezing her bones. "No, I ask you. I beg of you—"

"I don't care for beggars."

Her mouth shut, her teeth cracking hard together. Her eyes closed to the danger in front of her as she mentally counted the coin in the boot Juliet had pushed onto her foot in Edinburgh before she'd shoved her onto that mail coach. How long could she live off of those coins? Was it enough to get on a ship? Leave this land?

That was the only way to surely escape her husband. To disappear. But what then? She was trained to be a lady, nothing more. Could she take in sewing? Become a governess? Did they have governesses in the Americas?

Her look darted past Talen, skittering about the room.

Nothing. Where was her dress? Her cape? She didn't even have any damn clothes. For that matter, where were her boots—Juliet's boot with the coins in the heel?

The crushing panicked weight from the lack of a path forward descended over her and her breathing sped, almost out of control.

Gasping. Gasping, for no air could make way into her lungs.

"Juliet…" She had to suck in a frantic breath before every choked word she uttered. "But Juliet said you would keep me safe. Help me."

"Juliet oversteps."

Stumbling two steps backward, she sank back down onto the bed. Her breath gone. None going into her lungs.

None going out. The room spinning. Her right hand flew out, trying to catch her balance on the bed before she began to spin with the room and fall to the floor.

Her eyes squinted closed as she gasped again and again, trying to force air into her lungs.

An audible sigh reached her ears and his boots clunked across the floor and then back to her.

His fingers wrapped around her right wrist, lifting her hand from the bed, and she opened her eyes to find him shoving a tumbler of reddish-brown liquid into her fingers.

He stood straight, pointing to the glass in her hand. "Drink it."

Her hand quivering, she lifted the glass to her lips, then hesitated, doubting the liquid would go down her throat.

"Drink it."

She tilted the glass and the liquid burned a quick hole down her throat, and with it, air followed into her lungs. Brandy. She took another sip and another breath made it into her lungs. Five exhales and inhales and the room stopped spinning.

It took several long moments before her shoulders drooped, her hand clutching the tumbler dropping to her lap. She opened her mouth, though she couldn't lift her eyes to him. "You are right. I will leave. I will leave in the morning. I did not mean to burden. Juliet was positive you would help and I believed her. I should not have done so. It was silly, really. There is no reason for you to help me. May I ask for my clothes and my cloak? I know they were torn and a mess, but they are all I have. If you could be so kind as to have them delivered to the room or tell me where they

are, I can collect them. And my boots. I will need my boots, please."

"Stay."

Her look whipped up to him. "What?"

"Stay. Juliet told you I would protect you. Then I will. It's what she intended. But I'll not hear another word of this past you think exists but doesn't. You don't know me. Understood?"

She nodded, smothering the instinct to argue with him. If she had to keep her mouth shut on the matter for a safe roof over her head, she would do it.

She didn't have any other option.

She didn't even have her wits about her yet.

He moved forward and plucked the near-empty tumbler from her hand, then moved to a chest of drawers at the wall beside the door, setting the glass next to the decanter that sat lonely along the top.

Starting toward the door, he paused and looked back to her. "Your boots are under the bed. I imagined you would want them close by."

Her mouth went slightly agape. He knew exactly what was in the heel of one of those boots. Of course he did. The boots didn't match. One was hers, the other, Juliet's. He knew Juliet. Knew that Juliet never would have sent her to London without a coin to spare. Her voice came out in a grateful squeak. "I do. Thank you."

He offered a curt nod and opened the door, but then halted one more time and glanced back at her. "I've seen this. Seen women look at me like you did just now."

"Like what?"

His mouth pulled back on the right side—not a smile, more of obscure whimsy at a held secret playing at his lips. He shook his head. "Never mind."

She wouldn't let him escape so easily, her words barking out before he left the room. "Like what?"

He looked to the partially open window on the far wall as a heavy sigh lifted his chest. His ice blue eyes swung back to her, pinning her. "I'm not your hero, Ness."

She met his stare, stifling the exhausted chuckle in her throat. "I agree."

{ CHAPTER 5 }

Ness stared at the last page of the book—*A System of Sheep-Grazing and Management*—fingering the paper between her thumb and forefinger as her eyes read each word slowly, not wanting the book to end.

She'd read through the dreadful thing four times in the last three days. But it was late, the book and the light from the fire the only lifeline keeping her away from crawling into bed where the nightmares would start.

Sheep were infinitely more peaceful than the demons that visited her once her eyes closed. So given the choice, she would spend her time with the sheep.

Three days of sitting, locked, in this splendid room. Staring at the ceiling and the cherubs so long it seemed like they'd started to float about on their own. Staring out the window that looked directly out onto the brick building next to it. So close, if she stuck her arm out the window, she could touch the red pitted bricks. Truly, the window served the purpose of an excuse to hang long, light blue drapes in the room, much more so than to let air in and out.

Thus, the sheep book had been her only entertainment.

The only person in and out of the room had been Verity, the silent maid that came and went from the room, never saying anything and only nodding or shaking her head to Ness's questions. She'd helped Ness with her clothes and her hair, as Ness could manage very little with her left fingers barely jutting out from the top edge of the bandages.

Verity must have recognized Ness's restlessness and had brought the book in with dinner days ago. Though Ness couldn't complain. She would take anything at this point to keep her mind occupied and not drifting back to the horror of a week and a half ago.

Drifting back to what she had been willing to do to end it.

The key in the lock of the door behind her clicked and the door opened. It was late for Verity to be entering the room.

Talen stepped into the room, not asking permission, not hesitating at the door to see if she was properly dressed. She was accustomed to that. Her space, her body were not her own.

He strode across the room and stopped in front of her chair by the fireplace, his eyes raking her over from head to toe.

She hadn't seen him in days, so his sudden interest, this late in the eve, was disconcerting. She'd rather thought he'd completely forgotten about her. Which wasn't a bad thing, except for the fact that she'd been locked in the room.

Whatever he discovered in his assessment of her person, she couldn't read in his face.

He leaned forward and picked up the book from her lap. "*A System of Sheep-Grazing and Management.*" The edges of his lips quirked upward. "Engrossing reading?"

"Verity brought it in. It is the only thing available to read." She eyed the volume in Talen's hand. "I don't know why she thought I would be interested in sheep management."

"She cannot read." He flipped the book over in his hand, the rough rasp prevalent in his low voice strong tonight. "It has a pretty cover. Embossed trees and sheep and hills and some birds. I'm sure it seemed a fine choice to her."

Of course. Verity had been kind in bringing her the book and she'd been sour on it. Shameful. Her look lifted to his face. "Verity, can she speak? She hasn't said a word to me, she just motions."

"She's mute."

"It is kind of you to employ her."

He shrugged. "It also ensures she will not tell tales of what happens here in the rooms of the Alabaster House."

What seemed like kindness now reeked of a calculated choice. Every time she thought she saw the slightest glimmer of compassion in Talen, he quickly dissuaded her from the notion.

"That is what this place is called? The Alabaster House?" She'd never been sure if that was a nickname because of the building or the real name of the establishment.

"Aye." He set the book onto the gilded side table by the chair.

She nodded, more to herself than to him. "What are you doing in here?"

"I came to check on the progress of your healing."

"You didn't expect me to be sleeping?"

"I can look you over asleep or awake."

"You've been in here while I was asleep?"

"Aye."

A shiver skittered down her spine. Heaven to hell, why had Juliet sent her to this man? Had she just traded one overbearing ogre for another? "So, what is your assessment?"

"The bruises are fading and the swelling has mostly subsided about your face. You heal fast." He took a step to the side, turning away from her to assess the room. "Why is it that you aren't already asleep?"

"My mind is restless and I cannot sleep."

He looked over his shoulder at her. "Do the sounds from below keep you awake?"

"No. Fear. The past. Those things keep me awake." Her gaze landed on his light blue eyes and her breath caught in her throat. It was hard to look at him and not obsess upon the fact that he was Conner.

She was sure of it. Sure of it still. More sure than she'd been days ago when her mind had still been hazy and she could only see out of one eye.

Not that she dared to bring up the topic again. She wasn't yet ready to get kicked out of this place and be on her own. She had to make plans first. Plans as to what she would do next.

Talen turned fully toward her. "You don't think you're safe here?"

It took her a long second to realize the offense on his face. She shook her head. "No, you mistake me. It is not a fear of this place. I do feel safe here. And the food has been most tasty and this room is grand, so I have nothing to complain upon."

His lips quirked to the side. "But you have a complaint?"

She stood, her hand flattening across her stomach. "I haven't been out of this room in days. I am starting to imagine I'm going mad, trapped in a room like this with nothing but my thoughts and the cherubs above and the *System of Sheep-Grazing and Management.*"

The slightest chuckle passed his lips. "It can be stimulating reading. Do you agree with the Romney Marsh system or the traditional method?"

"The Romney Marsh system by far. It seems to spare the trauma of the ewes, especially if there is a lost lamb but a suitable replacement when twins are born by another ewe. With some centered attention on lambing, one gets happy ewes. Happy ewes make happy lambs."

A smile actually took root across his face and he took a step closer to her. His right hand lifted, his fingertips going onto the bandages that wrapped her left arm in place along the splint. "Are you going to tell me who broke you like this?"

Her mouth pulled into a tight line. Of course. This again. He wasn't just there to check on her healing, he was there to demand answers from her. She shook her head.

For a long moment he stared at her, his gaze searing into her. The smile vanished from his face with a sigh. "What am I to do with you?"

"You don't need to do anything with me, Mr. Blackstone."

"Except I do. And it's Talen." His hand lifted farther and the knuckle of his finger stroked the side of her cheek. "Your cheeks have healed—I can see your face, your eyes, now."

She bit her tongue, holding in the scream that was threatening to escape. He could see her face, her eyes, so why didn't he recognize her? Why didn't he remember her?

"You understand that until I know what I'm protecting you from, I cannot let you leave this room?"

Her lips pulled inward, her teeth clamping tight on the inner skin as she nodded.

His hand dropped away from her face. "So, if you won't tell me who did this to you, why don't you tell me what is it that you want most in life?"

An odd change of topic. But a question she could at least answer.

Her lips parted. "I want to be strong."

His head snapped back, his brow furrowed. "Strong?"

"I want to be strong." She nodded, taking a tiny step toward him. "To know that if I fight back, I can survive on my terms. Not because I was weak. Not because I curled up in a ball and took a beating like a coward. I want to be strong."

Silence stretched into the room. Talen's blue eyes had locked onto her, his face an impenetrable mask. Silence that stretched for so long, she regretted the words. Regretted ever uttering them out loud.

The smallest smile suddenly curved onto the corners of his lips. "I can make you strong."

That, she hadn't expected from him. But she was one to recognize an opportunity when she saw it.

Determination set into her features. "I want to start tonight. Now."

He shook his head. "I can't teach you anything with your arm broken. It will have to wait."

She jumped another step forward, almost bumping into him. "But what better time than now? That's exactly why I want to start tonight. If I can fend off an attack with one arm broken, imagine what I could do with two working arms."

He laughed, a deep chortle that held remnants of the cadence of the laugh from the boy she once knew. His right brow arched. "You are positive you are up to it?"

She pointed to her face. "I can see out of both eyes. I can breathe. Move. The bruises may still ache, but the sharp pain is gone. If you can teach me, I can learn. I swear I can."

He stared at her for an excruciating moment—judging her words, her worth.

Decision made, he sighed. "Come with me."

{ CHAPTER 6 }

As much as he wanted to, Talen refused to look over his shoulder at Ness trailing behind him through the halls of the Alabaster.

She was either following or she wasn't, either action would tell him volumes.

She wanted to be strong.

What woman wanted that? Women wanted safety. Food. Clothing. Shelter. Children. That was what women wanted.

They wanted a champion. They didn't want to be strong.

Yet here was this sprite of a woman, following in his footsteps, looking for that very thing. To meet life on her own terms, as preposterous a notion as that was. Though his respect for her just increased tenfold.

This, he could work with.

He set the key into the lock of his office and opened the door, ushering her past him before closing the door behind them.

As she moved into the room, Ness's gaze centered on the long wall of windows, eight of them, that looked down into the main gaming room of the Alabaster. She walked past the long length of his desk to look out the far right one.

The patronage below would be in full debauchery mode by now. With the constant hum of the many voices,

the smoke of cheroots hung thick in the air directly in front of the windows and the alcohol flowed freely at this time of night.

Her gaze remained on the gambling several floors below. "What is this room?"

"My office."

"An office where you spy on people?"

"I watch over my business. I make no apology for it."

She nodded and turned around to him, shifting the braid of her thick, deep brown hair behind her shoulder, and her right hand smoothed down the front of her simple pale yellow muslin dress. Curious that was what Verity had found for her to wear. Something so…innocent.

"I am ready."

His eyebrow arched. "Ready for what?"

"For you to start teaching me."

Right to it, then.

Talen stifled a smile and moved across the room to stand in front of her. "You are positive you want to do this?"

"Positive."

"On with it, then. I am about to attack you." His left hand lifted and he motioned about them. "Look around—what weapons do you see?"

A flicker of fear sparked in her eyes and her look shifted off of his face to search past his shoulder. Chairs, desk, chests, fireplace. Her amber eyes snapped back to him. "None."

He studied the unease in her face. "Look again. There must be something solid to get into your hand. Can you injure me with something on the desk? Something on the floor?"

Her arm flew up, her forefinger pointing toward the fireplace. "The fire poker."

He nodded, turning sideways from her to look at the heavy black fire iron hanging beside the fireplace. "You think?"

Her bottom lip disappeared between her teeth and then she nodded. "Yes."

He motioned toward it. "Then grab it. Attack me. Hit me with it."

She glanced at him, her brows drawn together. "You want me to do what?"

"Attack me with the poker. People learn best by doing, so do."

Hesitant for a long moment, she took a deep breath and scampered past him toward the fireplace and took the fire poker from the wall, then turned back to him.

"Now attack me."

Her cheeks cringing, she lifted the tip of the poker until it was higher than her head and swung it toward his shoulder. Swung it slow.

He easily caught the length of the black iron in the air and yanked it from her hand.

"Oh." She stumbled a step forward.

He held the handle of the poker out to her. "Do it again. Harder."

Her lips drawing into a determined line, she snatched the poker from him and swung it down faster.

He caught it mid-swing but didn't pull it from her grasp. He released it. "Again."

She took a step to the right, swinging sideways toward him at a lower angle. He caught the iron. "Again."

She huffed a breath of annoyance, then swung quickly, hard.

He caught it. "Harder."

Again and again, from all angles, she swung and he caught the poker until she was panting, her face red with frustration.

A screech ripped from her mouth on the last swing. He caught the poker just before it slammed into his shoulder and he yanked it from her hand.

Heaving, she jabbed several steps away from him until her hip ran into the side of his desk. She stopped, her glare pinning him with every heavy breath, her right hand clutching her side as heat flushed her face with a tinge of pink through the fading bruises.

He inclined his head to her. "That didn't work."

"So what were you trying to prove?" she spat out. "Just how weak—how slow I am?"

"No—only that your choice of weapons matters."

She shook her head, looking away from him, fire crackling in her amber eyes as they stared at the door. She was debating. Debating on the wisdom of what she'd just started.

He didn't want her to give up on herself so easily.

"Look around again, Ness. What else can you attack me with?"

She glanced around, frantic, her right hand flying up, palm to the ceiling. "I—I don't know."

Talen moved across the room to her, stopped, then leaned past her to set the fire iron onto his desk, his chest brushing her shoulder.

Damn. He was too close to her. Too close with her chest heaving, her eyes blazing and the smell of apricots drifting up from her hair. The swelling had abated on her face and he'd realized days ago that she was pretty—beautiful, even. That was when he'd started locking her door. The Alabaster was no place for a beautiful woman.

But why in the hell did she smell like apricots?

Verity. Verity would have found and brought up some odd mish-mash of soap from the kitchens for her. For as silent as she was, Verity was far too good to any guest they had here at the Alabaster.

He took a step backward. Out of Ness's air.

It took him a full second to refocus on the task at hand. "Here's the truth. You're small, Ness. Wielding something big like a fire poker isn't your best option. Someone is attacking you? Your goal isn't to fight back and win. Your goal is to get away. Injure your attacker enough to run. Injure him enough to make sure that even if you are chased, he'll never catch up to you. No matter what, stay alive. You're small so you need to be fast."

His chin tilted down as his look pinned her. "You're small so you need small weapons that you can wield efficiently. Ones that don't tire you out. Ones that aren't going to be turned against you. I would have crushed your skull in with that poker after ripping it from you."

Her jaw dropped.

"Now is not the moment for delicacy. This is reality and that's what you wanted." He shook his head and walked around his desk, picking up his silver letter opener with a dragon relief in the gold, coin-sized round at the top of

the handle. The first thing he'd won off a peer years ago—a win that had opened his eyes to the lucrative possibilities in London.

He flipped it into the air and caught it by the tip, then held it out to her. "Here's your weapon."

"But it has no blade."

"The tip can impale just as easily as a dagger." He wiggled it and she took it from his hand. "You impale, you draw blood, and then you escape. You won't slit a throat with it, but it will damage. Damage equals escape."

He walked back around the desk to stand in front of her. "Attack me again. See how fast you can be."

Before his words even finished, she'd jumped to her left and jabbed the tip at his upper arm. A rip of fabric and the point of the opener hit skin and nicked him.

Blast, she could be quick.

He spun to the side just as she went for another swing at his shoulder and he caught her wrist. Wedging her arm up, he grabbed her opposite shoulder and shoved her backward until she ran into the wall. He slammed her right hand against the wall, making the opener fall from her grasp.

Her eyes flew wide, instant panic in them as her body curled against his hold, her eyes closing as she tried to make herself small.

"You're cowering. Stop." His words barked, harsh, into her face.

She shook her head, refusing to open her eyes to him.

He notched his voice down. "I'm not going to hurt you, Ness. But you need to feel the panic—this panic—

know exactly what it is so you can identify it, overcome it. Stay alive."

Slowly, her eyes opened, though the cringe about her eyes stayed determinedly in place. She nodded.

"Good. Now I have you pinned—what do you do now?"

"I don't know." Her voice came out in a squeak.

A squeak he didn't like. He liked it when her voice was strong. Determined.

"What weapons do you have?

"None, you have my arm pinned against the wall." She lifted her left forearm. "And I can't move my other arm."

"You have two knees, Ness. You have heels. All of those work just fine." He leaned down, his face directly in front of hers, his look intense. "Your first move is to slam a knee up into my ballocks. Your next move is to crash your heel down on my instep. Hobble me. I will drop your arm."

"But that—that's underhanded."

"Underhanded saves lives. There's no politeness when it comes to your life, you understand? *Stay alive.*"

"I—I—"

Without another word, she rammed her knee up into his groin and then slammed her heel down onto his boot. Silent and vicious and just what he wanted from her.

He doubled over, spinning away, his hands dropping from her as instant pain swept his body.

He looked up to find her face horrified, her hand over her mouth as she watched him. He shook his head. "Shit, that hurt. But I'm still coming for you—look around, what else do you have?"

She glanced around for less than a second and then shook her head.

"Open your eyes, Ness. The decanter to your right—smash it over my head, hold onto the neck of the glass and then cut me with the raw edge that's left. Or grab a book, throw it into my face, slam it into my temple. You use anything you can get a hand on."

"But—but I don't want to wreck your things."

His hands on his knees, he grunted as he pushed himself upright enough to look her in the eye. "You're learning survival, stop worrying about my damn possessions."

A breath and he charged forward ready to pin her to the wall again. Her leg instantly flew up into his ballocks. Fine reward. A lamp smashed across the side of his head in the next second.

Bent over, he staggered three steps to the left, his brain stunned, not able to catch his balance.

She rushed forward, her right hand grabbing onto his shoulder, trying to steady him. "Oh, Talen—no—I'm sorry, so sorry. I didn't mean to—"

His hand flew up to her. "Don't be sorry. Good—that was good." He paused, tilting his head to the left and then to the right as he tried to still his brain in his skull. His left eye squinted closed and he glanced up at her with his right eye. "That would have given you enough time to run. Remember, you're never going to beat someone my size one-on-one. You fight like hell and then you run. Run and hide or run until you can get help. You understand? You understand now?"

Her hand tightened on his shoulder as though she wasn't sure if he would fall if she let him go. "I do. I wish I were bigger, stronger than I am, but I'm not. You're telling me what reality is, and how I can bend it to serve me if only I accept it."

With a deep heave of air into his lungs, he pushed himself upright. There would be shards of pain in his groin area for a stretch of time, but he'd hobbled through worse. He looked down at her, pleased she'd grasped what he was telling her so quickly. "Exactly."

Her eyes lifted to him, the gold streaks of her irises sparking, so vivid with pulsing fire that it nearly reached out, consuming him.

No. Eyes like that were dangerous. No good could come of it.

He tore his stare off her, looking at the windows at the end of the room. "You can't be bigger than you are, but you can be stronger."

"I can?"

"We can all be stronger." He stepped gingerly toward the bookcase filling the wall to the left of the fireplace. His eyes searching the shelves, he took his time in plucking an assortment of tomes from the bookcase. "To that end, I'm bringing you back to your room with a nice stack of books."

She moved next to him and neatly set the books on top of each other in a straight pile. "You're taking pity on me in that room with nothing to do?"

He gave her a sideways glance. "No, the books are for lifting. You need to get stronger. You're to balance these along your right arm and lift them, up and down, as many as you can do at a time. Then add another one. Then do the same thing with your legs. Lie down and balance them on your shins, lower and lift them. All of that will strengthen your muscles. If you were one of my men I would have you swinging an ax to chop wood, or pulling a stubborn ox along the road, or hauling carts of coal. But you're stuck in a room with little to stress your muscles."

She looked at the stack, her fingers running along several of the titles embossed along the sides of the leather jackets. "And they might just entertain me as well?"

"Will they?" His brows lifted. "If that is the case, then it is merely a fortunate happenstance."

He piled the rest of the books atop her stack and picked up the tower of them, then moved toward the door. She scooted in front of him and opened the door for him.

They walked through the corridors alongside each other, her a half step behind for she didn't know her way. Which was good. He didn't intend for her to ever be outside of her room or his office.

He stopped in front of her door and nudged it open with the toe of his boot.

She went into the chamber, quickly going to the small rosewood desk by the window and brushing aside the hairbrush and hair pins that sat scattered atop it.

He set the stack of books down and turned to her. "We're not done. We'll do this again, tomorrow if I've recovered by then. We'll see if you can best me once more."

She chuckled, the gentlest chime of laughter that struck a pang deep within him he couldn't identify.

"Thank you for letting me best you. You didn't have to do so." Her face grew serious. "And thank you for not dismissing me. For listening to me and not thinking me silly. I don't know that anyone has ever done that for me, save for Juliet."

The inexplicable but visceral need to protect this woman reared deep in his gut again and he forced his mouth closed for fear of what would come out of it. With a quick nod, he turned away from her and stepped out of the room into the hallway.

It wasn't until he'd closed her door and locked it that he exhaled the breath held in his lungs.

The best way to protect Ness was to teach her to protect herself. That was truth.

For he knew full well he couldn't be trusted to protect anyone.

{ CHAPTER 7 }

Ness looked up from the book she was reading and watched Verity come into the room and set a tray of roasted beef, bread, asparagus and parsnips on the small table. The food here at the Alabaster was always cooked to perfection, seasoned to make her tongue curl around the morsels, and heavy.

Men's food, thick in her stomach.

She'd already added a reasonable layer to her frame—the bones that had started to poke through her skin weeks ago after eating so little were now receding. Useful, for she didn't know what her future held and lean times could very well be her lot once she was safe to leave the Alabaster.

Ness smiled as Verity stood straight, smoothing her apron as she turned to the door. She liked the young woman—close to her age, if she were to guess. Verity had been nothing but kind to her, bringing her the finest soaps, ribbons and pins for her hair, a hairbrush, and books to read. She was always unassuming, but saw details that needed to be tended to.

Verity was pretty with delicate features—something one could only see when her head lifted from the bow she always held it in. Her green eyes were almost always downcast, and the first time that Ness had seen them straight on she'd been startled. A green so pure and bright it looked like a springtime field under the full sun. The dark cap she always wore on her head covered her hair

completely, but Ness had occasionally noticed a few strands of dark red hair poking out from under the brim of the cap. Verity would probably be not only pretty, but quite beautiful if her hair wasn't severely pulled out of view and the innate sadness lifted from her cheeks.

Ness stood from her chair by the fireplace, holding her book against her belly. "Verity, if I may?"

Verity stopped and turned around, her head tilted down but her look lifted to Ness with her eyebrows raised.

"I have a question about the Alabaster. Are there other women here?"

Verity's head tilted to the side, her eyebrows drawn together to indicate she didn't understand the question.

"Other women with big bosoms." Heavy with the splint and bandages that wrapped her elbow to palm, Ness's left arm lifted, the tips of her fingers motioning to the air in front of her own breasts.

Verity lifted her shoulders.

"Whores?" The word came sour off Ness's tongue, but she had no other name for it. She didn't want to use the word, as she'd been pondering it ever since she'd learned that Juliet had been the madame of a brothel. Knowing Juliet and where she'd come from, yet what a decent and kind woman she was, had made Ness start to rethink a lot of things she thought she knew about the workings of life. The word whore now seemed crass to Ness, a label uttered in haste as a slur against women who were, in reality, just trying to find a way to live into the next day with what little assets they had.

Verity's green eyes widened and she shook her head. Shook it vehemently.

Ness's forehead wrinkled. "No women work here for… sexual favors?"

Verity continued to shake her head.

Ness exhaled, nodding, confused. "I see."

What kind of a gaming hell didn't have women available for pleasure? She'd assumed all the women she could see in the main gaming room from high in Talen's office were for hire.

Maybe they were just for looks. Men did like women fawning over them. Genuine or not, men didn't seem to much care.

The door opened and a head poked into the room. Declan.

"Verity, I was looking for you. We need you in the fleur-de-lis room to ready the bed, if you would, please?"

Verity's head immediately bowed and she nodded toward the floor, stepping out past Declan into the hallway.

Confusion still etched Ness's brow. "Declan?" She blurted out before he closed the door and disappeared.

He half stepped into the room, the rest of his body staying behind the heavy wooden door. "Yes?"

She hadn't spoken much to Declan, but from what she had, she guessed that she might get answers from him that Talen had been vague about. "I was curious—I assumed this was a whorehouse as well as a gaming house, but then I guess I was wrong. Or am I right?"

The right side of his face pulled back into almost a cringe. "That would be a better question for Tal, Ness."

"But I'm asking you."

He shrugged his shoulders.

"Fine, then let me ask you a different question since you're here."

To her surprise, Declan didn't scamper from the chamber like he did every time she was in a room with Talen. In this bedroom, in Talen's office. Instead, he moved into the chamber, closing the door, and then sat on the arm of the plush chair by the doorway, his hands landing on his thighs. Not committing to staying for more than a moment, but at least giving her the courtesy of his attention.

That he did so reaffirmed her like of him. He was easier than Talen. Lighter.

His right hand on his thigh flipped up. "Hit me."

"You have known Talen for a long time?"

"Yes, since our time on the Royal Navy ship together."

"Were you there when he first appeared on the ship?"

Declan paused, his eyes slightly narrowing at her, instantly cautious. "Yes."

She ignored his guarded voice. "Where did he come from?"

He shrugged his shoulders. "Where do any of us come from? The streets. Parents that drop us off at the docks then never come back. Or stolen from a field and stuffed in a sack. We come from everywhere. We come from nowhere."

"How did you end up on the ship?"

His mouth closed, his stare went blank on her—not answering that question.

The exact same blank stare Talen gave her when she asked questions he wasn't going to answer. The two of them must have practiced the look at each other when they were young to have perfected it so.

She nodded to herself, turning half around to set the book on her chair, then spun back to him. "So Talen appeared and you became friends?"

An easy smile came to Declan's face. "I had to. No one can fight like him. I knew early on it'd be better to have him as my best friend than my enemy."

"You're scared of him?"

He chuckled, shaking his head. "No. Not now. Maybe once upon a time I was. But that was before I knew him. What he can destroy with his fists didn't much matter to me a long time ago. To me, he's just Tal and he's earned my loyalty a thousand times over in the years I've known him."

Her chest suddenly felt lighter.

For all she was trying to navigate just who exactly Talen was now, that he had at least one loyal friend made her breathe a bit easier.

Her breath wouldn't hitch at all if he would just admit he knew her once upon a time. She wasn't even sure if he was lying about remembering his past or not. But it made no sense to lie about it.

So that left her with one question. Why had Talen forgotten everything of who he was?

But his friend couldn't help her there.

She smiled at Declan. "Thank you. Thank you for staying for the moment and talking to me."

He inclined his head to her, then pushed off from the chair and left the room.

Ness stood, staring at the door for a long time.

There was only one person that could answer her questions about Talen's past.

Talen.

And he wasn't talking.

{ Chapter 8 }

"Take another drink, you're panting."

Ness gasped in a quick breath, licking her lips. "You're making me work hard." With pillow feathers still floating from high in the air down about her head, Talen watched Ness sit on the edge of a hard caned chair and pick up the teacup from the side table. The tea long since cooled, she took several sips, as proper as if she were poised in a Mayfair drawing room—not sitting above his gaming hell with tufts of white feathers landing starkly against her dark hair.

The pillow that she'd just destroyed against the blade Talen had approached her with had been a brilliant move. The pillow had protected her hand while snagging the dagger and giving her a chance to yank it out of his hand. Plus, an explosion of feathers had filled the air. More precious seconds for her to run from an attacker.

An odd mixture of pride and surprise filled him. She'd done well. Not enough to set her onto the streets of the rookeries, but she would be able to survive for far longer than she would have when they first started this. That was key.

She glanced to her left, plucking several feathers off her shoulder. Good thing there wasn't a mirror in his office or Talen would be watching her pluck feathers from her head for some time, for as many as had attached into her loose chignon.

She did that, he'd realized during the past days. She was always conscious of how she was presenting herself, how she looked. Innate movements she couldn't control. Whether or not she was sitting properly. How straight her spine was. How smooth her hair lay. Someone had trained her well long ago for a life of privilege. Someone else had demanded perfection of her since then.

His stare should have moved off of her seconds ago, but he couldn't quite do it.

It didn't help that she was entirely too fetching. She'd been a prize for some peer—probably the same man that had broken her. Though how any man could have bruised a face like hers was beyond him.

To destroy such beauty. Sacrilege.

And to see such beauty sitting in the mess of his office, her cheeks flush from training with him, her peculiar amber eyes aglow with adrenaline, feathers landing in her hair—all of it made the crux of him twinge alive when he needed to keep his cock down and on the narrow.

He didn't want her. Couldn't want her.

Juliet had sent Ness to him to protect. Not to bed.

He wasn't about to sabotage this mission, for heaven knows what Juliet would demand of him next time if he failed to keep Ness safe. And taking Ness into his bed would not be safe. For either of them.

Setting her cup down on the side table, she scooted deeper on the chair and leaned back, letting her shoulders touch the rear of the chair. The motion looked uncomfortable, even though he could see she was attempting to relax for a moment and catch her breath.

She looked up at him. "Why do you not let me from my room except when you come and get me? I am itching to escape those four walls, and while your office is a nice change of pace, it would be interesting to see what other rooms are in this building."

Stalling with conversation, as she liked to do. He liked to keep her on her toes, keep the blood pumping in her veins. She liked to take breaks and rest.

But there was no rest if someone was attacking you. He knew that well. A fact he hadn't been able to quite convince her of.

"The books have not kept you entertained?"

"I appreciate them, I do. But one can only stare at words on paper for so long. These training bouts with you are the only thing that has kept my mind from turning to complete porridge during these last days. It would just be nice to expand the tiny world my life has become."

"No." He shook his head, crossing his arms over his chest. "Your room. My office. That is the extent of your realm. The rest of this place—it is not for a woman such as yourself."

"Weak?"

"Innocent."

She sighed, her head angling to the side as she stared up at him. "I'm not as innocent as you believe."

"No?" All of the feathers had finally floated to the ground and he kicked through them on the floor until he found his dagger by the tattered remains of the blue silk pillow. He bent down to pick it up and slipped it into the sheath alongside his boot. "What's a drop-cove? What's

a skin? A gull? A bravo? A snaffler?" He stood straight, looking at her.

Her mouth quirked to the right side in an annoyed smile. She lifted her shoulders.

"Make no mistake, you're an innocent, Ness. And I know Juliet meant to keep you so. She may have sent you here, but she sure as hell didn't intend for you to be corrupted."

"Why did she send me to you?"

"Because she's smart. She knew I could do what she wanted."

A slow nod bobbed her head, then she stilled, her amber eyes suddenly searching his face. "Juliet—you are enamored with her?"

"A ridiculous question." Talen strode across the room and picked up the new decanter of brandy. The red-brown liquid slid along the inside of the smooth glass neck as he poured himself a drink and he realized he actually liked this decanter more than the one Ness broke the day before. Such fine brandy had spilled all over the floor. He'd been lucky that he'd dodged the swing of the decanter in time, or the cut glass would have sliced his forehead deep. He'd created somewhat of a monster in Ness. She now had no trouble in destroying everything in this room.

Except for the books. She'd never once endangered a book.

"Is it ridiculous?"

He picked up the glass tumbler with his left hand and turned back to Ness, leaning against the sideboard. "Isn't everyone that meets Juliet enamored with her?"

A chuckle escaped through a smile that turned her full lips soft. "Yes, I suppose. She has a genuine charm about her that wraps one up—her soul actually cares about others, and that is a rarity."

"Aye, it is."

Ness picked up her teacup and took another sip, her eyes intent on him over the lip of the china. "The favor she called in on me, what made you owe her? How did she help you?"

He stared at her for a long second, then took the tiniest sip of his brandy. "I'll tell you if you tell me."

"Tell you what?"

He wasn't about to let her play ignorant. "You know."

Her lips opened in a long exhale and she looked away from him at the line of windows. No activity below, as it would still be hours before the first patrons arrived for the evening's gaming.

A quick breath and she sighed out a whisper. "Fine."

"Fine?"

Her gaze swung back to him. "Fine." Her right hand holding the teacup fell to rest on her lap and her lips pulled inward for a long second. "It was my husband that did this to me, though I'm sure you already deduced that."

Her face had pinched at the words, a flush creeping into her cheeks. Shame.

The blood in his veins instantly boiled. Why innocent women always seemed to feel shame after being beaten by a man, he'd never been able to figure.

His suspicion that she was married confirmed. Another man's property. "Who is your husband?"

"Gilroy Docherty." Her look dropped from him to the floor in front of the fireplace. "He's the grandson of the Earl of Whetland and he's a vicious, evil bastard. I knew it within the first months of our marriage, but I was stuck in a cavernous, cold castle in Scotland with him. His power and reach stretch far and wide. There was no escape. He'd always been good at bruising me in places that were easily hidden by clothes. But the last time—this last time when he broke my arm and pummeled my face he didn't care. He didn't care what showed to the world for he was going to kill me anyway."

Talen's right hand curled into a fist. "The bastard was going to kill you?"

"He was done with me. I knew it days before he attacked me. What he was planning…I could see it in his eyes. He was a spider on a web, circling for days, deciding the best way it would be to dispose of me without anyone questioning it."

Her voice wavering, her chest lifted high. "Then when he attacked, he swore he was going to kill me. I was worthless to him, not able to give him a babe, an heir. I lost two—two in the last four years."

Her eyes filled with thick tears that overflowed quickly, uncontrolled streams down her cheeks as her voice dropped to a whisper. "The last one was formed, but he came too early. He was formed so well I could hold him. Hold him in my hand. He was so tiny, but everything was there. There for me to hold. I wanted him. Wanted him so badly."

She paused for a long moment, the tears ceasing before she drew in a sharp breath. "Losing that babe broke me so thoroughly I knew Gilroy could never truly hurt me again. And the only reason I was able to walk through that pain was because Juliet appeared. Appeared out of nowhere and walked with me, an angel pulling me away from the edge of hell. For days she sat by my side when I was willing myself to die. If not for her stubbornness, I doubt I ever would have moved from that bed."

A crack zigzagged down his chest, the pain he saw in her striking him raw. He'd seen pain like this before, but it had never moved into his own body like that, making him feel it just as keenly—the brokenness.

The lump in his throat raw, he had to take a sip of brandy before he could speak. "That is one of Juliet's magical traits. Stubbornness."

A sad smile flashed across Ness's face. "I don't know if she should have wasted her magic on me." Her shoulders lifted high. "Maybe I am worthless. Maybe I should have stayed and let Gilroy do what he was determined to. Maybe I shouldn't have let Juliet convince me there were more days to live where the pain wouldn't consume. Let her convince me there was an escape from him."

With each word, her voice sank into such defeat he wanted to shake her. Shake her until the fire and mirth she'd been in moments ago reappeared. Shake her until she looked around and saw there was still a world to live in— days where she could breathe and live and smile again.

He'd seen it in her, the smiles and laughter she was capable of. Smiles and laughter that had hidden all of this fear and terror from him for the last fortnight.

But at least now he finally had a name from her. The bastard she needed to be protected from.

His stare cut into her. "There is always an escape, Ness. You just need to know how to seize it."

"That's what you're teaching me?"

"I hope. There's always a way out. Always another day to live, as long as you trust it's there for you."

The fingertips of her left hand lifted to clear the wetness from her cheeks as her eyes lifted to him. "I am trying, Talen. I am. Even if it's other people's faith that I've been living upon these past weeks. Juliet's. Yours. You both have wills that can move mountains, spit at death."

He lifted his glass to her. "For good or for bad, sometimes. I don't know when to stop and I don't always know how it will turn out."

A sharp chuckle left her lips. "This is supposed to be the moment when you convince me I'm safe—that you know what you're doing. Not when you admit that you don't."

"Juliet sent you to me to protect, so let's just say that right now, I'm living off her faith on that point as well."

A wry smile crept across her face. "She better be as smart as I think she is."

"Exactly."

Ness took another sip of her tea and then looked at him, her voice steady once more. "Your turn. Why do you owe her?"

He didn't hesitate. A deal was a deal. "Juliet saved my life."

"How?"

"As in, she physically saved my life. A building was burning down around me and I had been knocked unconscious on the third floor. Juliet dragged me out of the building."

Her jaw dropping, Ness leaned forward in the chair. "She what? By herself?"

"Aye. By herself. No one was left in the building. She had gotten all the women out of the place and then came back in for me."

"That was the South Selkie brothel?"

He nodded.

Her eyes wide, she stared at him, her jaw still slack. "But Juliet is so small—taller than me, yes, but tiny compared to you. How did she manage that—getting you out when you were unconscious?"

"When I say dragged, I mean dragged. She dragged me down the stairs—I had a disjointed shoulder and the bruises from every step along the way to prove it." His right hand lifted, bumping along an imaginary line as though going down stairs.

He shrugged. "But she got me out. And she only singed the bottom of her skirts in the process. Then she was beyond irate with me, kicking me awake. I had been under strict orders not to go to the brothel without her, as I'd just purchased the building and the women there didn't quite trust me yet. But I went alone and brutes from a rival brothel were there. Nonsense ensued. Nonsense that Juliet would have mitigated. Regardless, I was knocked unconscious, and they set fire to the place."

Her head shook. Whether she believed the story or not, he wasn't quite sure. She truly had no knowledge of the machinations and danger of the underworld he thrived in.

Her look met his. "No wonder you love her."

His left eyebrow cocked. "Love her?"

Ness nodded. "Juliet. How could you not?"

His lips pursed for a moment. "Aye, I suppose I do. I love her as the sister I never had, as family."

Her forehead wrinkled. "You never wanted to be with her?"

"Bed her?" His head shook. "No, Juliet is worth far more to me as a friend than a bed partner. I respect her too much."

Her mouth opened as though she was about to say something, but the words stalled. It took her a moment of staring at him before she continued. "So, the women you do bed—you don't respect them?"

"How do you come by that conclusion?"

"I…" She shrugged.

Did he respect the women he bedded? Debatable. He kept his mouth clamped shut.

Her cheeks pinkened. "I…I just think that makes it wise for me to be your friend."

Talen took a swallow of his brandy and set it down on the sideboard. He turned back to her, a wicked gleam in his eye. "Usually, my friends offer me something in return, but you, dear Ness, have only taken thus far."

The insult hung between them, thickening the air for several pulsing seconds.

Until Ness jumped up from the chair, slamming the teacup down along the edge of the side table to break it, and then she ran at him, swinging the sharp shard of the porcelain still in her hand at his head.

With a laugh, he ducked. Baiting Ness was too easy. And he liked her angry. Coming at him.

He caught her elbow high in the air and twisted her arm outward as he wrapped his left arm around her waist and yanked her body hard onto the length of him.

With a fiery growl she wrenched her torso awkwardly to look up at him. Their faces only an inch apart, their hot breath entwined for far too long of a moment.

Excruciating.

The devil himself testing him—her body shifting against the front of him, the blasted scent of apricots in his nose, lips that screamed to be devoured.

Her mouth parted with an intake of breath as her amber eyes went wide. Wide, like she'd just seen down to the carnal core of him. Wide, like she wanted to explore that carnal darkness ready to escape.

All it would take was the slightest move of his head and her lips would be his. Tasting her. Molding her body to his. Dragging his hands down to the perfect mounds of her breasts.

But no.

No.

She was too wounded. Too married. Too much trouble that he didn't need.

Juliet had known that.

Protect her. That was all.

He jerked his head back, dropping his hands from her waist and wrist as he stabbed a step away. He forced another chuckle to cover all that he'd just imagined doing to her body. "Good, I like to see the fire in you when you're mad. Your angry swings are much better than your usual puny strikes."

A screech and she swung the shard of the teacup at his head again. He dodged it, jumping toward the fireplace and kicking up feathers.

The shard of the teacup high and aimed at him, she stalked him. "The one thing I can bring you, you don't want." She struck, the sharp edge of the broken porcelain nicking his ear.

His hand flicked up to his ear and then he looked at his fingertips. Blood. The minx had made contact. He looked to her. "Which is?"

"Your past."

His body instantly tightened at her words and his arm swung out, shoving her to the side as he stomped past her toward the door. His voice dropped, cold and vicious. "Aye, you're right. I don't want that. Don't need that. Because you don't know it."

"But maybe it wants you," she screamed, dropping the shard of the teacup and picking up the cane chair she'd been sitting in.

With a growl, her right arm swung back and she hurled it at him as hard as her small frame allowed. Except the chair went flying into the bookcase next to the fireplace because she released it too late, sending her into an out-of-control spin. A spin directly toward the protruding white stone mantel of the fireplace.

Her forehead didn't stand a chance and her skull crunched into it.

She instantly crumpled.

Talen leapt, mercifully able to get his arms under her, breaking her fall at the last instant.

Stretched out across the wooden planks, his arms under her, he froze for a long moment, waiting for her to wake up, to move. When she didn't, he set her long onto the floor and frantically moved next to her. His hand went onto her chest, his fingertips pressing down into the flesh just above her left breast.

A heartbeat. Lungs expanding.

Relief surged through his veins. She'd merely knocked herself into blackness. And she was going to have a walnut-sized lump on her head.

Exhaling his held breath, he stretched out along his side on the floor next to her. With his head propped on his left bicep, his right hand didn't move from her chest where he measured her heartbeat, her breaths.

He stared at her face, taking stock of the bruises quickly fading, only yellowish streaks left under the skin. The cuts about her lips had faded to faint pink streaks. Her left eye no longer swollen.

A sigh overtook him. "From a cocoon of bruises and pain, you emerge. What am I going to do with you?"

Tufts of feathers that had been kicked up still drifted in the air. Landing on her forehead, on her hair. He blew a

puff of breath sideways to dislodge a feather that landed on his cheek.

A knock and the door to his office cracked open behind him. Was there no blasted privacy in this place?

"Ye well, boss? All the noise stopped. Ye said not to bother ye no matter the noise. But now there's none."

He didn't bother to flip his head around to glance back at his man, Simon. "Aye. I'm well."

"The lady well?"

"Aye. She will be."

His fingers on her chest curled slightly.

She would be.

He would see to it.

{ CHAPTER 9 }

Leaning close to the small round mirror propped atop the rosewood desk in her room, Ness prodded at the lump on her forehead. Verity had been kind enough to set a simple braid into her hair before disappearing into the bowels of the Alabaster, and though removing all the pins in her hair had helped, it hadn't stopped the pain.

Her head had been pounding for hours and even the slightest touch of her fingertips along the lump sent sharp pangs into her skull. Her face had only just returned to its normal shape after the beating and now this.

She'd woken up on the floor of Talen's office to see him sitting next to her, his back against the wall, watching her. Concern evident on his face, his light blue eyes intent on her. His look almost making her squirm.

He didn't care for what had happened. It'd been her own fault, slamming into the mantel as she did. Stupid to not have her balance before she'd picked up that chair, but he'd made her so furious and the feathers were so slippery.

Everything was so easy for him, including baiting her into attacking him. And she fell for it every time. Though she was getting stronger. Smarter. Quicker. She could feel that in her bones. And her broken arm barely held her back anymore.

But the anger that tinged the corners of his eyes in that moment when she opened her eyes made him look dangerous. Dangerous in how he looked at her.

Odd, unless she'd misunderstood those few short seconds when she had been frozen in his arms, their lips near to touching. The man was too virile, and heaven help her, in those moments, she wanted everything that Talen was. The heat of him. His lips. His hands rough on her body.

All of him on her.

Yet he'd yanked himself away.

I'm not your hero.

His lips to her ears, the echo of those words haunting her.

And he didn't have any intention to become so. The anger lacing his eyes when she'd awoken proof of that.

Not that she needed a hero. She just needed a place to exist, to heal, to plan before she could move onward. If she'd learned one thing from Juliet, it was that she needed to be her own hero.

Walking out of his office, Ness had been startled at the destruction they'd caused. Feathers everywhere, two chairs broken, glass from a lamp scattered across the floor. Yet every time Talen brought her back into his office for another training bout, everything looked perfectly tidy and new and intact, as though the tornado of their training hadn't torn through the office the day before.

Talen was entirely too lenient with her in destroying his possessions.

She winced as her fingertip poked at the side of the lump in the direct center of her forehead. She needed something—anything—to get the swelling down. What was it her mother used to do when she had a lump on her knee from banging into something? Set cold to it. Ice, if they had it.

Surely there was an ice house adjacent to the kitchens here at the Alabaster. The cook in residence couldn't have made the apricot iced cream that had been sent up with her dinner two days ago without it.

Grabbing the key for her door that Talen had given her, she walked across the room. She'd been surprised when he'd handed her a copy of the key two days ago. She'd said she felt as though she was in prison, so he'd given her a key without argument, though made her promise that she would stay in her room. It was to be used in an emergency only.

Soothing the pounding red bump on her head seemed like an appropriate emergency. And how hard could it be to avoid people and find the kitchens?

Difficult, it turned out. She'd had to ask two different footmen she encountered as she'd slipped down the servant stairs and along the lower corridors the correct way to the kitchens. Not quite circular stairs, each level seemed to have a set of square stairs with four turns. And now she was lost on her way back to her room, standing in a stairwell by a doorway, ice wrapped in a cloth melting in her hand, trying to remember how many flights she'd just walked up.

The lump on her head had addled her brain.

But the one thing she couldn't do was step out into the main corridors where she could clearly hear men— too many men—laughing and arguing and carousing. It sounded like a very full gaming night. If Talen discovered she was lurking about the house, he'd kill her—but not

before taking away her key—the one small semblance of freedom she now had.

She lifted the ice wrapped in the linen cloth to her forehead, rubbing it about the lump as she closed her eyes, walking back up the stairs in her mind. One more level? No. She could hear what she assumed was the main gaming room on this level. That meant two, maybe three more sets of stairs to climb.

Her eyes opening, Ness continued up the staircase when the door behind her opened. She quickened her steps, hoping to avoid running into another servant. That she already encountered two footmen and three workers in the kitchens wasn't a good thing.

Footfalls thudded on the stairs behind her. Steps following her upward. Two sets of steps speeding up. She glanced over her shoulder. Two men and neither was a servant, both in expensive dark jackets. Their eyes blurry, their shoulders banging into the outer walls of the tight staircase. Soused. She'd had her fill of drunken asses— enough to last a lifetime.

She doubled her speed up the stairs.

The stout one closest to her reached up, catching the back of her skirts for a second before she kicked back, clearing his hand.

"Stop, little mouse." His feet on the stairs sped faster. "Are whores now at the Alabaster? Mr. Loggerton didn't tell us that. We've been asking for years now."

Hell.

Her look dodged upward. There. A door up at the top of this turn of stairwell. That was her escape.

She dropped the ice, her breath speeding as she tried
to gather up her skirts with her right hand to bound up the
stairs two at a time. Damn skirts in her legs. Tangled.

"Stop—stop—you little whore. We could use you."
The second man yelled at her, his shout echoing off the
walls of the staircase. "Stop. It'll only take a few minutes of
your time and we won't have to leave for the whorehouse
down the street. We'll make it worth your time. Stop her,
Harry. Stop her."

The door. Escape. That was what Talen had been
pounding into her head. Escape.

She reached the door, her right hand fumbling as she
tried to open it. It swung wide and she bolted into the
hallway. Her room. Her room at the end of the hallway.
Escape.

Her head jerked back suddenly, the braid of her hair
almost yanking from her skull. Her feet flew out from
under her and she crashed down onto her backside.

The man directly behind her laughed and then
wrenched her braid upward, dragging her up with it onto
her feet. Her right hand flew to the base of her braid, trying
to hold her hair from tearing out of her head.

"No—no—I'm not a whore. I'm not."

His laugh didn't stop as he twisted the braid around the
palm of his hand, pulling her closer to him. "I don't think
you get to tell us that, mouse. We get to decide what you
are. Filmore, you take a go at her while I have her stuck nice
and good—the tail of a little mouse."

The second man moved closer to her, trapping her
against the wall, already loosening the fall front of his

trousers. A gold chain dangled across his chest in front of her eyes, the gold flickering in the light of the sconce at the end of the hallway.

Her chest seized upon itself, clamping off all air to her lungs.

Panic. This was the panic Talen had been teaching her about.

Panic that she couldn't let take a hold of her.

Fight. Escape.

Whatever it took.

The world slowed as her right hand let go of her hair and she ignored the pain of her hair ripping from her scalp. The stout one had twisted her half in front of him, her head bent to the side. Which meant his ballocks were directly behind the stiff wooden splint wrapped onto her left arm. It would be brutal against the break, but the board was the only solid weapon she had. She had to save her knee for the one in front of her.

She went still for a long second, coiling her energy as the sounds of their laughter edged away, like they were in a far-off glen surrounded by trees.

One wild swing backward with her left arm, and she hit the stout man square on his already engorged member. Before he could even scream, she shifted her weight and viciously sent her right knee up into the groin of the man in front of her.

Screams erupted almost in unison as they both doubled over.

But the man behind her didn't release her hair, it was bound so tight around his palm. Instead, his fist at the back of her head punched downward, jerking her to the floor at his feet.

She kicked off from the wall, trying to tear his hand out of her hair. No luck. Their screams ended and she stared up at two raging monsters above her with brutal revenge in their eyes.

"You'll pay for that, you little bitch." The stout one lifted his fat hand, ready to swing down at her with the back of his ring-laden fingers.

But then his eyes popped wide, almost out of his head.

An arm flew across his neck, choking him. Choking him.

His right hand tangled in her hair fell to his side and she quickly reached up, ripping her braid from his palm.

A rush of legs jabbed about her in the tight hallway, boots barely missing her limbs as the stout man was yanked away and thrown to the floor.

Talen. Talen over the man, his fists flying into the troll's face as Declan slammed the other man ruthlessly into the wall.

Whimpers, squeals. The piercing crack of bones breaking.

And she sat in the middle. Blood splattering about her, arms and fists flying. She sat in the middle, perfectly still. Perfectly safe.

Safe because Talen was there and she knew it, just as Juliet had promised.

Knew it down to her bones.

Talen would keep her safe.

{ CHAPTER 10 }

"Talen—enough." Declan jumped over Ness on the floor of the hallway, screaming. "Enough. Stop."

He reached Talen, grabbing his left arm in mid swing and pulling him backward. Backward away from the sniveling bastard he was crushing. Backward from the red rage filling his mind, his sight.

Instinct had devoured him and the only thing he could do was swing. Swing and destroy.

"Talen—you need to stop. Stop." Declan yanked harder, sending the two of them slamming backward into the opposite wall.

It was just enough to snap him out of the rage. Just enough for him to look down and be able to see what he'd just done.

The man's face was mush. Cut after cut. A bloody mess. Bones clearly broken. No skin visible.

Shit. He hadn't just killed him?

The man twitched.

Not dead. Small favor.

"You know he's Baron Jaccard's youngest brother?" Declan's furious whisper rang in his ear. "What are you thinking, Tal?"

Talen nodded, his glare still pinned on the motionless man by his feet. He didn't care whose damned brother he was. He'd had his hands on Ness. About to hit her. He

deserved so much more than what Talen had just done to him.

"Talen." Ness's voice squeaked out and his glare shifted to her.

What in the deuced devil was she doing out of her room?

All the red rage reflooded his vision.

Talen yanked his left arm from Declan's grasp and moved to her, grabbing her about the waist and picking her up, carrying her over the other inert body on the hallway floor and into her room. He threw her onto the bed.

"Why in the almighty hell were you out of your room, Ness?" His hands went onto his own hipbones, his fingers gripping hard so that he wouldn't reach out and shake her. "Tell me they dragged you out there. Tell me you weren't out there on your own accord."

Her eyes wide and panicked, she looked up at him, then shifted her gaze to the doorway where Declan stood.

"No." He reached out and grabbed her chin, forcing her to look back to him. "Don't look at Dec. He's not going to save you. Tell me what you were doing."

Her fingers grabbed his wrist, pushing his hold off of her face. "I—I was—I was getting ice. Ice for my forehead." She pointed to the lump on the middle of her head.

"Ice?" His caustic chuckle cut into the room. "Ice? You needed ice? Where did you think you were going to get ice?"

"The kitchens. They had ice—I just wanted the swelling to go down so I thought I could use the servants' stairs—"

"You thought that traipsing all over the Alabaster was a fine idea?" His arm lurched up at his side. "What did I tell you? In this room. In my office. Nowhere else." He leaned over her, his words vicious. "What did I bloody well tell you?"

Her head bowed, her right fingers twisting in her muslin skirt on her lap as her voice came out small. "Stay in the room."

"Stay in the damn room." His arm swinging wide, he spun from her, his voice thundering. "You couldn't have gone down there without being seen. Now more people know about you. That was what was keeping you safe, Ness. No one knew you were here. No matter how long your husband's tentacles are, he couldn't reach you where he couldn't find you."

He whipped back around to her. "How many people saw you on the way to the kitchens?"

She glanced up at him, her shoulders lifting. "Just three, maybe four."

"Three, four? How many? What did they look like?"

She cringed, her eyes closing. "Two footmen, one had light blond hair, one had sandy blond hair. Both were lanky, but shorter than you. Two helpers in the kitchen, they were young—girls—one was peeling potatoes and the other was scaling fish. They pointed me toward the ice house. That was all. That was all, I swear. Except for the other girl in the kitchen—she was doing something on the floor, I don't know what, cleaning, maybe."

"Bloody hell—five?"

She cringed, nodding.

His glare didn't shift from her. "Declan."

"I'm on it." Declan left the room, closing the door behind him.

"What?" Ness jumped in place on the bed, looking ready to run out with Declan. "Where is he going?"

"To clean up the mess you just made. The mess I just made." He turned from her, his fist punching hard into the wall. Not that it mattered, his knuckles were already split. "Ice. Bloody damned ice."

He stepped away from the wall, his arms clamping across his chest as he moved in front of her once more. "Why in the hell didn't you just ask?"

She pointed toward the door, fear in her eyes. "But Declan—where is he going? He's not going to hurt them? The footmen, the girls?"

His head snapped back. "What do you think we are, Ness? Cutthroats? No. Declan is going to ensure their silence with few fat bags of coins." His eyes narrowed at her. "What in the blasted hell kind of man do you think I am?"

"I don't know—how should I know?" Her right hand waved manically in front of her. "You just pummeled a man in front of me. He looked dead—"

"He's not dead."

"He wasn't far from it—what if Declan hadn't pulled you off of him? What then? How do I know what you're capable of? You own this place. Half of the surrounding area from what I've gathered. Everyone is afraid of you. And what you did, it was…it was…it was vicious."

Talen had to take in a deep breath at the fear in her eyes. Breath that seethed back out through clenched teeth. "What they were about to do to you was vicious."

Her mouth clamped closed, her eyes dipping to the floor between them.

He attempted to rein in the rage in his voice. "I'll make no apologies for it, Ness. They deserved every blow that was laid."

There it was. The exact man he was. The reality of it hanging in the air between them. Vicious. Cold. Brutal.

Better that she knew.

Silence for the longest stretch, her gaze solidly on the floor. A minute, probably more. But he wasn't about to apologize for the very thing that was keeping her safe.

"I tried." The smallest whisper eked from her lips, yet her eyes didn't lift upward.

"What?"

"I tried." Her look, skittish, ventured up, but only to his chest. "Thank you. Thank you for coming. I tried. I tried to get away, tried everything you taught me. I was desperate and going to try to sweep his feet next. But the lock he had on my hair was too harsh. But I was trying."

It was small, but he heard it, the quiver in her voice. A quiver that made him pause. Pause and really look at her without rage tingeing his eyesight red.

Her dark hair was askew, the thick braid her hair was often in half undone. Tufts of hair errantly floating about her face. A tear in the right sleeve of her dress. Her breathing still ragged.

"Hell, Ness, are you okay?"

Her chest lifted in a deep breath and she finally met his gaze. "I—I am. I am fine, nothing more than bruises, and my arm survived the impact."

His look jumped to her left arm. "Wait. What?"

She looked down, dropping her left arm along her skirts and angling her body slightly to the side to hide her left arm. "Nothing. I am fine. It is nothing."

He took a step toward her. "What impact did your arm survive?"

She sighed. "My arm. The splint board broke when I slammed it into the groin of the one that had my hair. The one you pummeled."

His brow furrowed. "You what?"

Her gaze went evasive. "I crushed it—the board—into his…uh…protruding member."

"You what?" An instant chuckle vibrated up from his chest. "Well done." But then his hand dragged down over his face, his head shaking. "No. Dangerous. You shouldn't have put your arm through that—you could lose it, lose your whole arm if you injure it again and it becomes infected."

Her glare met his. "I didn't have anything else to grab to help me—no weapon. There was nothing in the hallway. The board was the only thing hard I could use because I had to save my knee for the other one's ballocks."

The laughter took him over again before he could look at her. "Again, well done. But dangerous—did you look at your arm? Does it hurt? It could be out of alignment."

"I haven't had a chance to look at it."

He moved forward, dropping to balance on his heels in front of her. Snatching a pillow from the head of the bed, he set it on her lap and then gently grabbed her left arm from where she had hidden it and he set it atop the pillow.

Silently, a smile still playing at his lips, his attention stayed on her arm as he loosened the white linen bandaging that bound her broken arm to the splint. "You fought."

"I did. For what little good it did."

"It bought you time." He glanced up at her, then looked back down to her arm. "What if Declan and I had been a minute later? What would have happened then? Seconds count, Ness. People think they are nothing. They wile them away. But they count. They always do. Seconds can be the most important thing."

She inhaled a deep breath, her chest lifting in front of him. "It makes me sad to think of all the seconds that have been wasted in my life. Too many to count. Too many spent accepting what was around me instead of devising a way to take them for myself, to make them my seconds to do with what I will."

He tugged free the last of the linen strip away from her arm and set it on the bed, leaving her forearm balanced upon the broken plank of wood. He looked up at her, their eyes almost level. "That must mean you are now devising a new life for yourself?"

Her right shoulder shrugged. "Possibly."

"Then I can only imagine it includes *A System of Sheep-Grazing and Management*."

An instant smile broke her face wide and her laughter floated into the air, her head tilting back. Magic, the sound

of it, the way it lit up her face and the air about her. Magic he would capture and bottle if he could.

Twinkling, her amber eyes centered on him. "I do believe I may have overlooked that option for my future. Something I will have to consider."

The air between them hard to breathe for how light it was, his lungs were suddenly starving for air.

He rocked up from his heels and stood, going to the chest of drawers by the door. He pulled the second to top drawer open and pulled out a new splint and a fat rolled strip of white linen bandages. "Mrs. Jenkins left two other splints here in case they were needed."

"That was forward thinking of her."

"She's thorough and the best bonesetter for a reason. Though the most cantankerous woman that I've ever known. You should have seen her scowl when she first saw you. She thought I was the cause of your injuries."

Ness laughed. "I don't imagine you took that well?"

"Why don't you imagine it?"

"You are not one to let misconceptions hang out in the open without correction."

She had that right about him. "No, I don't suppose I am." He paused for a moment as he shut the drawer, taking a steadying breath of air that actually reached his lungs.

He walked back to her, dropping down to his knees as he studied her arm. Still black and blue, and the skin was shriveled from being under the bandages, but her forearm looked straight, solid. There was no tinge of green to the skin and the scabs had healed over, which was promising.

"Does it hurt?"

She shook her head.

He wasn't certain of her motion, but let it pass. Of course it would be hurting. Of course she wouldn't admit to it. She was stubborn, just like him.

His fingertips went gently to the spot on her forearm where the break had happened. "It's healing well. You're lucky it was a clean break."

"It didn't feel like a clean break at the time."

"Nor I imagine in the days after before it was set properly."

A frown set onto her lips, her face darkening. "No, I don't think anything started to heal until I arrived here."

He instantly regretted bringing up the past. The past that was still too raw and painful for her. Better topics. He needed better topics, but his mind was blank.

Talen cleared his throat, glancing up at her, spurting out the only thing that popped into his mind before he could stop himself. "Why did you hate that boy?"

"Which boy?" Her brows lifted.

"That boy that you think I am—which I'm not. Conner, that was his name?" He lifted her wrist and slowly started to slip the new splint in between her arm and the broken board below it.

Her head tilted to the side as she looked at him oddly for a long second, but then a half smile lifted the right side of her face. "I hated him for good reason."

"Which was?"

"He was keen on putting toads in my slippers."

Talen laughed. "Seems appropriate. Funny, though."

"Was it? Of anything, toads in my shoes? They are infinitely worse than frogs in one's slippers."

"What's wrong with toads?" His attention stayed downward on her arm as he finished sliding the new splint into place. "They aren't slimy. Just kind of lumpy."

"Which is exactly their folly. One's toes sink deeper into the slippers, because there isn't the instant reaction to the frog slime. It isn't until the flesh of the toad squishes against your toes that you realize." She shuddered. "Infinitely worse."

He chuckled as he picked up the fresh bandage and lifted her wrist and the splint to start the wrapping. "Whoever that boy was—he was devilishly conniving."

"That boy was you, Talen."

His hands paused and he looked up at her sharply, though he should have known she wouldn't leave it be. What she thought the past was, and what the truth of it was, were very different things.

"That boy wasn't me." His words spat out, clipped. "And I'll not have you keep up this farce of how you know me. I'm helping you, Ness. You know that. You don't have to pretend that you once knew me in order to gain my assistance."

His attention went back to wrapping her arm tight against the new splint.

She puffed a sigh. "Then tell me—tell me who you were when you were six. When you were eight. When you were ten."

"No."

Her left fingers twitched. "I can't feel my fingers."

Too damn tight. He stifled a growl and reversed course on the wrapping, loosening it until he was back at her wrist again. He started around her arm, looser this time. Or as much as the suddenly vexed blood pumping through his veins allowed.

"Tell me."

"No."

"Why?"

He shook his head. "Because I can't. I don't remember that time, but I sure as hell don't have any memories of toads."

"You don't remember?" Sudden excitement made her words vibrate. "Well, what memories do you have?"

His mouth clamped closed.

"Tell me. What memories do you have?"

He looked up at her, his voice a growl. "None before the ship."

Her mouth dropped open. "You have no memories before being on the ship?"

"Don't look at me like that."

The excitement had crept from her voice into her eyes, making them glow. "But that just proves it."

"It proves nothing."

Her right hand lifted in exasperation. "It proves it's a possibility. A possibility that you are Conner. Don't you see? Why can't you remember?"

His jaw tightened, his words seething. "I am not your dead friend, Ness. And I'll not go through this with you again."

His head ducked and he finished wrapping her arm to the splint, tying it off. At least she was smart enough to keep her mouth shut.

A knock echoed into the room and the door opened.

"Tal. A word." Declan's face was serious. Deadly serious.

Without a word to Ness, he stood and went to the door, following Declan into the hallway. The two men that had attacked Ness had already been dragged out of there. Better their arses in the gutter. Dropping them face down, if his men were smart. He pulled the door closed with a snap. "What is it?"

"Jasper from the Den of Diablo just stopped by. He said there were four men there, looking for a small woman with dark hair and amber eyes."

"What?" Ice snaked down his spine.

Declan gave him a curt nod. "They mentioned Juliet like they knew her, but Jasper said these were not the type of men Juliet would have dealings with."

"Shit."

"Exactly. He just wanted you to be aware, as he hasn't heard from Juliet in weeks. He's sent word north to his cousin in Scotland to have him ask her about it. But he wondered if we'd heard from Juliet."

"You didn't tell him anything?"

"No. Of course not."

"Good. But dammit."

Declan nodded.

His heart started thudding hard in his chest, a pit of fear expanding upward from his gut.

Fear? He didn't feel fear.

Not since he'd been a whelp on the ship.

But there it was, a rising tide in his lungs.

He needed to find out the true reach of Ness's husband. Clearly, Gilroy had connections to the London Underground if he had men sniffing about the Den of Diablo.

Damn. Why had she picked tonight, of all nights, to show herself to far too many people in the house?

He needed to find out exactly who the men were that were searching for Ness. The sooner the better. How many. Where they were from.

And in the meantime, he had to get her somewhere impenetrable.

The Alabaster was no longer safe.

{ CHAPTER 11 }

"You are positive this is safe?" Ness leaned forward in the carriage, pulling the dark curtain open a crack to find sheep dotting a hillside. "Oh, we are in the countryside."

Talen swatted her hand away from the window and the curtain swung back into place. "You need to trust me on this. It is the safest thing I could think of."

She looked at him. Studied the hard set of his jawline. The dark stubble that had appeared overnight. A night with no sleep, she'd deduced.

He'd found out last night about the men looking for her, but he didn't tell her until this morning. He'd said he'd wanted her to sleep soundly after the attack in the hallway. Yet the look on his face when he'd woken her soon after dawn had said volumes. He'd told her about the men searching for her, that they had yet to be found, and then he'd set Verity onto her to get her ready to leave.

She'd been fighting waves of panic ever since.

As expected, Gilroy had sent men after her. She was his property. And he hated nothing more in this world than losing what was his. She'd thought she would be safe at the Alabaster under Talen's watch, but she'd been silly to think it would be that easy to escape Gilroy. If his men were at the place where Juliet had worked, then they were only streets away from finding her.

The wheels crushing on gravel, the carriage lurched to a stop.

"Stay in here." Talen shifted forward from his seat, reaching around her head to tug the hood of her cloak up and around her face. "Declan came out ahead of us to arrange privacy as we entered, but I need to verify it before you set one foot out of this carriage. Trust me on this."

His look met hers, his light blue eyes indomitable. She trusted him. How could she not? He'd kept her safe thus far, just as he'd sworn he would.

She nodded.

Talen opened the carriage door and the bright light of the day flooded the interior of the coach for the seconds it took for him to alight. She was still blinking the white splotches out of her eyes when he reappeared, opening the door and holding his hand up to her. "Pull the hood as much as you can over your face and keep your head down. Look at your feet, nowhere else."

A fresh wave of terror gripping her, she did as bade, the hood of the dark grey cloak taking away all but a narrow slice of the world in front of her. She set her right hand into Talen's grip and stepped down from the carriage.

His arm went around her shoulders and he ushered her forward. Her focus stayed on the tips of her boots peeking out from under her skirts with every step, their feet crunching along the grey gravel until they came to the wide, cream stone steps. Up and into a cavernous foyer—she could tell by the hollow echo of their footsteps—and then Talen turned her to the right, prodding her up two levels of stairs.

It wasn't until they'd walked along a long hallway where she could hear people—some singing, some talking, some yelling—that he steered her into a room.

The door clicked closed, but she still kept her head down.

"You can look up now, Ness," Talen said.

Her head lifted slowly, her hand pushing back the hood away from her face and onto her shoulders.

A room. A simple room with gauzy curtains pulled in front of the windows. A bed with thin wooden rails sufficing as the head and foot boards. White sheets and coverlet. Empty walls. One wooden chair by the fireplace. That was all.

Not the luxury that had been surrounding her at the Alabaster house, but she didn't need luxury. She needed somewhere safe to hide.

She looked to Talen. "Where are we?"

"Somewhere safe. Somewhere no one will look for you."

She nodded, moving over to the window and she pulled aside the gauzy white curtain.

Black iron bars crossed the window.

No in. No out.

How had she not realized it?

The sounds she'd heard on the way in. People in all states.

Mad people.

She doubled over slightly, pain seizing her gut, all the air leaving her as though she'd just been punched. Her fingers crumpled the curtain in her hand and she looked

back at Talen, her voice nothing but a whisper. "Wh—where are we?"

His left hand lifted, palm toward her to calm. "It's an asylum, but it's the safest place there is, Ness. No one will think to search for you here."

The world started spinning around her.

No. No. No. He couldn't leave her here. *Not here.*

She forcibly stretched her fingers, letting go of the curtain, and rushed across the room to him. "No—no, please don't do this. Please." Her right hand grabbed the lapel of his jacket, tugging it, her voice pitching high and fast. "Please don't leave me here, Talen. I can't. I can't. Please don't leave me."

His head snapped back, confusion creasing his brow. "But it's perfect. We're outside of London and it's the safest place for you. No one will find you here, Ness. I swear it."

"No, please. Please." She yanked on the front of his coat, words heaving from her chest. "Not here. Anywhere but here. Please, please. There has to be somewhere else. There has to be. Please."

He caught her wrist, stilling her frantic hand as he ripped her grip from his coat. "Now you're the one acting quite mad."

She gasped back a sob that threatened with his words and her legs buckled under. She dropped onto her knees in front of him, her neck craned to look up at his face, her panic taking her breath as her manic words barely squeezed through her throat. "No—I swear, I swear I'm not crazy, Talen. I swear it. Is this because I think you're Conner? Because I won't believe you? I'll believe you. I'll do it. I'll stop. I'll stop insisting you're him. You're not. You're Talen. Only Talen."

She grabbed the bottom hem of his coat, tugging at it as she begged. "Please, just don't leave me here. I'll never say another word about the past. Never. Talen. Talen Blackstone. That is who you are. I can do it. I'm not mad. I swear I'm not."

His forehead still wrinkled, he looked down at her, his light blue eyes searching her face for understanding as to why she was suddenly acting insane.

Blast.

She *was* acting like a mad woman. Falling to the floor. Begging. Of course he would think this of her.

His mouth pulled to the side as he tried to figure her. "Ness, this doesn't have anything to do with who you think I am. You're only here because this is where I need you to be."

With the softest of motions, his fingers sank into the side of her hair. Far too gentle, like his own hand disagreed with his words, battling them. "This is how I keep you safe."

He wasn't listening to her. Not hearing her. Her fingers curled into a death grip on his coat. "But no. You don't understand. You cannot leave me here. You cannot."

His hand pulled away from her hair, his voice going gruff. "No, I have to leave now. I can't afford any more time here. Someone may see me that shouldn't. I'll be back once I've found those men searching for you, I swear it."

He grabbed her right hand and had to peel back her fingers, one by one, to disengage her clamp on his coat. Free from her, he took a step toward the door.

Her heart thundering in her chest, she crumpled in that instant, defeat overtaking her voice, sobs starting. "Don't leave me here, Talen. Please. Please, not like my mother, please." Her sight blurry with tears, she reached out, grabbing furiously at his retreating feet. Black boots moving out of her grasp. "Please, Talen. Please don't do this. Please."

The boots stopped for a long second at the door and she looked up, searching for his face through the shield of tears clouding her eyes.

"We covered this." He stared down at her, his face hard as granite. "I'm not your hero, Ness."

Before she could blink, he was out the door.

The clink of the lock set in place.

{ CHAPTER 12 }

It was what needed to be done.

He'd panicked, true. And this had been the first place he could think of where Ness would be free from harm. The last place anyone would look for her.

Above everything else, she needed to be safe.

Leaning forward, Talen pulled aside the curtain in the carriage and watched the retreating large, pale pink monstrosity of a building. A giant rectangle, pink stone. Even the outside of the place looked like it was trying to pretend everything was fine.

When it wasn't.

That had been clear the moment Ness had figured out where he'd brought her.

Her reaction? That wasn't fine. Not in the slightest.

And it had him staring at the building quickly shifting out of view.

Everything that he knew of Ness had just been flipped. She had inhuman ability to withstand the worst pain. She was strong. Or wanted to be. That she'd even admitted to wanting to be strong had taken courage he hadn't thought she possessed.

And he'd seen, day after day, what she was willing to do to make that happen—doing everything he asked of her.

Lift books to strengthen her muscles? He'd walked into her room several times a day, only to find her stretched out on the floor, doing that very thing.

Come directly at a blade instead of cowering from it? Again and again she'd lurched toward him, hitting his arm from the side before he could take a swing.

Smash every movable item in his office across his head? That…that she probably actually enjoyed.

All of it was against her nature, but she did it. Did it because she'd discovered a well of courage deep within. Did it because she refused to ever be a victim to her own inaction again.

Her fight against the two fops cornering her in the hallway at the Alabaster was testament to the fierce spirit within her that had been unleashed.

But there—in that retreating building, she wasn't fine. All of her courage had deserted her, turning her into a blubbering mess, begging on the floor.

The asylum slipped out of view and he let the curtain fall back into place.

Ness would be safe in the madhouse. Her arm would finish healing. No one would find her. It was the best place for her at the moment. The room had been simple, but private, far from the sounds of the other patients. And he'd paid handsomely to have her taken care of well, her every need more than met. He only needed a few days, a week at most, to find the men that had been looking for her and either turn them against her husband, or have them removed from England, or dispose of them, if that's what it took.

Above all else, Ness would be protected.

Still, four little words she'd uttered haunted him.

Not like my mother.

She'd said the words brutally, like she'd dredged them up from a raw, deep wound that she'd had to tear open. Tear open for him.

And the despair that had been in her eyes had pinpointed onto him, as though he was the one that had just inflicted some horrifying terror upon her.

He didn't care for it. He wasn't the one looking to own her, to kill her. He was the one wanting to keep her safe.

But the accusation had been there in her eyes. How could he do this when he knew full well he was the only person she trusted at the moment?

How could he do this—*of all things*—to her?

It didn't make any sense. He shook his head, the drama of her reaction worming far too fast into his head when he'd already made up his mind.

Stay the course.

It was just a room he'd put her in. A simple room where she would be taken care of. Warmth, food, drink. All of her basic needs met. Everything she had at the Alabaster, though not as opulent.

He'd even had his driver bring into the caretaker a crate of the books Ness had been reading. Strips of ribbons marking pages in a dozen books. She wouldn't be bored.

Sure, the adjoining rooms were full of the mad and insane, but she had to see that this was the safest place for her. Didn't she?

He closed his eyes and the instant image of her betrayed, tear-filled eyes engulfed his mind.

He held the image in his head for a long moment, then inhaled a deep breath, capturing it in his chest before it escaped in a long sigh.

His eyes opened and he shifted, banging on the top of the carriage.

"Bring it back around, Tom," he shouted, and the carriage instantly slowed.

"Right away, sir."

Talen sat back against the cushions as Tom went a stretch farther before he could turn the carriage about.

Dread filled his chest with every clomp of the horses' hooves on the gravel of the drive back to the asylum.

There was one other place he could take her.

He didn't want to do it. Shouldn't do it. Hell, it was idiotic to do so. But she'd be safe there.

Within minutes he was back at her door in the asylum, watching the caretaker turn the key in the lock. He pushed past the older woman as soon as the lock cleared and strode into the room.

Ness sat on the floor, unmoved from where he'd left her, now crumpled into a ball, her face hidden under her right arm, sobbing to herself.

She didn't even bother to look up at the sound of his footfalls by her head.

He dropped down to rest on his heels, his fingers dropping, drifting lightly into her hair along the side of her head.

She jerked into herself, then shifted her arm covering her face, peering up at him with visceral terror in her amber eyes.

She blinked hard, disbelieving it was him.

He held his open palm out to her right hand. "Come."

It took her three full breaths before she lifted her hand, her fingers shaking as she set them into his grasp.

What he was doing was stupid. But stupid had its place. And apparently, this was it.

{ CHAPTER 13 }

"This is your house?"

"Aye."

Ness looked up at the four-story townhouse as she stepped down from the carriage. Her fingers tightened around Talen's grip as she studied the building.

After riding in the carriage in silence for the last two hours, she couldn't be sure he wasn't just delivering her to another madhouse. A double-wide townhouse, the front façade was a deep red brick with bright white triangular pediments over the symmetrical windows. A deep blue double door centered the building. Impeccably neat and tidy in the twilight. Not even a stray leaf marred the wide marble steps leading up to the house.

"Head down." He reached out and tugged the hood forward along her face that had fallen backward as she gawked upward, then stepped away to talk to his driver.

The carriage rolled away as he stepped back to her side. "Let's go in."

She hadn't expected this. Hadn't expected this quiet street in the middle of London. What little she'd seen of the city was loud and dirty with squalor overwhelming. This was the opposite. A peaceful park centered the middle of the square with the sound of children laughing twinkling in the air.

She stole a glance at him as they stepped up to the house. "I thought you lived at the Alabaster."

"Why would you think that?"

"Why would I not? You were there all the time as far as I could deduce."

"Aye. I do spend far too much time at the Alabaster, and I do have a room there as well." He set his hand on the small of her back and ushered her through the entrance of the house, setting her in the middle of the foyer as he went back to the door.

The large entryway soared three stories upward along a gilded spiraling banister. Impressive. But something was off. It wasn't until she looked to her left that she realized it was the drawing room. The well-furnished but eerily cold drawing room. She studied it for a long moment then glanced over her shoulder at Talen. "No one uses the drawing room?"

"Why do you say that?" Talen turned around to her after locking the door.

"Everything is perfectly positioned within it. No books. No drinks on the sideboard, not even a water ring stain on the wood. Just the gleaming furniture with perfectly plump cushions that appear as though they've never been sat in."

His mouth quirked to the side. "Your eye for detail is interesting."

"Interesting how?"

"Interesting as in you're right. No one uses the drawing room. No one uses any of the rooms here. They are dusted and cleaned. That is all."

"What?"

He crooked his finger over his shoulder to her. "Follow me."

Talen walked along the main corridor that led into the depth of the townhouse, not waiting and not looking back at her.

With a quick hop, she hurried behind him. "But you just said this is your house."

"It is. That doesn't mean I use it."

He opened the rear door of the townhouse and stepped down onto wide marble steps that led to a picturesque courtyard. Hedges surrounded all sides and rows of flower beds held roses that had started to go dormant in the fall weather.

He shifted to the side, waiting for her to exit the house before closing and locking the door behind her.

He tucked the key into an inner pocket of his dark coat. "We should wait until darkness full descends, but dusk will have to do."

"Do for what?"

"We aren't staying here, Ness."

Her forehead wrinkled, fully flummoxed. "We aren't? Where are we going? I thought you sent your driver onward?"

"I did." His voice dropped to a whisper. "I need you to be quiet now. I'll answer your questions in a few minutes." He held his left elbow out to her. "In the meantime, take my arm and keep your head down.

Her lips pursed, she set her fingers along the crook of his elbow and they walked down the three steps to the garden, weaved past the rosebushes and exited out the rear wrought-iron gate to the mews.

Talen tugged her hood farther down over her brow, glanced to the right and left, and then started forward, straight through the coach house. After walking past stalls and carriages, they slipped out a back door onto the mews behind another row of townhouses. In silence, he ushered them to the left, walking along the shadows of the cobblestoned passage and crossing three streets before he turned to the right to lead her through another passage where he opened a tall metal gate at the rear of a townhouse.

Into the wide gardens—double the size of the gardens at the first house they'd walked through—he brought her up to the rear door and quickly set key into lock.

Ness only managed to keep her mouth shut until they were both inside and the door was firmly closed behind him. "Where are we?" She didn't care for the slight shake of fear in her voice, but couldn't quite control it.

"This is where I actually wanted to take you. The last house was the home everyone thinks I live at when I'm not at the Alabaster. Including my driver."

She pushed the hood off her head and peered down the dark hallway to her right. "But you don't live there?"

"No. I live here. No one knows this place exists."

Her look snapped to him. "No one knows of this place?"

He shook his head. "No one except for Declan. That's it."

Her jaw dropped, gaping for several seconds. "But why?"

In the dim light still eking into the hallway through a window beside the doorway, his icy blue eyes looked even chillier. "There are plenty of people that wish me dead, Ness. This is the only safe haven I have."

"What? Who wants you dead? Why?"

He moved past her, walking along the main corridor. "People I have destroyed. People that want revenge. And I have power. Other people want that. The world has never been any different." He shrugged as though that simple answer satisfied him.

It didn't satisfy her. "So, you own one home that you don't use, except to stroll through on the way to your real home? A home that's hidden because you cannot sleep peacefully when you're exposed?"

"Yes." He stopped in the front foyer, went to a side table and lit a lantern.

The flicker of the flame lit the area about her. The last home they had been in had been grand. But this was palatial, if the imperial staircase that cascaded down from the level above was any indication.

Her look fixed on the marble stairs as she shook her head. "It just seems like such a…"

"Waste?"

"Yes."

"It is." He moved to the right arm of the staircase and swept his hand upward to move her along. "But this place fell into my lap and I like having a place where no one knows me. Where no one wants anything from me."

Picking up the front of her skirts, Ness moved up the staircase in front of him. "What about neighbors?"

"The house to the left belongs to an earl that is never in town and there was a house being built on the other side, but the family ran out of money to finish it. They made it all the way to the full exterior, but have never been able to scrape the funding together to finish the interior and furnish it. Yet they refuse to give it up. Either way, this street is empty and it suits my needs perfectly."

She glanced back at him. "And how did this place 'fall into your lap'?"

"There was a duke with a son with a rather large debt run up at the Alabaster. The duke didn't have the resources to pay the debt, so I accepted the house as payment."

"And no one knows of it?"

"I used a solicitor that only serves…clients of a certain esteem."

"Wealthy ones?"

"Yes. He deals in secrets knowing that his life is forfeit if he spills said secrets. The man knows I received it from the duke for an undisclosed sum, but he doesn't know the business I am in. Declan knows. And now you know."

Ness paused at the landing at the top of the staircase. "But this townhouse, I can hear the echoes of my footsteps up the walls, it's monstrous. You must have staff here?"

"Just a maid that comes and cleans every week. She doesn't know who lives here. And a cook drops off salted beef, biscuits, and brandy in the kitchens twice a week. It's all I need here as I usually eat at the Alabaster."

He halted at the top of the stairs, his right foot atop the landing and his left foot on the last step. Even at that, he was still taller than her. "I didn't think about food. You'll probably need more than some tough meat and bread. And I can't have you soused all the time."

She glanced away from him, spying what looked to be a wide ballroom to her right. "So, this is where I am staying?"

"Yes. It's the only other place that I trust to be safe, Ness. No one knows of it, so no one would ever find you here. You could, quite frankly, grow old and die here, and someone would find your bones tucked into a bed a hundred years from now when the building is torn down."

She chuckled, unease in the sound. But as long as she wasn't locked in an insane asylum, she was grateful. "Please tell me that is not my fate. Please tell me there is another way." She exhaled a quivering breath. "Another way to be free of Gilroy. I can't live hidden away forever, Talen. I cannot."

His gaze locked onto hers, the rasp in his voice dropping to a low rumble, both calming and determined. "Once I find the men looking for you, we will figure out a path forward, I swear it."

She held his stare for a long moment, trying to judge the sincerity of it. Trying to not break under the weight of the fear that had crippled her bones for the past four years. She wanted to believe him. Wanted so much to believe Gilroy wouldn't find her—couldn't find her.

But what then? He would always send more. And this was no life. Hidden away in an empty, cavernous house.

She straightened her spine. Patience.

A path forward would reveal itself eventually, she just had to be patient. Patient and quiet and hidden away from everything and everyone.

A prison of a different sort, just not the terrifying one she'd existed in under Gilroy's thumb.

Her bottom lip jutting upward, she nodded.

{ Chapter 14 }

"Oh, you are up here." Surprise sent Ness's hand flying onto her bare chest above her chemise, the wide silk sleeve of Talen's dark blue banyan slipping far down her arm. He'd given it to her earlier in the night, promising to bring her more clothes from the Alabaster in the coming days.

His feet swinging down to the floor next to a lantern, Talen sat up from the long wooden chaise longue he'd been stretched out flat upon, his right forearm propped under his head. "How did you find your way up here?"

Ness looked from him to the roofs of the buildings surrounding them, lower than the top of Talen's house. Lights as far as the eye could see, glowing orange in the night. The city streets far below were busy at this time of night, though the stark noise of it didn't reach up to her ears, just the fat echoes of the many wheels and hooves on the cobblestones.

Her gaze shifted back to him. "I couldn't sleep. I tried, tried for hours, but then I heard sounds, sounds from above so I followed them. It took me a while to find the staircase next to that last room in the attic."

He pointed to a dark corner of the rooftop terrace. "You probably heard Cat."

"Cat?" She took a step closer to the corner he pointed to and saw a black tail twitch in the dark. A black cat with two white paws sat eating something from a bowl, paying her no mind. "You have a cat?"

He shrugged. "More of a visitor that visited often enough I finally began to feed it."

Her lips pulled to the side in a wry smile.

She hadn't figured him as an animal person. Especially not one that would take in a tiny cat. A lion. Maybe. Or a dragon. Definitely.

She turned around in the dark, surveying the rooftop oasis that sat atop his townhouse. Taller than all the surrounding buildings in every direction, the rooftop terrace held several benches, the chaise longue Talen sat on, chairs and a table. Vines grew from planters along the edges of the space, curling up onto the wrought iron railing that topped the half-wall surrounding the terrace.

"You really shouldn't be poking around other people's houses, Ness."

"You didn't lock my room, didn't tell me to stay in one place for a change, so I took advantage." She walked over to the edge of the rooftop, setting her right hand on the iron railing. The view stretched to street after street, full of busy coaches, all black and shiny with the finest dressed people within, rolling to and fro through the maze of the lanes below. Lights glowed in the many townhouses around them—a thousand flickers of flames that warmed the city, almost making it charming for the late hour. She'd heard that London was active during much different times than in Scotland, but had never been able to judge it according to the Alabaster. It was a gaming hell, after all.

Talen cleared his throat. "Then this is me telling you to stay in place. Your room. Up here. That is the extent of where you can go. I cannot afford anyone discovering you are here."

Without turning around to him, she offered him a slight nod.

"Promise me, Ness. Don't make me sink to locking you in your room again."

She looked over her shoulder at him. "But at the Alabaster you did that to lock others out, not me in."

"Yes. But I also wouldn't think twice about locking you in your room below for your own good. You know I will do it." The hard cut of his voice sliced into the night, making her cringe.

He would do it, she didn't have a doubt.

"I promise." She turned back to the street, leaning forward, her right arm long along the railing propping her up as she watched the carriages below. She would promise him anything at this point. He'd brought her here instead of leaving her in that madhouse. It was better than she could have hoped for.

"Thank you for not leaving me there." She said the words softly, letting them drift off into the night air of the city, not sure he even heard her.

"What did you mean at the asylum when you said, 'not like your mother'?"

Her mouth clamped shut as she stilled in place. The gratitude hadn't been an invitation for questions, but she should have been prepared for Talen to be curious. She'd acted like a madwoman when he'd left her there. Now he wanted to know why.

Her look trained on a woman in a glowing silver gown floating down the street at the arm of a gentleman. So simple. So light. A burn deep in her chest seared with envy. She would never be a woman like that. Light. Easy. Not a care in the world.

That sort of freedom was stolen from her long ago, so what did it matter now if she talked of her mother? Who was there to judge?

Her mouth opened, hanging agape for long seconds before she could form words. "My mother was the finest woman. A lady, through and through, the fourth daughter of a baron. She loved me so much. Loved my father." Her head shook, the darkness of the night sinking into her lungs.

"But?"

She turned around to look at him and leaned back against the railing. The black cat with two white paws had moved from the corner, curling in and out of his legs, though Talen's attention was solely on her. His forearms balanced on his thighs, he stroked its back, sending warbling purring that sounded more like a mouse squeaking into the night air.

"But my father tired of her. Tired of her by the time I was ten. To be honest, I don't know that he ever cared much for her. Not for how he treated her. Treated me. Still, it took him years to get rid of her."

"How did he do that?"

"When I was fourteen he wanted to have his mistress move into our estate in Cumberland, so he placed my mother in an insane asylum." Her right hand moved to clutch the front of his banyan higher over her bare chest to cut the chill invading her. "He committed her to the asylum and my mother wasn't mad. She was sad. Sad that her husband had no regard for her. But she was always sane. And once she realized she was in there for good, with no escape, she was even sadder."

"Could you visit her?"

"I was allowed to see her once a month and I lived for those days, for she would always brighten when she would see me. Sing me songs she used to sing to me when I was child. Like she could send time back to where I would crawl in her lap and she would sing to me. I think she thought I wouldn't notice the marks on her arms if she was singing. The marks set onto her arms by her own fingernails. The gaping wounds where she'd gouged out her own skin."

Even with the scant light from the lantern, she could see his eyes darken. "Yet she was sane?"

"Too sane. And it was more painful—harder—because she was. If she were mad…it would have been easier. But she wasn't." Her bottom lip pulled under her top teeth for a long moment as she choked back tears. "I would ask father to bring her home. Beg him. Beg him for hours on end. He would do nothing but laugh at me." Her hand curled onto the folds of the banyan at her chest, her knuckles near to popping. "Every time, he would laugh. Until he didn't."

"He stopped?"

"He did. That was the day he told me he'd found a new place for me to live. He was done with me. That I was to marry Gilroy. I didn't even know the man. But Gilroy had seen me at our estate, reading in the gazebo. Father said

Gilroy offered him a healthy sum for me, and he sold me. Sold me to him like a sack of grain."

"Did you not have a dowry?" His forefinger twirled around the cat's half-missing left ear.

"Why waste a dowry when he could get paid instead?" She unclenched her hand from the banyan, flattening her hand on the slope of her chest. "I fought him on it for a week, refusing to marry Gilroy. I had never stood up to him until that moment, and I paid for it. Paid for it with bloody lips and bruised cheeks until he finally gave me an ultimatum—my choices were marriage to Gilroy or marriage to a lecherous old marquess looking for his fourth wife, or exile, or the madhouse."

A shudder ran through her and she exhaled a long breath. "I chose Gilroy. So I was sent to Whetland Castle in Scotland with my maid. Married within a day. It was its own exile that I never saw coming."

"Why?"

"There were no women at Whetland. Only a few maids. A cold castle. An even colder man that was my husband."

His head shook and he looked down at the cat wrapped around his left leg, scuffing its chin against his calf. He scratched it behind the ears for a long moment before looking up at her. "Your mother, is she still in the hospital?"

Her mouth opened as she sucked in a hiccupped breath. She shook her head, her eyes closing, fighting the tears that threatened. No matter how many years had passed, the images in her mind stayed vibrant, as though they were happening in front of her in that very moment.

"I was allowed to visit her one more time before I left for Whetland and I was the one that found her, a sheet wrapped around her neck and tied to the railing of the bed. She looked so peaceful, like the sadness couldn't get to her anymore. It was all I wanted, month after month, to see her happy, at peace. But not like that."

A sob gargled up her throat as she buried her face in her right hand for a long moment. Her voice reclaimed, she looked at Talen. "Not like that. I don't know if she knew I was leaving her behind. She lived for those visits with me, and if she knew they were ending…"

Her right arm wrapped across her ribcage, her gaze going to the left, locking onto the greenery wrapping up the trellis in the corner. "They said she killed herself. I never believed it. She would hurt herself, bleed her arms, yes, but to kill herself? No. She believed in the sanctity of heaven and hell. She would never."

The same visceral rage from when she'd first heard those words spoken—that her mother had killed herself—surged in her gut. Surged to the point of almost exploding when she was always so good at tamping down the anger.

What the hell was happening with her? She excelled at controlling the rage. The pain. Holding back tears. But now, in the last few weeks, it was all she could do to hold onto the slightest remnants of sanity.

Sanity.

Tight control.

Always tight control, or she was two steps away from belonging in a madhouse herself.

She swatted away the tears that had escaped onto her cheeks and turned away from Talen, staring out at the rooftops. Gagging downward the spiked ball of rage stuck in her throat, she heaved a breath—it usually wasn't that painful, ripping at her throat like that.

Her look glazed over and she forced her voice to as neutral a tone as possible. "But then again, my mother wasn't insane when my father stuck her in that place. Maybe it did eventually drive her mad." Her shoulders lifted. "I don't know. I don't know anything."

"I'm sorry." Talen had stood and moved directly behind her, making her jump as his words drifted soft into the air about her right ear. "I didn't know. I never would have brought you there—much less left you there had I known." The odd rasp in his voice wrapped around her chest, making her heart constrict.

"There was no way you could have known."

"Except there was a way I could have known." He moved to her left side, setting his hand on the railing, his eyes searching her face. "I could have asked you questions. Could have listened to your answers. I could have known what happened to your mother and this whole day would have been avoided. But I've been avoiding asking you questions for days now, and that is my own failing."

"Your failing? No. That is ridiculous to put that upon yourself." She turned toward him, her eyebrows lifting. "But why have you not wanted to ask me questions?"

His lips pursed for a long moment, hedging his reply. Measured. He was always so measured around her it was no wonder she secretly celebrated breaking through his granite facade when he smiled or chuckled.

"I had originally thought that the less I knew of you, the better. You were a job Juliet sent to me." His mouth pulled into a tight line, fighting what he didn't want to say. "But then I did want to know more about you—every damn minute we've spent together has only stoked that thirst. But I knew full well I couldn't act upon it. Juliet sent you to me to protect. Nothing more."

"You've wanted more?"

"Honestly, I don't know what I want when I'm with you." His head shook slightly. "I want to know everything about you. I want to know nothing. Neither is a path I should take."

She froze, her eyes fixed onto his. "Why can't you want to know more?"

"You want the thousand reasons why not? You're an innocent. You're married. You think I'm someone that I'm not. Juliet explicitly told me to keep my hands to myself."

His right hand flipped up as his shoulder lifted. "I can't afford the complications in my life that come with someone like you. Yet Juliet set you in front of me."

His words stole the breath from her lungs. She was a burden. He'd been taking pity upon her. She'd known it from the start.

Except that wasn't all of it. Every one of the glances that she'd seen from him when he thought she wasn't looking. He'd stare at her, his jaw flexing back and forth. She'd thought he'd been working out how to get rid of her from the Alabaster.

But it hadn't been a detached scowl in his eyes. It'd been heat.

He'd been thinking about complications. About whether she'd be worth it.

Her voice shook. "Which means that you were considering those complications?"

He leaned forward, setting his cheek next to hers, his words a whisper in her ear, though there was no one there to overhear them. "I've thought about your lips under mine, yes. My hands dragging down your body. Tasting your skin. Pulling your skirts up and slipping into you and watching your face as I do, the innocence in your eyes turning into raw heat. I've thought about how your mewls would sound in my ears, your gasps for breath. I've thought about watching the pleasure roll through your face, pleasure like you've never felt before—never felt what your body can truly do, can truly be."

Her eyes closed, and her body swayed slightly, sending her leaning into him.

He didn't pull away, his breath still heating her cheek. "I've thought about it all, Ness. All of it. All of what it would mean. And it would mean too much. You can't handle what I want from you right now. And I can't do that to you."

He pulled up slightly and her eyes popped open, only to see the width of his chest taking up her world. Her gaze lifted, finding the scant moonlight reflecting in his light blue eyes. "You can't do it to me because?"

"Because I respect you."

"Are you saying you respect me like you do Juliet?" Her words were incredulous. No man had ever bothered to actually respect her. Certainly not her father. Certainly not Gilroy. "That we are friends?"

The slightest smile came to his lips and he bent down, farther this time, to where his lips were almost brushing her neck. "I have never wanted to do to Juliet what I want to do to you. But I do hold you in the highest esteem. Your spirit. Your courage. Your tolerance for pain." The rasp in his voice rough, his breath stayed hot on her skin. "So just turn away, Ness. Turn away and make this easier on both of us. I don't want you. Can't want you."

She stood as still as a statue for far too many thumps of her heartbeat, until she caught her breath and her forehead wrinkled. Her movements wooden, she shuffled a step away from him and turned to look down on the city, her right hand gripping the railing, the only thing keeping her upright. For a full minute, she'd begun to think he wanted her. Wanted her beyond the unwanted burden she was on him.

And she rather liked the idea of it.

But he didn't want her. Anything to do with her, really. Fine.

She was perfectly adept at making benign conversation.

Her forefinger flung out from the railing into the night air. "This house is so much taller than the rest in this area. Do you like it up here because you get to look down on everyone?"

He chuckled as he turned toward the street and set his forearms upon the railing. "No. I have several reasons. That is not one of them."

"Tell me one of them." She couldn't look at him, her stare firmly fixed on the cobblestones below.

"I kept this townhouse for its height—but it's not so I can look down on everyone, it's so no one can look down on me. No one can see me. I like to be anonymous, but I find that hard to come by with the business I am in."

"Reasonable. If I recall correctly, when I first arrived in London, I merely uttered the name Blackstone and people's eyes went wide. Everyone had heard of you. Feared you." She glanced at him. "I envy you this."

"What?"

"You know who you are, where you belong, who you can depend upon. I've never had that. Not since my mother was sent away. Since then, there hasn't been a place for me in this world. A true place for me. A place without fear. A place with simplicity."

"You can have that here, for as long as you need to."

"Thank you." Her mouth quirked to the side. "But I'm allowed my room. This terrace. That is it. This isn't simplicity, Talen. This isn't normal. None of it is."

"What if I brought Verity over? Aside from Declan she's the only other person I would trust with knowing this place exists."

"No—I don't want to jeopardize your anonymity here."

"I trust her." He shrugged. "She would never let it be known."

"You would do that?"

"If it would stop you from sulking about, then yes. It may even squeak a smile out of you."

She smiled at him, meeting his look. "Don't think me ungrateful, because I am. I'm grateful for everything you've done for me when I was nothing but a stranger dumped upon your doorstep."

"I wouldn't say dumped. Juliet is smart. She would never dump anyone."

"She is that. Regardless, you took me on when you had no reason to. You're more of a hero than you give yourself credit for."

"Ness—"

"So tell me another reason you like it up here." She pointed outward into the night air as she cut him off, knowing what he was going to say. He wasn't her hero. That was his opinion. Her opinion, she was beginning to suspect, was very different.

"Another reason?" He turned toward her, leaving his left arm draped across the railing, and pointed upward. "The stars. Up here on clear nights, I'm above the lights so I can make out the stars."

She glanced upward. The sky was clear and the stars were shining brightly. That's what he'd been doing lying on the chaise longue when she'd stumbled upon him. "You like the stars?"

"I do."

"Why?"

"From my years at sea. I learned to navigate by them, though I wasn't very good at it. Declan was always better. But truly, I always liked the mystery of the stars more than

the practicality of them—fixed stones in the sky, marking the way, yet always moving. Always moving." He looked up, his eyes shifting across the night sky. "Look at that one."

She followed to where his finger pointed, turning her back toward him to do so. "Which one?"

"Actually, look at those three—the three in a tight line, together. That is Orion's belt. He just made it into the sky here in London."

"Orion?"

"Do you know mythology?"

She shook her head as her neck craned her face to the sky.

"Orion was a great huntsman that Zeus placed into the stars as a constellation after a scorpion stung and killed him. The scorpion constellation—Scorpius—will never be in the sky at the same time, as they chase each other around the world." Over her shoulder, his pointer finger shifted up and down. "See how those three stars make a belt? His head is up there. And coming off the belt are three stars that are his sword. On either side are his legs. One arm is held high, the other holding an animal hide. On that side, Taurus the bull is snorting, charging him. Those two have always been my favorite."

She chuckled. "I don't think I'm seeing what you're seeing."

"Come over here." He set his hand on the small of her back and ushered her to the wide wooden chaise longue. "Lie down."

Her eyebrows cocked at him.

"Trust me. It's easier here."

She sat, then stretched her legs long onto the chaise. Talen squeezed in next to her, careful to not bump her left forearm and the splint, and then slid his arm under her head for a pillow as they both reclined flat on the bench.

Far too intimate, yet she couldn't excuse herself. She had barely two slips of cloth on her skin and he was so warm in the chilly air. And smelled too good, something that always unsettled her, how she so liked the scent of him. How it made her chest tighten every time she was near him.

His body next to her a rock of strength, the whole of him a haven. A solid, begrudgingly accommodating haven from the pain and the turmoil her life had become. She didn't want to leave it. Leave him.

"Now look." His left arm went up toward the sky, his forefinger wagging towards a clump of stars. "There is a V-shaped star cluster, that's the bull's snorting snout. You follow those to the left and those are his horns, ready to impale."

"That is a snorting snout?"

"If you use your imagination, it is." The cat jumped up onto the chaise and picked its way to a spot in between Talen's calves. He let it paw at his trousers for a moment as it nestled in, then continued. "We have a cat and Orion has a dog, Sirius, there, the brightest star in the sky. And here is a nice trick—from that star on the belt through his arm you can draw a line to the south."

"These stars guided you on the sea?"

"Aye."

"You've seen faraway lands, haven't you?"

"I have."

"I wish you could remember the time before the ship."

He stiffened, his bicep clenching under the back of her head. "Does it even matter, Ness?"

"No. No, I guess it does not. We are where we are." Her right hand flicked up toward the sky. "What other tales are up there in the sky?"

"Too many to count. I spent years listening to grizzled old sailors speaking of the stars."

She pointed upward in the sky to a bright star. "What's there?"

"You just found the north star in the little bear, a tale of its own."

The odd rasp in his voice suited the air about them, nothing but the dark and the stars above them. Low and gravelly, and lulling her to sleep with tales of bears that saved Zeus from his father.

Sleep with only one thought on her mind.

She'd never felt safer.

{ CHAPTER 15 }

Ness nudged open the door of Talen's study slowly, letting the door creak on its hinges as she peered into the room. Two large windows at the back of the chamber lent moonlight to the space. This floor was off limits to her. But this was necessary and she would be quick.

Seven days of wandering between her room and the rooftop terrace and Ness was near to going out of her skin. For as much as Gilroy held her in a tight cage at Whetland Castle, she'd been free to walk the grounds, and she'd had her maid, Gertie, to talk with.

Verity was sweet, ever attentive, and Ness was happy for her company, but the hours when Talen was not at the townhouse stretched long, and she could only read for so long, day after day.

So it had been a fine idea to go searching for a quill and an inkwell. She'd found paper in the secretary in her room, but nothing to write with. If she could jot a letter to Juliet—whether or not Talen would actually allow her to post it, it would ease all of the madcap thoughts running about in a circle in her brain.

What she should do next. How she could ever find a life away from Gilroy. Her attraction to Talen and everything he was—though she fought against it every day.

He didn't want her. He'd made that clear. Insisted she turn away.

Yet he would still arrive at the townhouse deep into every night after the business of the Alabaster was done, bringing her something—a dessert, a new book, a map of the stars. They would train. Then eat. Then sit on the terrace looking at the stars until the first rays of dawn streaked into the sky. He lived his life opposite the sun, and she'd flipped her own schedule so that she could spend as much time as possible with him.

Something she should cease, if she was smart.

But she was quickly deducing that when it came to Talen, she wasn't thinking straight.

She needed to tell all of this to someone, and Juliet was her only option, whether or not the letter was actually sent.

Ness stepped into the study, quickly spying an inkwell at the top left corner of the desk. Perfect. Now she just needed a quill.

No quills were next to the inkwell so she rounded the desk, quickly pulling open the set of drawers on the left side. Papers, a letter opener, but no quills. Onto the middle drawer. Three were lined up neatly with sharp nibs ready for writing. She pulled two free and her eye caught the red wax of a broken seal on a letter in the drawer.

She paused. A seal she knew. The distinctive north tower of a castle with garland curling up the sides. The Whetland Castle seal.

Her eyebrows drawing together, she fingered the edge of the paper. Juliet had said she would send a letter posthaste after Ness left Edinburgh, but she wouldn't have had access to the Whetland seal—they had brought nothing

with them to the city besides the clothes on their backs and
the coins in the heels of Juliet's boots.

Juliet must be back at the castle.

Good.

Relief flooded Ness. She had been in fear that she'd
destroyed everything between Juliet and her brother-in-law,
Evander, with how they'd escaped from the estate.

Ness set the quill down and picked up the tightly
folded letter. Talen hadn't said anything about a letter from
Juliet, aside from mentioning the first letter he'd received
from her a day after Ness had arrived at the Alabaster. She
flipped it over and saw her name on the outer swatch of
paper.

Her name. Not Talen's. Her letter. Not his.

Her hands shaking, she unfolded the letter, quickly
scanning the contents.

Then scanned them again.

Then sank onto the chair behind the desk, studying
each word in Juliet's elegant script.

…Gilroy is dead…

…Come back to Whetland…

*…Evan has written to your father of Gilroy's death and he
travelled here to collect you…*

*… I told them you were visiting a friend in London. For
appearances sake, it would do well for you to travel up here if
you are feeling well enough…*

She stared at the letter, frozen in place for far too long.
Hours. Hours she sat with the letter in her lap, rereading
the words over and over.

Gilroy was dead. Dead. She was free.

She stayed frozen in place, staring at those words, her mind not able to move past that one line. *Gilroy was dead.*

Frozen, until she heard the rear door open and close on the floor below her. Talen's heavy footsteps walking along the main corridor below. Up the stairs, passing by the first floor and continuing upward.

The echo of his footsteps a level above, steady, then quickening, disappearing higher to where she could no longer hear them.

It wasn't a full minute before they thundered down the stairs, the pace of them frantic as they moved from room to room above her.

Out back to the stairs. Down to the drawing room. The ballroom. The dining room. The respite room.

And still she couldn't move.

The door to the study swung open with a thud and the footsteps stopped.

His breath heaving, Talen found her sitting behind his desk in the moonlight, instant fury on his face, his words thundering. "What in the hell are you thinking, Ness? I couldn't find you—couldn't find you and you were in here. Sitting in here the whole damn time?"

"Don't yell at me." She didn't look up at him as her words came out measured and wooden against his anger.

He stormed into the room, his arm swinging in the air. "Your room. The terrace. That was the agreement. You promised."

"Yes, well, I needed ink and a quill. I waited until twilight. Didn't even light a candle. Then I snuck down here like a good little mouse that would never be found."

"Why are you talking like that?" He took two more steps forward. "Look at me, Ness. Look at me."

Her eyes slowly lifted to him. "How long have you had it?"

"Had what?"

She lifted the letter from her lap, dropping it onto the desk.

"Shit."

Her eyes closed as she drew in a deep breath, then she stood, her knuckles landing on the desk as she leaned toward him, a bitter edge she couldn't control lacing her rising voice. "How long have you had it?"

He exhaled, straightening his spine as he glared at her. "Days. But that's no reason to sca—"

"No reason to what? To scare you? I have been terrified of my husband finding me for almost a month—terrified. Every single day. Every hour. Terrified. And you knew this?" Her hand slammed down onto the letter. "You've known this for days? Days and you haven't told me."

"You don't understand, Ness."

"What don't I understand? That Juliet sent me a letter that you deemed you should open before me? That you deemed should be hidden from me? I trusted you, Talen. Trusted you when I had no reason to. I trusted you and this is what you do to me? What else are you keeping from me? I could have left days ago, but you've kept me here in a prison of your own design."

Her right hand flew through the air. "Buy me off with a few books and treats and stars and I'll just stay here, no questions asked?"

His left hand curled into a fist at his side. "You don't understand."

"What don't I understand?"

"The men are still out there. The ones looking for you." The words barked from his mouth, the ire in his voice palpable. "They're still searching for you. We found one of them but not the other three. You think they got a letter from Juliet? You think someone told them Gilroy was dead and they wouldn't get paid even if they managed to find you and bring you back to Whetland? They're still after you, Ness. You're still not safe."

"But why not tell me?"

His voice notched louder. "You want me to talk about the danger you're in? Talk about what men like this will do to you if they find you? They find you, they bring you back to Whetland, and I promise you that journey will not be pleasant for you. Men like this will abuse you to no end. You are nothing more than flesh to toy with as long as they have you in their possession."

He moved around the desk and captured her face in his hands, his ice blue eyes intense in the shards of moonlight. "Is that what you wanted to hear? For me to add more fear into your eyes? There is already so much that haunts you why would I ever want to add more to it?"

All her anger deflated from her chest as her right hand lifted, gripping his wrist. "But if I had known Gilroy was dead…"

"What?" His fingers tightened along her cheeks.

"That would have been something, Talen. Something to hold onto." She blinked hard, her head shaking against his hold on her face. "But what happens to those men once you find them? What's to stop them?"

His hands dropped away from her face. "With Gilroy's death, there will be no payout so they'll drop the matter if they know what's good for them."

"And if they don't?"

He took a step backward, setting space between them. "They will be dealt with."

She swallowed back the sick lump forming in her throat. "The last thing I want is blood on my hands."

"It's not on your hands, Ness. It's on mine. And I don't mind blood."

"But—"

"Correction." His right hand lifted and he set his palm along her neck. "I mind your blood. I mind your blood spilling. I mind it a lot. Would you rather be accosted?"

"No."

"I'd rather it not as well, so let me handle this, Ness."

"All part of keeping me safe?" The tightness in her chest didn't ease. She hated this. Hated all of it.

"I promised I would, and I intend to keep that promise." His hand dropped away from her neck and he moved toward the door. "Get into your room and don't leave it until I'm back."

"Where are you going?"

"To take care of it. The less you know, the better."

"But, wait, don't leave yet." Her hand flew up to stop him as her mind started working again.

His fingers twitched, anxious to be gone. "I have to Ness. This has gone on long enough. The one man we have isn't talking and that's about to change."

"But my father." Her gut suddenly sank, her fingers going to her mouth as new terror seized her. "Oh, no—my father—"

He shook his head, turning away from her. "I don't have time for your father right now, Ness. I need to find out if Declan is any closer to learning the location of the other men."

Talen was gone in the next instant, his footsteps retreating quickly downward in the house until they disappeared out the rear door.

Her hands quivering, Ness sank into the chair behind the desk.

Her father.

Her fingers reached out, shaking so badly she couldn't hold the letter from Juliet, so she let it fall to the desk, her stare on the ink, rereading Juliet's words. Again and again and again.

Her father had already shown up to claim her.

Her father.

She hadn't thought past the fact that Talen had kept this letter from her. Hadn't thought past Gilroy's death. Hadn't thought past her fury.

But hell and damnation.

Her father.

She curled her right fist into her belly, trying to stop the tremble in her hand, trying to quell the bile quickly turning over in her stomach.

Her father.

She'd been afraid of Gilroy, but with him dead, that meant she'd be shuffled back under the reign of her father.

No. No. No.

Her gut roiled, ice freezing her veins.

This wasn't freedom—this was a completely different prison she was destined for.

For her father terrified her more than anything else.

More than Gilroy ever had.

{ CHAPTER 16 }

The bloody docks.

The damn bloody docks.

Talen jumped out of the hack before it even started to slow, running toward the pier where Ness had been spotted.

He prayed it was her. It had to be.

How many dark-haired, broken-armed, innocent waifs travelled in this area at night?

None.

His feet thundering through the muck covering the cobblestone street, he slowed with heaving breath as he passed the last warehouse and could see the pier with several ships docked.

Swinging lanterns dotted the darkness. Men busy loading the last of goods onto two ships ready to depart with the tide.

His heart pounding, he rushed into the bustling crowd, searching faces, searching for someone short, probably with the dark hood of a cloak covering her face. That was if she knew what was good for her.

If she knew what was good for her? Laughable. If she was down here, she didn't have the first clue what was good for her.

There.

Straight ahead by the closest gangplank. A tiny figure faced away from him in the middle of three men looming over her.

Shit.

His arms flying, shoving men out of his way, Talen tore along the fat wooden boards of the pier.

Before the three men saw him coming, he reached past the closest man and grabbed the arm of the small figure, yanking her body toward him.

The hood of the cloak fell from her face and Ness's startled eyes found him.

"Talen?"

The first real breath he'd had since returning to his townhouse only to find Ness had disappeared sank down into his lungs. He'd just tortured a man to within a hair of his life and all he'd wanted was to see Ness. To let her smiling face when she saw him wipe free the echoes of the man's cries from his mind.

But she was gone.

With another seething inhale, he stepped in front of the man to the side of her, creating a wall.

"What the blazes, ye scalawag?" The man to Ness's right grabbed his arm, ripping away his grip on Ness. "This little piece is joining our ship."

Talen's foot instantly swung out, kicking out the knee of the man and sending him hobbling, holding his leg, howling at Talen. "Ye bloody maggot."

Talen set his glare on the man between Ness and the gangplank. "Don't touch her." He looked down at the top of her head. "Ness, don't even think to encourage what they're trying to sell you."

"Who do ye think ye are?" The man behind him shoved him in the middle of his back and Talen stumbled a step forward, falling into Ness but managing to grab her about the waist and keep both of their balances.

Talen spun around, fury spiking on his face.

The man met his eyes and his look went wide, his mouth gaping like a fish for a full second. "Ah, so sorry, Mr. Blackstone. I didn't see that it was ye. Pardon our enthusiasm for the young lady's…business. She thought to join our voyage to Caribbean waters."

"She did?" He glanced at Ness, his rage directed fully at her after reaching a boiling point in his limbs. He needed to crush something. Anything. He looked back to the man, leveling his voice. "The islands, you say?"

"Aye. Then onto America. We'll be out with the tide in the hour. The lass be lucky to catch it with us, for how much she said she needed to leave."

Talen jabbed a step forward to the right, grabbing the man's arm and twisting it behind his back, sending him doubling over. He leaned over the man, his words violent. "She isn't going with you and I will forgive this incident on one condition."

The man flailed for a second, trying to escape Talen's hold on his arm to no avail. "Anything. Anything, sir."

"You never saw me. You never saw her." He yanked the man's hand higher up his back. "Understand?"

He howled in pain. "Aye. Yes, yes, yes."

Talen looked up at the other two men. "That goes for all of you. Understood?"

Both men nodded, their hands lifting, waving in surrender.

Talen shoved the man away, making the man stumble onto his knees.

His left arm swung out and he wrapped it around Ness's shoulders, the grip on her upper left arm harsh and probably jostling the broken part of her forearm out of place. Not that he could help himself. Not when what he really wanted to do was throttle her.

Half picking her up, he stormed his way through the men scurrying about the pier moving barrels and crates onto ships, and then up through the streets.

The hack he'd jumped from still sat on the street and he dragged her toward it. Without even looking at the driver he flung the door open and tossed her into the interior— there was no other word for it and for the life of him he couldn't find gentleness at the moment.

She landed in a heap, quickly trying to right herself on the bench.

He tossed a couple coins up at the driver, told him the address and jumped into the decrepit old coach, slamming the door shut behind him.

"Talen—"

"Don't." The one word was a bark, a command that vibrated the air around them. "Don't speak another word."

The one horse moved forth and the wheels of the coach started to roll.

He heaved breath after breath. Staring at her. Staring at her staring at the floor by his feet.

What the deuce had she been thinking? Did she think? Think at all?

Leaving the townhouse. No note. Nothing. Just gone.

A ghost that never was.

Blasted woman.

The silence sat so thick in the cab of the coach that she opened her mouth several times, sneaking a glance at him. Each time he shook his head slightly, his lip snarling.

She shut her mouth, time and again, her look skittering back to the floor.

A street away from his townhouse, he banged on the roof of the cab and the driver pulled the horse to a stop.

He jumped out of the carriage and didn't pull the steps, instead grabbing Ness around the waist the second she'd half-stood from the bench, and he pulled her free of the coach.

Dropping her onto the ground, he gripped her upper right arm, a tight clamp that wasn't about to let her escape, then pulled her along the streets, her feet not able to keep up with his long strides.

"Tal—"

"Not a word."

"But."

"Not. A. Word."

She stumbled, but he paid no heed, dragging her through the mews and into the back of his townhouse. He didn't release her until he had her upstairs and in her room where he spun her away from him at the doorway.

He needed to leave the room.

Leave her.

He didn't trust himself to be with her at the moment.

She left him.

Left him without a damn word.

He took a step backward, turning away from her as he fished into his inner right pocket for the key to her room.

"Talen."

Her voice stopped him.

Small and pitiful and tinged with fear. It was the fear that stopped him.

Fear of him?

"What in the almighty hell were you thinking?" He turned halfway back toward her, every word punctuated with rage. "Why would you leave like that? To the docks of all places? You damn well disappeared without a bloody word."

She took a step backward, her hands lifting to him, even though her left hand was awkward with the bandaging on the splint wrapped up and around her palm. "Talen, stop. I cannot stay. But I didn't…didn't want to leave. Leave here. Leave you."

"But. You. Did."

Her right hand flew high beside her head, her words in a frenzy. "I panicked—I am weak and I panicked. But it was all I could think to do. Run. Terror-stricken. I had to run fast, get out—leave London. Don't you see? There is no other choice, not now. I have to leave England and the docks were the only place to do that. I had to leave now, tonight. I still do. I have to get back to the docks before the tide. I have to. You have to let me go."

"You're not going anywhere near the damn docks." His words seethed, vicious. He turned away from her, looking out the open door, sucking in a breath. A modicum of control over his voice returned and his head swiveled back to her. "By Zeus's tooth, why in the hell do you think you need to leave England?"

Her head shook, her eyes wide to him. "You don't understand what's coming for me, Talen."

"Gilroy is dead." All control lost again, his words shook the air.

"But my father is not." Her foot stomped into the carpet as she shouted, matching his anger. "My father is very much alive and four years ago he made me choose between a lecherous old marquess and Gilroy, and the only grace of it was that I was able to choose the lessor of the two evils. I won't get another chance to escape. Not once he has me again. I guarantee you he is coming for me and is about to sell me off again. He wouldn't have travelled to Whetland Castle to collect me if that wasn't the case. That's what Juliet's note said—he came for me—he couldn't have come to collect me any quicker."

"You don't know that. You don't know what he wanted." He snapped the words, even though the manic fear in her eyes should have curbed his volume. But at least her fear wasn't at him.

"I do. My father never cared for me one way or another, where I was, what I was doing, save for the time that he wanted to make coin from selling my body off. I was sold like a whore, nothing more."

He tried to level his voice. "So what were you thinking you would do?"

"Leave. Leave England as soon as I possibly could. Leave before you could stop me. Get on a ship and leave."

"And then what? What was the plan?"

Her palm flew up. "I don't know. I was working on that part. It would have depended upon where the ship landed in port. If it was in a big city, I could look for work as a governess. I could take in sewing. I don't exactly know, but I was working on it. But I needed to disappear first."

He took a step toward her, yelling, his fist punching into the air at his side. "You were already disappeared, Ness. No one knew you were here. Beyond Verity, Declan and me, you are nothing but a ghost. No—you were nothing but a ghost—no one could find you, not even your father. But now…"

His words cut off, his fist unfurling and curling again and again.

"Now what?" Her hand went flat onto her belly, her face paling.

He expelled a sigh, his fingers running through his hair. "Now everyone knows of you—do you have any idea how many people I had looking for you?"

"You…you sent people to find me?"

"Too many to count. In every street and alley. And one of my men spotted you by the docks. Everyone knows you're connected to me now."

She swayed slightly. Her fingers pushed into the dark blue muslin on her gut, looking to hold back a retch, her breath speeding. "So that means my father will find me."

He nodded, his look grave. "It won't be hard."

"I am sorry I panicked." Her head started to shake. "But you didn't need to find me. You could have just let me go…disappear. Why didn't you just let me go? You told me to just turn away—I've been nothing but a burden to you."

His eyes closed for an elongated breath as he attempted once more to temper the anger still speeding through his veins. "I swore I would protect you, Ness, and the last thing I was about to do was leave you to whatever fate it was that tore you out of this house. I didn't know how you left here—I thought you were taken. I never imagined it was your hare-brained idea to leave on your own volition."

Her head dropped, her gaze fixed on the floor for a long moment. "I didn't want to leave you, Talen. And not just because you keep me safe. I didn't want to leave here… you." Her chest lifted in a deep sigh as her gaze moved up to him. "But now. Now I truly do have to disappear. My father will find me and I cannot live with being sold to another brutal man. I refuse it."

The way she stated her refusal—such finality in her voice—made him pause, wondering how very far she would go to avoid a repeat of her fate under her father's control.

"We'll figure out another way." He took a step toward her. "One that doesn't have you sailing off to a distant land with a hundred people on a ship that could identify you if your father got even a sniff of where you went. One that doesn't have you taking in laundry in a strange country."

Her eyes closed. "But there is no other way."

"There is one that will cut your father off at the knees."

Her eyes cracked open to him. "What?"

"You could marry."

"Marry?" Her voice pitched high. "I just rid myself of one brutal husband and I don't intend to ever take that path again." Her head shook. "You're mad to even suggest it."

"Am I? If you're married your father cannot touch you."

Her head tilted to the side, barely restrained panic taking a hold of her voice. "Talen, no. I cannot. I cannot marry—I can never be under another man's fist again."

"But I can think of several men that are kind and wealthy enough and would never hurt you."

She stumbled several steps backward, her hand waving in front of her. "No. Don't even suggest it. I will never be able to trust a man again. Never enough to marry."

"Or…"

"Or what?"

"Or you marry one you already trust."

Shaking her head, her forehead wrinkled. Then her eyes suddenly went wide, her stare locking onto him. "No… no…"

"You trust me, don't you?"

She gaped at him, frozen.

"Do you trust me?"

Reluctance vibrated in her amber eyes, but she wasn't about to lie to him, he knew that of her. She nodded.

"Then marry me, Ness. Marry me. I can keep you safe."

"But…"

"We marry. We marry before your father finds you and he cannot touch you."

Words he never could have imagined uttering a month ago flew from his mouth. He wasn't looking for a wife—couldn't even fathom the thought of one—but his jaw still prattled on, trying to convince this one maddening woman that she should marry him for her own good. "Even better, we marry in Scotland, and should it suit you, you can always exit the marriage well after he is dead and cannot hurt you."

Her hand flew up between them. "No. No, you cannot possibly think…"

"Do you have a better suggestion?

"No—I—"

"Your father threw your mother into a madhouse, Ness. What do you think he'll do to you if you don't listen to him?"

Her lips drew inward, her eyebrows pulling tightly together.

"Exactly. Let me protect you from this. Let me do this. You say you once knew me. You say the sun revolved around me when we were children. Yet I was awful to you. Let this be my amends. Let me give you this. Protection."

Her eyes closed for a long moment, her fingers rubbing her forehead, and she looked to be drawing upon a well of patience. But there was the slightest crack in her facade. She was considering it.

And hell, he wanted her to consider it. Wanted her to say yes. He'd never even contemplated it, but suddenly, poised in front of him, the thought of marrying Ness was maddeningly attractive.

He wanted her.

Wanted her for a wife as long as she would have him.

Her amber eyes opened to him. "Sneaking toads into my slippers does not require a marriage proposal, Talen. You don't even remember me from that time."

"But you remember me, and I trust you."

"You do?" Her right eyebrow arched.

"Aye."

"Why?"

"Frankly, you have no reason to lie on the matter. You never did. I was going to protect you no matter what because Juliet asked me to. It was that simple." He shrugged. "And the fact that you bring absolutely nothing to the marriage should assuage you of any apprehension you have on my motives."

A breathless chuckle left her lips. "I bring nothing?"

His chin jutted out, nodding to her. "You bring you."

"But that, that is nothing."

He took a step toward her, so close now he could feel the panic and fear and hope vibrating off of her.

He needed her to choose the hope.

His hand lifted to drag his knuckles along her cheekbone. "I'd say that is everything. And I would never demand anything from you. Nothing that you didn't want to give me."

Her breath caught in an audible hiccup. She stared at him for long seconds, scrutinizing him. Scrutinizing his intentions.

He held her gaze, not flinching under her assessment.

"But this isn't fair to you." One last futile argument against what she was being swept into. Admirable.

"Does it matter? You'll live life on your terms, away from your father's clutches."

Her right hand lifted, her fingers settling on his chest. "It matters. It does. What you want matters. What if you meet a woman you truly want as your wife?"

"I want you, Ness. I didn't imagine this when you first appeared at the Alabaster. I didn't imagine it in the first, the second week. But I came back here and you were gone."

He paused, his look going to the ceiling as his head shook. "I was going to tear London apart to find you."

"You were?"

His gaze dropped to her, his stare piercing. "I was."

Her lips closed tightly as she stared at him. Stared at him for the longest moment, disbelief lacing her eyes. But then a flicker. Heat lighting to flame in the amber of her eyes. Fire that made him want her all the more.

Her full lips finally parted. "What if I want you, as well?"

{ Chapter 17 }

The words had barely left her mouth and he was on her, his lips finding hers, his hands wrapping around her ribcage, her back, pulling her into him.

Not tentative, his fierce intensity enveloped her, heat and lust descending from him, parting her lips, consuming her every nerve. The whole of the onslaught creating an insistent, pounding thunder in the core of her.

This was what it felt like.

To truly want someone, deep in the depths of her soul. She'd never experienced this raw, brutal yearning that was consuming her from the inside out.

Except in her dreams.

Dreams she'd had one too many times in the past weeks. Talen's body over her. His skin on hers. His tongue dragging along her shoulder. For all the thoughts she'd refused to allow to worm into her mind when she was awake, in her sleep his naked body was painfully vibrant. How he would cup her breasts, set his mouth to taste the crux of her neck, crush her body into him. Too many times she'd woken in a thin sheen of sweat, panting, her body aching for his touch.

Dreams she would force out of her mind the second her eyes opened.

Unrequited lust was not going to help her move on with her life.

But now this.

She wanted him, and it was the first time she'd let herself think that thought while fully conscious. The first time she could acknowledge it.

She wanted Talen.

She wanted him, wanted everything about him on her, in her, making her feel the exact opposite of everything that had swamped her soul these past weeks. Despair. Fear. Anger. All of that bounded up and discarded by the carnal craving ripping through her body.

His tongue explored her mouth, demanding everything he could reach, his breath hot on her skin. The scent of him sent her head light, spice and evergreen and smoke and something she couldn't quite identify, could only classify it as man—as Talen.

The kiss wasn't enough. She wanted—needed—more.

Her tongue warring with his, her hands lifted up along his chest, sliding under his coat and pushing it off of his shoulders. She popped buttons on his waistcoat free. Not fast enough, for all she wanted was to touch his skin, slide her palms against the smooth expanse of his back, his arms.

She tugged upward on his lawn shirt, pulling her mouth away from his to rip it over his head.

His shirt on the floor, he paused as he looked down at her, his crystal blue eyes cutting directly to her soul.

Everything she wanted from him, he wanted from her tenfold. All of it pulsated in his eyes. Harder, faster—he wanted to ravage her head to toe.

Her breath caught at his stare, instant panic that she wasn't enough for him spiking through her chest.

Panic he didn't give air to breathe, for his lips captured hers again, the kiss battering any misgivings into oblivion.

Her head spinning, she grasped onto him, her nails raking his back as she fought to stay upright.

He pulled up slightly, his eyes searching her face, a grin playing at the corners of his mouth. A grin that belied the desperate heat in his voice. "You don't owe me anything, Ness. We can stop anytime."

In that moment, she realized her dress and chemise had slipped down about her waist, her stays long since dropped to the floor. Her back was arched toward him, her right breast fully encapsulated by his hand, his fingers rolling her nipple into taut submission.

A sorcerer.

When had he even managed all of that? She'd been so focused on him—on touching his body—she hadn't even considered her own until that second.

And now that she did—blast—the sweet agony shooting through her body from her nipple sent a thirst she couldn't control into her throat.

He was waiting for an answer, his mouth not moving back down to her, and for the life of her, she couldn't form words, the thirst holding her tongue hostage.

She could only nod as she reached up and wrapped her right hand around his neck, yanking his head downward, first to her mouth, then he drifted lower, devouring every speck of her skin from her mouth to her left nipple. Pulling, sucking, rocking the nub back and forth between his teeth. A fine line between pain and pleasure, and he walked it with

aplomb, never letting the pain last long enough to really hurt, the pleasure sending guttural moans into her throat.

Awkward as it was with the bottom half of her left hand wrapped with the splint bandages, her hands went to work on his trousers, clearing the buttons of the fall front and shoving the black fabric down his legs, her hands skimming across the hair along his thighs, the muscles underneath tensing at her touch.

His head at her breast, she couldn't see downward. So she moved her right hand inward, brushing along his shaft. Brushing again until she could grab a hold of him, dragging her fingers along the smooth span of his member. Heaven help her, there was no way they would fit together. Not with the girth. The length.

"Damn, Ness." A guttural rumble vibrated his tongue as he swirled it about her breast and his hands ran down to her thighs, sending shivers along her skin in the wake.

Her dress was gone. Her chemise as well. She needed to pay more attention to the clothes stripping off her body.

Talen kicked his way out of his boots and trousers and then set his hands under her backside. His fingers clenched into her skin as he picked her up and she wrapped her legs around him.

His cock suddenly long and hard along the crux of her made the insistent throbbing in her folds spike. His hips grinded, teasing his length against her, and her breath lodged in her chest.

With a crushing kiss, he barged four steps forward and her back hit the wall through the long drapes alongside the window. Velvet dragged along her back, cushioning her from the hard plane of the wall.

He pulled away, yet his teeth stayed attached to her bottom lip, nipping, tugging. Talen liked to skirt to the edge of pain and she wondered just how much he liked it.

The second his bite let her free, she returned in kind, raking his lower lip between her teeth. Too hard. The metallic taste of blood touched her mouth—not her own. It only sent a growl ripping through him and he attacked her neck with a fury, dancing to that edge of pain again.

So much energy swirling within her from a thousand directions. His mouth. His hands. His cock pressing along her folds.

"Forward?" His voice raw, the one-word question rumbled into her neck.

"Yes." The word came out weak, already wearied. "Yes." She repeated, full force, almost a scream as his fingers twisted her right nipple, sending shockwaves down to her core. If she was going into this, she was going into it with genuine intention.

He exhaled like a tiny death had embraced him, pausing for a moment, his breath on her neck, his muscles twinging before he moved again.

Holding her up against the wall with his left hand under her, Talen angled his hips slightly away, grabbing his shaft and positioning it at her entrance, ready to plunge.

She tilted her head back, her eyes closing with a grimace, bracing herself.

He stopped, the whole of him frozen in motion. "What are you doing?"

His words cut through the haze muddling her mind and she dropped her chin and opened her eyes to him. "What?"

"The grimace on your face that just traveled through your entire body."

Her eyes dipped down between them. She'd meant to hide it. "This part hurts."

"Hurts? Hell, Ness." He reached up with his right hand, lifting her chin so she looked at him. "It hurts?" His eyes searched her face.

She nodded, sudden heat flaming her cheeks. "It always does." Her fingernails clawed into his back. "I don't care, I want you. Want you inside of me. Even with the pain."

With a shake of his head, his hands dropped her backside downward, setting her feet onto the floor.

For a full second, he looked to leave her. Abandon her with this throbbing, aching need for him that needed to be sated.

Instead, he dropped down onto his knees in front of her, his mouth going to her upper belly, the edge of his top teeth raking across her skin. "Devil take it, you taste so good. Every part of you." He worked his way downward past her belly button.

Without warning, his finger slipped in between her folds and she went up on her toes, the shock of him finding her nubbin sending her body into a quiver. She could feel him smile against her lower abdomen.

Dragging his fingers deep along her folds, seeking, he dipped his middle finger into her. "You're already so wet for me."

Hell, that was what that was? For as many times as Gilroy had battered into her, she'd never felt this. Her body had never once reacted this way.

"But we can do better." The rasp in his voice dripped with arrogance.

His thumbs traced inward along her thighs and he spread her legs slightly, his mouth finding the crux of her. His tongue slipped out, following the same path that his finger had forged.

Shock jerked her body farther up the wall, her right hand pushing off from his shoulder.

Heaven to hell, what he was doing was torture. Pure, unadulterated, delicious torture.

His tongue swirled around her swollen nub and then his lips locked onto it, rolling it back and forth.

Death, death was coming for her and her screams told him exactly that. Her fingernails dug so far into his shoulder she could feel the warmth of blood seeping out.

He sucked until her body started to shudder, a barrage of nonsensical words flying in a scream.

He pulled away, looking up at her with devil eyes, his chin dipping into her folds, rubbing with the rough stubble that had appeared on his face during the last day. "You like the edge, Ness?"

"Wh—what edge?" She formed the words, but they didn't sound right in her own mind.

"This one." He dragged her left leg up and over his shoulder, then dipped down to suck her nubbin again, his tongue swirling hard.

Saints and demons. The edge—the damn edge she needed to go over. He knew exactly how to make her body bend to him. Beg for more. Her right hand still locked on his shoulder, her left fingers moved to his hair, clutching his head as her body pleaded for more. But how could there possibly be more than this? More than this painful, glorious, raw pleasure that she wasn't sure what to do with.

But her body knew. Her body wanted him inside of her.

Freeing her leg from his shoulder, she dropped, sliding down, her breasts dragging against his mouth and then chest. Further down until the tip of his shaft reached her folds and she wrapped her legs around him. Balanced on his knees, he chuckled, his mouth finding his way to her neck as his hands wrapped around her waist, holding her steady.

She plunged, sending the full length of him deep up into her.

Ballocks. It didn't hurt.

His cock slid up into her—tight, filling her—but it didn't hurt. The exact opposite. How could it be that this was exactly what her body had been pushing for, begging for?

He lifted her, sliding her up along his member, then let her crash back into him. Yes. Hell, yes. Again and again and the edge was back, the very edge he had goaded her to with his tongue.

Up and down, the hard length of him reaching deeper with each thrust.

"I can't hold it—I need to pull out, N—"

She slammed her hips down onto him, not thinking, trading any rational thought for her body to go over this edge she so desperately needed.

A growl ripped through his chest and his cock expanded deep within her, warmth flooding her and spiraling her over that very edge. A cry ripped from her lips, her body fracturing into streaks of pleasure burning straight from the sun. Even as she gasped for air, her body jerked, curling into him as burst after burst vibrated through her core, contracting viciously around his hard shaft.

A limp rag against him, she couldn't move, couldn't think, only the comforting peace of utter blackness filling her head.

Talen collapsed backward onto the carpet, dragging her body down with him.

She stayed in that position for far too long, her forehead and nose buried into his chest that moved up and down, her lips gasping for breath after breath. Her muscles unable to relax enough to fully collapse down onto him. What in the good earth had Talen just done to her? Demons and angels had just warred in her body and she had come out the victor.

His hand moved upward from the small of her back and he nudged her downward, making her body cover his, every inch of her skin that could be touching him, on him. She needed the prodding for she couldn't move on her own.

Her body eased into a puddle on top of him and his hand moved farther up along her spine, his fingers entwining in her hair that had lost its pins long ago.

When her breath finally came back to her, her right hand drifted up along his chest in front of her face, watching the muscles under his skin flicker alive at her fingertips. For as much as she now dared to want more— want this with Talen, when she never could have imagined it hours ago—she had to speak to the one thought festering in her brain. "Talen, this…marriage…it is too much. You do not have to sacrifice yourself for me."

His fingers twisting strands, entangled in her hair, stilled. "Why do you insist this is a sacrifice I am undertaking?"

"Because it is. You are free and now you won't be." She shifted her head along his chest to look at his eyes.

He tucked his free arm under his head to see her better. "Or is it that you are the one worried that you won't be free? You said you trusted me, Ness."

"I do." Her head shifted down, her cheek brushing his chest as she nodded. "I do." She repeated, more to convince herself than him.

"Then we get married in Scotland—it's the quickest choice and it will get you out of London. We marry in Scotland and you can always seek to end the marriage in the future, should you want to. Either way, I will ensure you are taken care of."

All of this, his generosity, was too much to believe in, to trust in from where she was a month ago. She wedged her right hand onto the carpet and pushed herself up, hovering above him, her gaze pinning him. "Why would you do this for me?"

"Honestly?"

She nodded.

"I don't know, Ness. I don't know what it is about you, but from the first moment I saw you, even bruised and battered, you were someone that I knew, instinctively, that I needed to protect. I cannot explain it and I have not been able to place that compulsion. And then the more time I spent with you, the more I have come to want you just for you, beyond protecting you."

Honest. Not a declaration of love, not that she was looking for one. Love was the last thing she needed at the moment. Her brow furrowed. "So if we did marry, how would we…I mean—us—you and me…" The heat of a blush crawled up her neck. "How would we live? Where?"

"We will figure that out."

"Will we?"

His look centered on her, his light blue eyes untroubled. "We only need to worry about one thing at this moment, and that is get to Scotland as soon as possible. That is the first order of business. The rest of…everything… we will figure out."

"Am I still in danger from Gilroy's men?"

"When are you not in danger?"

She laughed. "True."

"Your husband's men. Your father. Random fops at the Alabaster. You collect danger like posies."

Her smile faded away. "This isn't fair. What I have brought you, the mess that I am, what it has made you do—spill blood."

"Spilling blood means we now have information on the men Gilroy hired. Declan is on it and I imagine they will be

found tonight." His right cheek pulled back in a half smile, his fingers brushing the hair along her temple. "Plus, I don't mind blood. Don't mind any of the harsh realities of kill or be killed."

He said the words so casually, her heart twisted at the thought of the boy she once knew becoming a man as hard and calloused as the mighty Talen Blackstone.

Her hand lifted, her fingertips tracing the line of his collarbone. "How was it that you became this?"

"Became what?"

"Harsh. Deadly."

He stilled for a long moment, then his chest lifted in a deep breath. "The road to hell is littered with good intentions. It's as simple as that."

"Or as complicated. Something made you into this man—and I don't judge you for it. I am not so daft that I do not realize that the man you are has saved me numerous times in the last month. But something built you into this man from the boy I once knew, and I worry on that. What happened to you?"

He shrugged. "I toiled for years on that first Royal Navy ship—it was where I met Declan. Those were harsh times and both of us were skinny whelps, prime for whippings. The war, what we saw. We were nothing in those days, so it was about survival."

She winced, the thought of a cracking of a cat o' nine tails across his back filling her brain. "And you did survive."

"Aye, we did. After the war we eventually made it onto a privateering ship, the *Firehawk*, and after a number of years, we left the ship in London with a meager fortune.

Declan and I pooled our money and we purchased a gaming hell by the docks. Then another one. Then another one. We moved the business farther into London. He took care of our people and I took care of the numbers. We both took care of any threats. And we hired the best men we could find—those that knew how to inflict pain, but were principled men." His right hand ran through his hair. "It wasn't long before our men became feared, which presented its own opportunities by the docks—acquaintances wanted our men to see to the safe delivery of certain goods."

Her eyes went wide. "Smuggled goods?"

His look shifted from her to the ceiling. "The less you know, the better."

"Or the more I know the better?"

His gaze dropped down to her, his look severe as he shook his head. "No."

She gave him an exasperated smile. "So, you expanded your business."

"We did. In those early days it was a scrabble for every coin, every speck of power. Lots of blood was spilled, territories carved out. But it worked. We earned our corner of London. A better life for me. For my men."

His mouth closed in a long pause and she could see his mind drift to the past. "Then some of the men wanted to marry. Wanted families. Wanted better lives for their loved ones. Good intentions drove all of it. A slippery slope to what we did to expand. Little by little, morals slid away. There was always a reason. Johnson's wife was sick and needed medicine and a home in the countryside to get her out of the London air. Tiller's oldest boy needed a stash to go to America and buy land. Perkins's family in Scotland

was destitute, all of his twelve younger siblings due to the workhouse after his father died. Noble causes, all of it. All of us wanted better for those that depended on us. The ill-gotten measures to those goals became normal. Normal became moral. And that is where things stand today."

She met his look, her bottom lip jutting up at the harshness of what she had to ask. "Are you a bad man, Talen?"

He paused for a long moment, his look on the soft cream ceiling—no cherubs, just simple, elegant coving along the edges of the room. "I don't think so. But there will be plenty to tell you otherwise."

"Who did you do it for? You say it was driven by wanting better for your men's families, but who were you doing it for?"

"Nobody." He stopped, shaking his head. "No. My men. Their happiness was what was important. Loyalty dictated it. Their loyalty to me, my loyalty to them."

Her head curled down along his chest as her arm slid around his torso. "I am sad for the loss of your innocence. The loss of the boy you once were."

"I don't remember that boy, Ness."

She held in a sigh. "Then there is nothing to grieve."

"Exactly."

She exhaled a long breath.

Maybe he'd been right all along. He wasn't that boy. Hadn't been him for a very long time.

So did it even matter if he remembered or not?

And why was it so bloody important to her?

{ CHAPTER 18 }

"I know this place."

Talen looked across the carriage at Ness as she scooted forward on the cushion, her right hand going to the bottom of the window.

The devil take it, she was beautiful. A ray of sunlight angled in across her eyes, making them glow like molten gold. Excitement clear on her face as she searched the countryside along the edge of the village that they'd just passed through.

Four nights with her in his bed and where he should well be tired of her, his infatuation had only grown. Four nights in bed, with every waking moment spent with her on this journey north to Scotland, and his body, his mind should be sated of her.

But he wasn't.

Infatuation? Hell, he was obsessed. Obsessed like a scrawny teenage whelp who'd just strolled past his first whorehouse with his mouth agape at the breasts and nipples stuffed high above corsets.

Except Talen's obsession was centered on one woman, one body. Ness's.

This was the longest continuous stretch of time he'd ever spent with one person. Declan and he had grown up together on the ships, but they'd always been busy, always working, always scraping. This—this had been a purity of time. No emergencies. No demands. No piles of ledgers to

go through. No bones to bust. Just sitting across from Ness in the carriage, whiling away the hours with laughter and stories.

His chest at ease, when his chest was never at ease. The only thing in the last days that had made his chest tighten, his blood rush, was the moment when they would escape into a room at a coaching inn and her fingers would slip along the bodice of her deep blue traveling dress, nudging it off her shoulder, insistent that he help her undress.

He shifted slightly on his seat, trying to calm his cock that became ornery and demanding at any thought of some part of her body sans clothes. It didn't matter which part. Her knee. Her shoulder. The spot just above her hip bone where he liked to set his lips to her skin and tickle her. Those images crept into his mind and the blood rushed straight to the very appendage he could do very little about in the carriage in the middle of the day.

The excitement on Ness's face boiled to a pitch and she jumped up from the rear bench and banged on the ceiling of the carriage with the side of her fist. "Go left at the next crossroad," she shouted at the top of her lungs to the driver.

A muffled "Aye," came down to them.

Talen grabbed her wrist as she started to sit back down. "What the hell are you doing?"

"This is it—don't you see? Look." She wedged her right hand away from his grip and pointed, her finger wagging toward the window as words flew frantic out of her mouth. "Just look. This is it. This is where you lived or at least where you lived when I knew you. This is where your family's estate is. This is where you grew up and where my family visited yours. This is it. I know because I recognized that church at the edge of that last village and then the old gnarled oak tree that is half alive and half dead with its crooked branches that I always thought were going to snatch me out of the carriage as we went by. This is it. We would take a left and I knew I was safe from the tree because we were so close to your family's estate. I remember it so distinctly. The turn is not too much farther up the road, maybe a mile or two. We are so close. We have to turn. We have to go there."

An icy chill ran down his spine. "We don't have to do anything."

She slumped onto the bench, her head shaking at him. "Why don't you believe I knew you when we were young?"

"Does it even matter if I do or do not believe it?"

"Yes. It would seem to me, yes." She reached forward, grabbing his knee. "You were buried, Talen. Buried with your parents. A third coffin, laid into the ground. But you weren't in it. You were alive. Don't you want to know why?"

"Whatever you think you know…" His words stopped as his gaze drifted to the window. Why did she keep up this inane insistence that he remember the past? The past meant nothing to him. It never had. "No. My life is what it is now."

Her hand on his knee clutched hard. "What if I could prove it to you—prove to you who you are?"

"Leave it, Ness. Just leave it." His hand jutted upward and he clunked on the ceiling with his knuckles. "Stay the course to Scotland."

Another "Aye" echoed down to them.

Her look pinned him. "Why do you not want to know? Why won't you even give it a chance—to know who you are, where you came from? How can you live with this blank space in your life?"

"Because it wasn't good, Ness." His words snapped. "Whatever it is that I can't remember. It wasn't good. It was bad. It would have to be or I would remember it. And I already live in darkness. I don't need more."

She crumpled back against the cushions, her right arm curling across her stomach. "You live in darkness?"

He stared at her for a long moment, his jaw flexing hard. "People that I've destroyed. Killed. Sins I've had to come to terms with. There is already so much darkness that permeates my world that it is hard enough to live in. I don't need to add to it. I don't want to know what happened to me. Where I came from."

Her jaw dropped, her amber eyes stunned.

Good. She would drop it.

Her mouth closed for a breath, but then her lips parted, not quite defeated. "Knowing the past would make who you are now worse?" She leaned forward. "Or could it make everything better?"

His head instantly shook. "That is optimism not becoming of you. You've lived through the end of innocence. Is it worth knowing what you were when you compare it to what you've become?"

A frown set deep on her face. Worry. But not worry for herself. Worry for him. Worry so deep it made the corners of her eyes wrinkle as she looked at him.

He wouldn't take her pity.

"We need to make it to Scotland, Ness. Your safety depends on it. We need to wed before anything else."

She exhaled a long sigh, her voice quiet. "You don't understand, do you?"

"Understand what?" This woman was intent on driving him to Bedlam.

"That I want you to know who you are before you marry me."

"Why?" His hand flipped upward. "It won't make a difference to me. I could learn I was the King of England and still the only thing I would be concentrating on is getting you across the border in front of a blacksmith with me."

"But it will make a difference to me." Her palm landed flat on her chest. "I want you to know who you are. This isn't for you—it's for me. So you don't think you're marrying a woman who is insane."

"I don't think that."

"I know how marriages work in Scotland, Talen. The reasons it takes to get out of one. Believe me, I know." Her knuckles set upon her lips as her stare fell to the floor of the carriage by his feet. "Adultery or desertion is primarily needed for a divorce. But an annulment may be pushed through if one party is insane or lied about one's identity. Both of which are very relevant in our case. Both reasons which my father could manipulate to rip me away from you, and I don't want to give him that chance."

"How do you know so much about it?"

Her look snapped up to him for a second before her mouth clamped shut, and her stare shifted to the window.

"Ness."

She kept her gaze trained at the window. "I inquired into it years ago when I still had hope of getting out of my marriage with Gilroy. We had married in Scotland and I knew the laws were different, but I didn't know what they were. So I had to find out." She paused for moment as her lips pulled inward. "And I ended up paying dearly for that knowledge."

Instant rage coursed into his veins and he leaned forward, setting his face in her view, only barely able to keep his voice to a low rumble. "How did Gilroy find out? What did the bastard do?"

"The clergyman told him of my inquiry. That was when I realized I was truly alone up there. I was rewarded with a jaw pummeled so far out of place I couldn't eat solid food for a month. So I know. I know what my father can use against me. Us."

Never in his life had he wanted someone who was dead, so much alive. He wanted Gilroy alive. Alive so he could tear the bastard apart with his own hands. Limb by limb. Scream by scream.

He couldn't do that, but he could give this one simple thing to Ness.

He shifted backward onto his bench, his words coming out through gritted teeth, the rasp in his voice rougher than usual. "Fine. We'll go."

He slammed a fist up onto the ceiling. "Take the left turn."

In a minute, the carriage swayed with the turn, bringing him closer to the very thing he vowed he'd never do.

Learn his past.

{ CHAPTER 19 }

Talen watched the back of Ness's dark blue skirt swing in front of him, the bottom hem dusting along the overgrown grasses half-dormant along the hillside.

"Not too much farther." She looked over her shoulder at him, a half-smile on her face meant to encourage or placate him, he couldn't read.

Fifteen more steps and she crested the top of the hill, pulling to a stop at a wrought iron fence that he hadn't been able to see from the angle they walked up the hill. The fence encircled a plot of land dotted with headstones.

The heavy rocks already rolling about in his gut multiplied. He didn't want to do this. Didn't want to do this with every fiber of his being.

He needed to leave. Leave now. And at the exact moment he started to turn on his heel to do just that, he caught sight of Ness's gaze on him.

Intent, worried, needing this.

Needing it more than he needed to escape. She needed this to move forward with him, so he would give it to her. He would look at a couple headstones and then they could be on their way.

Easy enough.

Hunks of granite with names emblazoned on them couldn't conjure memories that were long since forgotten.

Her look darted away from him. "Over there is the gate." She pointed to the far side of the iron fence. "We

must have come up the back way, but it was the only way I knew of. That sheep field below is where we would escape to, your cousin, Harriet, and I liked the lambs and you liked chasing the sheep. Harriet always used to yell at you for making the ewes nervous. And you liked to tell us ghost stories of who was buried up here on the hill. So when it was near to dark, we used to dare each other to come up here."

His gaze went back to the long pasture they'd trekked across, several sheep moving slowly in the distance along the stone fence they'd crawled over. Grey skies above threatened rain. None of it looked familiar. His bottom lip jutted upward. Just another memory he didn't have.

"My mother said we couldn't come to the burial—that was men's work. But Harriet and I snuck out of the manor house and watched them lower you into the ground from over there." She pointed to her left at a long bank of trees, oaks with crispy, russet-hued leaves still stubbornly holding onto the limbs.

"This isn't right, Ness."

She stepped toward him and took the shovel that they'd borrowed from a farmer along the way from his hand. "I don't want to disturb the dead any more than you do. But I don't know that there's another way. You need to know. I need to know." Before he could snatch the shovel away from her, she moved away from him, her gaze determined on the iron gate opposite them.

Talen followed her, a new fear burning down his chest. Fear of what this would do to Ness if she was wrong about this grave. His grave.

Half of him wanted her to be wrong for his sake. Half of him wanted her to be right for her sake.

Pulling a hard breath into his lungs, he followed her around the fence to the front of the cemetery. It was private at least. The site nestled between three hills. No one around for miles. It'd taken a full half hour to walk here from the road where they'd left their driver and carriage and if they didn't hurry, twilight would be upon them before they finished the business of this.

By the time he caught up to her, Ness had already wedged the point of the shovel into the ground by a headstone on the far left of the graveyard. Her movements were awkward with her left hand and arm still wrapped along the splint gently trying to help balance the handle as she dug her heel onto the back of the metal spade.

He stopped directly behind her, his hands slowly going around her waist as he slipped the shovel out of her hands. "I'll do it, Ness. This isn't work for you. I shouldn't have even let you come up here."

"You know I need to be here, just the same as you." She turned around in between his arms, her hand on his chest, her look lifting to him. "I need you to look at the headstone. Your headstone. Your name. This is where I lost you. Where we all lost you."

His gaze left her face, going over her shoulder to the weathered grey stone with a rounded top sticking out of the ground, leaning slightly to the left.

Beloved son, Conner J. B. F. Burton.

Nothing. No recognition. No sudden memory.

He looked down at Ness, his head shaking.

"Nothing?" she asked, worrying her lip.

"No." His right hand dropped from around her waist and he shifted to her side, driving the spade into the ground with his boot. "So we dig."

Three shovelfuls of dirt moved and Talen glanced up as Ness moved to the next headstone over, her fingers touching the top of it. A tall classical panel with side pillars and a pediment atop, the flowers etched into the stone were only partially worn with time. His gaze moved down the front of it.

Beloved wife, daughter, mother, Mariana Burton.
Mariana Burton.

The shovel fell at his side and he moved forward, his legs wooden and barely able to carry his weight. An uncontrollable shake set into his hands, but it didn't stop him from bending and reaching out, tracing the letters etched deep into the stone. Once, twice, three times over her name.

"Mariana." His lips moved, the faintest breath of a whisper forming the word.

His eyes closed with the name spoken to the wind and a blinding light filled his head, so bright it felt as though his brain was about to explode from the inside out.

And then nothing.

Nothing but blackness.

Blackness and one thing—the echo of a voice from long ago.

"My merry Mariana." He whispered the words, afraid to set them into the air for fear his head would truly rupture.

Ness's hand landed on his arm, worry in her voice. "Talen, what did you say?"

"My merry Mariana." He swayed slightly with the words, trying not to lose them into the blackness. "My merry Mariana."

His eyes opened to Ness. "My merry Mariana."

The words didn't leave him. Instead, they only grew stronger in his mind, a seed with a thousand tiny sprouts flashing all at once.

He closed his eyes, trying to stem the flow, trying to stem everything that was entangled with them.

"Talen?" Ness's hand tightened on his arm.

The words. Concentrate on the words.

"My merry Mariana. It's what my father used to call my mother. My merry Mariana. All the time. *My merry Mariana.*"

"You remember?" Her breathless words drifted into his ears.

His eyes flew open, searching for her, searching for her eyes. "Your face—when you showed up at the Alabaster for me beaten to all hell."

She blinked hard, her head shaking. "What?"

His entire adult life instantly made sense.

Why he could never stomach a bruise on a woman.

Why he could never dabble in brothels in his holdings.

Why he cringed every time he heard a gun clicking on an empty barrel.

"They killed my father immediately—even though she fought them—he fought them. She went crazy. Pure vicious madness. Scratching their eyes. Biting their arms." His words flew in a torrent, his eyes closing as the scene—arms

and legs and terror flying in puzzle pieces in his mind. "I fought them. I did too. But my father was the first to go. Quick. Merciless. One gunshot and he went down. They turned on me next, setting a pistol to my head. And then a click, the trigger pulled." He had to gasp in a breath.

"They shot you?"

"No. The gun didn't have a bullet. Just the click. So they took to their fists. Pummeling me, my head, my stomach, my chest. Fist after fist crushing into my face. So much blood I couldn't see past the red in my eyes. They dropped me to the floor when they grew tired, thinking I was dead. I thought I was dead. In and out of blackness."

"But you weren't."

Both of his hands went to his face, the butt of his palms crushing into his eyes, trying to wipe free the images. Images he didn't want to see. "They moved onto my mother." His hands pulled away from his eyes with a growl and he found Ness's face.

"Hell, you. This is what you looked like. It's why I first felt the need to protect you, Ness—that first day when you came to me. I could never stand a woman with a bruise on her face—but yours, yours was horrific. It looked just like my mother's as she took her last breath."

Her face crumpled, horrified, her hold on his arm bruising. "What?"

His eyes squinted close as image after image flooded his mind. "But only…only after the hours—the night of the horrors of being half alive, hearing her screams, what they did to her. I could only watch through blood streaming in my eyes. I couldn't move. When they finally let her body drop to the floor, she looked at me."

He collapsed onto his heels, his knees hitting the ground, his shoulders dropping. "And I saw only one of her eyes looking at me. Everything was in that eye. Still blue. Crystal clear blue. She could see I was still alive. And everything was in her eye. What she wanted for me. The future. For me to live. Giving me the strength to keep breathing. She wouldn't look anywhere but at me. Willing me to live."

Ness's hand, gentle, slid along the back of his neck. "And you did."

The blackness invaded, wiping free the images.

He shook his head. Trying to get them back. Trying to banish them back into the void. An anguished roar left him, his mind battling itself.

"You lived, Talen."

His body buckled forward, all air leaving his lungs, his knuckles digging into the dirt. "I did, but I do not know how." His voice rough, words choked out. "The next thing I remember, I was waking up on that ship, Declan shoving a mop into my hand, yanking me out of bed because he was sick of swabbing the decks alone."

His body swayed, his mind fighting itself with every second.

Fighting until he was numb, losing track of place and time.

Fighting until he didn't exist, not even in his own mind.

{ CHAPTER 20 }

Heaven help her, what had she done?

She'd wanted—needed—Talen to remember his past, to remember her. To know that she wasn't mad and destined for an asylum. But this—she'd never meant to send *him* into madness.

She hadn't wanted this. Not the horror of what had happened to him. Not for him to leave this world even as he left his body behind.

He'd warned her and she hadn't listened. She'd let her own blasted self-doubt demand this of him.

Rain had started, heavy rain, but even that hadn't nudged Talen from where he'd frozen in place. Poised on his knees in front of his mother's grave, not moving, his eyes open but not seeing anything.

She'd yelled his name, over and over again, but she couldn't get him to flinch, to move. A granite statue she couldn't budge.

Wedging herself between him and the headstone, she bent down in front of him, her right hand fully on his cheek, her left fingertips cradling the other side of his jaw. The rain was coming vicious now, slashing across her cheeks, drowning his face in rivers that ran from his dark blond hair.

"Talen—Talen—look at me, please. Just look at me." Not that her face could pull him from the monstrosity of

what he must be feeling at the moment, reliving the deaths of his parents.

Not that anything could pull him back.

Her hands tightened around his face. "Talen, please."

No reaction, not even the slightest blink. Panic set deep into her bones. His eyes were glassy, so like her mother's often were when she'd visit her in the asylum.

She couldn't lose him. Not now.

What the hell had she done?

"Apologies for the interruption, but the rain has started in earnest."

Ness tore her gaze away from Talen to crane her neck and look at the driver they'd hired in Birmingham at the far side of the iron fence. She had to lift her voice to be heard over the downpour. "The rain, it is already mucking the roads, isn't it?"

"It is, miss. We need to leave before the carriage gets stuck. I moved it closer along the lane."

She straightened, her right hand moving to grip the side of Talen's neck. "Help me. Help me get him back down to the carriage."

The driver hustled along the side of the fence until he could enter the cemetery. "What is wrong with him?"

"He's had a shock. That is all. But your arm around him from one side and mine on the other should suffice."

The driver nodded, quickly slipping his hold along Talen's back and prodding him upright onto his feet as Ness did the same on Talen's left side.

Thank the heavens, Talen held the bulk of his weight on his own, and they managed to get him to take steps forward, though much of his heft still crushed down onto her shoulder. Again and again as they moved down the hillside, she tried to shift Talen over slightly, so he would lean more against the driver, but he would take a step and then lean back onto her.

But she would bear the weight. Bear anything for him.

She hadn't realized until that slog down the hill, how much he truly meant to her. How she would trade everything—make a deal with the devil—if only he would come back to her.

Her right shoulder near to cracking, they finally got Talen down the hillside and across the field to the coach.

When they stopped at the open door of the carriage, Talen's eyes were still glassy, unfocused, as Ness implored him, "Two steps up, Talen, please. Just two steps up and into the coach."

An exhale of relief flew from her mouth as his right leg lifted, then his left. Up and into the carriage.

So he hadn't completely left her. Not yet.

She jumped up into the coach behind him, prodding him toward the bench before she turned back to the driver. "How far is the nearest coaching inn?"

"There was one in the village we passed several miles back in Calthwaite."

She waved her hand toward that general direction. "Please, then, to there, posthaste."

He gave her a nod and closed the carriage door, the coach shifting to the side as his weight scampered up onto the driver's seat.

The ride back to the village was agonizingly slow with the muck of the road sucking at the wheels with every turn and stopping the coach twice, but within two hours they had a room in a coaching inn and Ness was teetering on the side of the bed, biting her bottom lip. She stared at Talen sitting on a chair, facing the fire, his eyes still glossed over. No words, no movement.

Nothing from him even as she'd pulled off his sopping coat, waistcoat and lawn shirt, and pulled off his boots. Even with as wet as they were, she left his trousers in place. She doubted she could get him up off the chair enough to remove them.

Then she'd sent a tumbler of brandy down his throat in hopes that might numb whatever had seized him, but there was no change.

As she'd stripped off her own wet dress, leaving in place her damp shift, she'd kept up steady chatter about inane things like the birds most common in Scotland, the types of moss present on the ancient stones around Whetland Castle, and the lambing of ewes.

Anything to keep her mouth moving and her thoughts off the possibility that she'd broken his mind with their trip to the Washburn estate.

Not that he heard any of it. But she couldn't leave him alone in the silence. Silence with nothing to bring him back to the present.

But now she was waning, her words faltering, tears threatening.

Watching the agony he was in had shattered her heart. That she had done that to him. Make him suffer as he did. She would never forgive herself for this.

He would never forgive her for this.

With her shoulders slumped, she scooted along the bed toward the bedside table and grabbed the decanter of brandy, pouring it into the tumbler that sat next to it until it was half full. She rarely drank brandy, but now was the time to start if there ever was one.

One sip. Two. Both gulps sending fire across her tongue and deep into her throat. What she deserved.

A third sip at her lips and Talen jerked, his body suddenly moving where there had only been stillness.

The jerk and then he stood slowly, rising from the chair as his eyes came back into focus, though he didn't look at her, his gaze solidly trained on the fire.

She jumped to her feet, setting the glass on the table and moving to stand in front of him.

Staring at him. Silent. Waiting. Excruciating.

"Hell. All of this." The words eked out rough along his tongue, a raw whisper.

Her lips parted, but she had no words. No words for this. No words to make this better. To soothe the pain.

His eyes slowly shifted up to her from the fire. "Dammit, this is why I froze. This is why I'm not fit to protect you, Ness. Not fit for anything but death and disaster."

{ CHAPTER 21 }

"Not fit to protect…" Her head shook, her forehead wrinkling against the worry that had lined her face. "What are you talking about, Talen?"

Immersed deep in a pit of darkness and suddenly, there was Ness, in the light, bringing him back to reality. Back to the present.

He blinked hard, his stare finally able to focus on her. On the terror on her face.

Blast, where were they? A coaching inn? How had they gotten there? Where were his clothes, his boots?

He blinked again, the one revelation he'd forged in that well of blackness hammered into his brain, unable to let go of him. "Death follows me, Ness. Death. Destruction. You need to get away. Get away from me now."

"What? No." Her head flew back and forth. "No. I don't need to get away. You're not death, Talen. You're the farthest thing from it."

"I froze, Ness. I froze." He sucked in a breath that only partially made its way down his tight throat. "I freeze and I fail. I am death. Death for sure, for you."

She stilled in front of him and Talen could see her slipping, slipping away from him. Whether she wanted to or not, she was recoiling.

Her arms drew inward across her body, her right arm cradling the bandage wrapped along her left arm. She wore only her shift. What had happened to her clothes?

Her eyes wide orbs, she stared at him. "You froze? When?"

"The brothel that burned down—the one Juliet saved me from."

"The Selkie South Brothel?"

"Yes." He nodded, his look dropping to the fire just beyond her skirts, not able to keep the long-held shame from his voice. "There was a reason it was set aflame. I had taken over the house, adding to it a cadre of women enticed over from a brothel across the river. I told you of them. All wanted to join my house, it was clean, they would be paid well, and I'd hired Juliet to see to all of that and she did an admirable job of making sure every girl wanted to be there and was content."

His voice became wooden, hollow to his own ears. "But I needed a shining star, a woman men would clamor to see, to be with. So I stole one. Layla Hodwell. A beauty. Charming. Men would extol on her theatrics in the bed all about town. She was the shining star I needed, but she was also the property of Filmore Bloodwater, a wretched, toothless cur. I convinced Layla to come to my house, paid off her debt to Bloodwater, and told her she would be safe with me. I would protect her. Except I didn't. I couldn't. A month after she came to the brothel, Bloodwater came for her. He got to her in the Selkie South when I wasn't there. By the time I'd arrived, rushed into her room, Bloodwater and two of his cutthroats had already severely beaten her."

Ness's fingers lifted, pressing against her mouth.

"I could have saved her. I had the brawn, the skill. But I didn't save her. I froze. I had a split second to act when I walked into that room and I didn't—couldn't do it. I saw her face, the brutality of what he'd done to her, and my body locked up upon itself. I couldn't move my arms, my legs. I froze and I couldn't control it."

"Talen—"

"I failed her. I told her I would protect her from Bloodwater—swore it—but I didn't. And I never knew why I froze like I did. It had never happened before. But it makes sense now—her face…her face was what happened. The blood, the pus, how she could only see out of one eye."

His words choked, he had to pause, running a hand over his eyes, as though bitter hope promised he could erase the past with just one swipe. "It was the same thing I felt when I first saw you. I froze then, too, when you stumbled into the room. You didn't see it, didn't know it, but I froze. I froze because you and Layla looked just as my mother did at the end—face crushed, one eye open, staring at me."

He swallowed hard, his voice catching. "I froze that day and Bloodwater's men jumped on me before I could recover. I'm deadly because I'm fast and that day…that day I was nothing. They beat me into unconsciousness. Juliet pulled me from that building—saved me, saved all the girls, but Layla…"

His head shook as his fingers curled into fists. "They took her away and I never saw her again. Never heard of her. No one did. She was just gone. Dead."

"But you didn't kill her."

"I did just as much as if I'd slipped a blade into her gut." His stare lifted to Ness, self-loathing eating away at his chest. "I was the one to convince her to come to my house.

I was the one that swore to protect her. And I didn't. After that, I swore off anything to do with whores and brothels. The women at the Alabaster come and go on their own accord. We have rooms available if the man wants to pay for it—and my men oftentimes have to step in when there's danger to a woman from men that are out of control on our property. But I will never be the cause of another woman dead because of me."

"Talen…"

"It's why you need to get away from me, Ness." His legs suddenly useless, unable to hold him, he wanted to sink back down to the chair. But Ness needed to hear this, understand it, and she only would if he was looking down at her. His lips pulled into a terse line. "I am death. I can't be trusted to protect anyone, especially you."

"Except you aren't death and I'm not going anywhere." She didn't even blink at his words.

His head cocked to the side, his voice low. "Ness—"

"No. I won't hear such ridiculousness from you." Her arms unfolded and she reached out, her fingers wrapping around his forearm. "You are not death because of a few short minutes in an entire lifetime. Those moments in the whorehouse, those moments that your parents died—they aren't everything, Talen. They're not all of you. You have always been so much more."

His mouth clamped closed. She was denying what he knew full well. "You don't know what you're talking about."

"I do." She nodded, her face solemn as her hand fell away from his arm. "I know because I touched death.

Touched it on my own accord. And those minutes do not define me. They can't."

His breath stilled in his chest. "Ness, what did you do?"

She let out a breathless scoff, the side of her mouth pulling into a strained smile. "You weren't the only one that Juliet saved."

"What happened?" His voice hard, he didn't want to know what she'd done to herself. Yet he *had* to know.

Her head bowed, her shoulders sank as remorse washed over her small frame. "It was just after Gilroy had broken my arm, broken me. Broke me so completely, set so much pain into my body that it was all I thought I had left. My own death. My own death, under my control. My room was high—so high in that castle. I climbed up onto the window and at the very moment I let myself go, falling to freedom, Juliet tackled me away, pulling me back into the room. Pulling me back into life. Yet I still didn't want it. Hated what she'd done. Hated her actions until…"

His eyes closed for long seconds. To imagine her drowning so far in that pain that she would leave this earth on her own volition set agony deep into his own chest. Her scars, so deep and wounding becoming his own.

His eyes opened and he stared at the top of her bowed head, wanting nothing more than to erase the past for her but knowing he couldn't. Instead, he prodded her onward. There was nowhere to go but forward. "Until what?"

Her eyes slowly lifted to him, the golden strands in her irises glowing with intensity, a sheen of tears glossing them. "Until I opened my eyes and you were there. You were dead. Long dead. But then you weren't. You were alive, breathing

when you shouldn't have been. I know death, Talen. And you. You are not death. You are the opposite. You are life. You brought me back to life."

She stepped closer to him as her chin lifted, her stare desperate as it pinned him. "When you were young, you were funny and smart and mostly kind, except when you got that wicked gleam in your eye and wanted to make me squeal. But your heart…your heart has always beaten gold, no matter the iron you've since shackled it in. It is still in you. I've seen it. I've felt it."

He closed his eyes to her. "But I don't remember that—what I was. I don't remember anything more."

"Nothing else?"

"I only remember that night. That one night." His hand lifted, his fingers rubbing across his forehead and eyes. "Why can't I remember more?"

"I don't know. But if you remember the worst of it, maybe the rest will follow."

"And if it doesn't?"

She worried her lip for long seconds. "Did you recall anything more from that night? What happened after your mother dropped in front of you?"

He shook his head slightly, his eyes still covered, then he shrugged. "Just that I was choked. I remember that. After my mother died, they found out I was alive and I was choked."

She gasped. "It's the rasp in your voice. It was never there before. But it is now. I thought it odd, but it makes sense that is where it came from."

His hand dropped away from his face and he found her eyes. "I couldn't speak for a long time on the ship. Weeks it took, my throat barely able to let breath in and out, much less talk. That's how I became Talen. Talen Blackstone. Some old sailor named me because he was sick of calling me boy and he said I had eyes like a hawk—watching everything with intent to strike."

His eyes opened wider and he swayed, the blackness he'd just emerged from suddenly threatening to swallow him again. "I never remembered that. Never. The memories of it, of my first days on the ship. All of it just slipped away. Forgotten when it never should have been. I should have remembered. Remembered everything."

He swayed again, his body threatening to collapse and she stepped into him, wrapping her arms around him to balance him, the splint on her left arm jutting into his side.

So unsteady, his body wavering, shards of black cutting across his vision.

His face buried into the top of her head, drowning himself in her scent. "Hold me. Hold me against this. I can't go into the blackness again."

Her arms tightened around him. It had to pain her left arm, but dammit, he needed this. Needed her to keep him from slipping away again.

"I have you, Talen. I do. Always." She pulled her head away from his chest so she could look up at him.

Worry strained her face. Worry he hated. She shouldn't have to worry, not on him.

But he didn't know how to stop the blackness from taking over again. How to stay here with her when his mind

was determined to make him abandon everything around him.

Abandon her.

Her amber eyes pinned him. "Even if you slip away, I am here. Waiting."

His left hand moved up and he found her jawline, holding onto her, her face cutting through the black shards cutting across his vision.

She could hold him here. Hold him in the present.

His head dipped, his mouth finding hers, his kiss desperate and pleading.

He pulled slightly to the left, his lips still brushing against the skin of her cheek.

"I never needed anything from you, from anyone. But I need this, Ness. Need this to ground me in reality. Need you. Need you to keep me here, where I am. Not where I was."

Without a word her lips moved to his, kissing him. Her mouth parted, immediately demanding more from him, her tongue flickering against his. A force he was not about to deny, his cock already an iron rod throbbing for her.

This was what he needed. Nothing but her. Her hands on his body. Her mouth on his. His body consumed with possessing her, the taste of her—leaving no space for anything else in his mind.

No memories. No anger. Just Ness.

Ness and the sweetness of her lips, her breath steamy fire on his skin, her sultry moans filling his ears when he set his hand behind her neck, tilting her head to deepen the kiss.

Sinking into everything she was. Hiding from everything he couldn't control.

Without breaking the kiss, the tips of her left fingers fumbled in trying to help her right hand with the fall front of his trousers, nudging him backward as she worked the buttons. He was naked by the time his calves hit the side of the bed and her shift had fallen to the floor.

She broke the kiss and pushed his shoulders back and down, sending him flat onto the bed, then crawled in after him, straddling his thighs.

The blood in his cock pounding, he stared up at her as she hovered over him for a long breath, her golden eyes fixed on him, making sure he didn't think to leave her again. The tips of her left fingers went along his cheek, her nails sinking into his skin. "You are here with me, Talen. Here."

Then she lifted her hips, grabbing his shaft to center him and drove downward in one harsh motion. It pulled him into her, into a world where there was nothing but his cock buried deep in her tightness. The exquisite sensation of her muscles contracting around him.

With a gasp at her lips, she lifted up, and sank down again and again. His eyes locked onto her face, the gyration of her hips driving him to madness in less than a minute.

As if he could be anywhere else when she was on top of him.

He reached up and grabbed the back of her head, burying his fingers deep into the thick of her dark hair. Pins flew and strands fell about her as he yanked her downward, his mouth taking hers. Ravaging her lips, he buried himself in the soul of her. Her hips kept gyrating, lifting,

descending. Furious and fast, her body pitching herself to the edge.

Her teeth bit his tongue as she slammed down onto him, sending her into a writhing orgasm with a scream. All of her muscles hardened under his touch, her body clenching viciously around his cock, drawing him deeper with every wave storming her muscles.

His mind consumed, his body desperate to devour her, he flipped her onto her back, slamming into her in time with every contraction of her orgasm. Thrusting until he was frantic, pummeling her so hard he was sure he was hurting her when all she did was scream, "More."

Every piercing drive into her, "More."

His hips moved in a fury until he lost his bloody mind, his body going carnal, his teeth raking over the skin on her neck, one of his hands holding her arms high above her head so her body stretched to accommodate the full length of him. His other hand gripped her breast as her hips bucked, meeting him with every thrust. And still she begged for more, her back arching, needing all of him.

It hit him in a furious landslide, his muscles shaking as he came into her, his seed spurting so brutally he lost all sense of time and place except for his cock buried deep in her. Her body taking everything he needed to expel in that moment.

Fury and anger and confusion and anguish.

She took at all. Willingly, not buckling under the onslaught.

Before he could breathe, before he could think, he wrapped an arm around her and spun onto his back, dragging her body with him, capturing her fully between his legs. He wasn't going to let her go.

Probably never.

He'd long since reconciled the fact that he had no control over himself when it came to his cock deep in her. He was a damned mess, never pulling out of her when he needed to. It didn't matter. He was ready for the consequences. He'd been ready from the first moment he'd set his naked body to hers, whether or not he'd admitted it to himself.

His breath rasping in his throat, he searched for some semblance of sanity. Worried that the last he'd known of it was in the second before Ness had appeared at the Alabaster.

She'd gone limp atop him, her cheek nestled in the center crook of his chest, her body exhausted but her breath still gasping for normalcy. His arms stayed locked in place around her, not letting her roll off of him. He needed her there, atop him. The weight of her continuing to ground him to the present, if not sanity.

Her breathing finally evened out, each inhale sinking deep into her lungs.

Asleep.

He reached over on the bed and grabbed the sheet, pulling it up over her rear so she didn't get chilled, not that it was possible for how hot his skin was on her.

She rustled slightly, all of her limbs stretching for a moment before she snuggled back into him. Her voice, raspy with sleep, whispered into his chest. "You're not death, Talen. You aren't. And I'm not going anywhere."

He didn't believe her.

But for that that moment, that night, he'd not argue it. Let it be.

For he'd never been at such peace.

{ CHAPTER 22 }

"This is where you lived, or at least where you lived when I knew you." From atop her horse, Ness pointed to the right with her left hand, the motion in her fingers not causing the slightest discomfort along her arm. She probably didn't even need the splint attached to her forearm anymore, though Talen insisted on keeping it on her, patiently rewrapping her arm three times a day so her skin didn't rot against the splint or itch too much.

She warily looked at Talen on his horse. The knuckles of his hand holding the reins were strained to white.

He didn't want to be here.

But he'd come because she'd insisted. She was pushing too hard and she knew it, but she couldn't stop herself. He'd been the one to teach her how to fight, so that's what she was doing.

Fighting to get him to remember. Remember her. Remember his past so that he could believe in himself. In the good that he held within him. Because right now, he still thought he was death. Death to her.

He may have stopped saying it, but he still believed it. She saw it in his eyes. In the angst etched deep in his blue irises.

His look flicked from Washburn Manor to her. "We should be headed north right now, Ness. Not on some fool's errand to look at a monstrosity of wealth and privilege."

She glanced to her right. The main house was a bit much. It had been a grand palace of fun when she was young. Portland stone graced all sides of the manor house. Fat and wide and perfectly symmetrical. A beacon of light against the green surrounding it.

Wide green lawns unfurled in every direction until meeting with the forest on the back side and grazing fields on the right and left. The lawn held perfectly manicured evergreens all about, a labyrinth, several ponds and a multitude of gardens where one could easily get lost. The stables were beyond a swath of forest in the rear, five barns that had, at some point, housed some of the finest breeding horses in England, if she correctly recalled what her father had once said.

Grandeur and pomposity oozed in every direction. But that had been Talen's childhood. A childhood she knew he'd been happy in. Happiness he could take solace in, happiness that could steal some of the pain away from what he'd remembered.

She cleared her throat and looked to him. "The coach got stuck twice yesterday on the way back to the village, and the driver said the roads were much worse this morning. So our options are to sleep on the roadside tonight when we get stuck halfway to the border because you are too insistent on leaving, or to spend the day here in the area. And there is no harm in visiting the estate—it may help you to remember more."

His stare had moved off of her to fix on the manor house, his jaw shifting back and forth. "I don't know that I want to remember more. Yesterday was enough." His head swiveled, his wide eyes finding her. "The coach got stuck twice yesterday? How did you get it out?"

"The driver and I both pushed on the rear corner of the carriage as he turned the horses with a long lead rope."

His brows lifted. "And I sat inside the coach the whole time?"

She didn't try to hide her grin. "You did."

"Pathetic." He exhaled, his head shaking. "Well, I am back in the land of the living, you can be assured of that."

A wanton smile crossed her face. "Anytime you need me to ground you to the present time and place, I am more than willing."

A chuckle rumbled from his chest. "I may black out more often if that is my reward."

She motioned with her left hand that had been resting in her lap. "Shall we at least go up the drive? We don't have to inquire about going inside or meeting anyone in residence. Just poke about."

He looked up the long gravel drive, staring at it for a long moment before nodding his head.

She flicked her reins with her right hand, sending her mare into motion next to his horse. They moved slowly, Talen's eyes shifting across the landscape, the land unfurling out from the manor house, the lane lined on one side with majestic oaks about to drop their leaves.

His focus landed on the manor house up the hill, his eyes squinting at the structure. "Who are these people that I come from?"

Her lips drew inward for a long moment as her heart sank.

He really hadn't remembered anything past the night his parents died. She'd hoped sleep would help him. He'd been so quiet the previous night about everything that was going on in his mind, that she hadn't wanted to badger him with a lot of questions about what he did and did not remember.

She forced a neutral smile on her face. "You were one of the grandsons of the Earl of Washburn. Your cousin, Harriet, she was my friend, and she was why I would always be so happy to visit this place. I'm sorry, but I don't recall how many grandchildren there were or who her parents were or who your parents were—I was so young and I didn't pay attention to all the adults. And then after your parents' funeral, we no longer visited. I do not know why we stopped. I wish I had paid more attention, could remember more to help."

His eyes closed for a long moment as he nodded. His face suddenly scrunched tight in a long wince. "My father—there was a uniform."

Ness looked to the manor house, searching her memory. There had been so many adults there when her family visited and the adults rarely interacted with the children.

A faint recollection perked into her mind. "Yes, maybe. I partly remember a man in a red uniform. I believe he may have been in the army?"

Her head shook as her eyes closed. "I'm sorry I don't remember more. I remember the funeral for the three of you, we traveled here for that, but there were so many hushed tones of people talking about what happened to

your family, and I didn't understand any of it. Just that
Harriet was so sad and scared she barely spoke two words
to me. I never heard what happened to you three, just that
you all died in a horrible accident. We didn't visit again.
And I missed it, missed Harriet, missed you. I'm trying to
remember more and I hate that I cannot."

"It's not up to you to piece my life back together for
me, Ness."

She opened her eyes to find him staring at her, worry
on his face. Worry for her when he should only be worried
about his own mind.

She gave him a bright smile. "I just want you to
know where your place in the world once was. That you
were happy here. I knew that about you. You laughed too
easily back then to have been troubled. Real laughter. Your
laughter was so light and carefree. It was a rare thing. Even I
understood that at that age. Wondered at it."

A distance in front of them, a carriage pulled up from
the far side of the manor house and stopped at the front
door of the home. Anyone exiting the manor house was
blocked from view, but Ness could see through the open
space under the carriage dark boots and skirts shuffling
about. Then the coach was on the move, clipping down the
drive toward them.

Talen shifted his horse off to the side of the lane and
Ness followed suit, tightening the reins to still her horse
until the carriage passed.

The finest of carriages with a partially faded coat of
arms—a lion opposite a dragon surrounded the shield—
passed Ness and Talen with the curtain drawn. Just as she

was about to nudge her mount forward, the coach stopped abruptly, sending the team of horses neighing, pawing at the ground at the intrusion to their pace down the hillside.

The driver turned around in his perch and motioned to Talen and Ness to move to the coach.

Talen gave Ness a sidelong glance with a raised eyebrow, then clicked his horse into motion to align next to the carriage.

The curtain pulled aside and the small window slipped open. An elderly woman with a turquoise turban wrapped atop her head, but not covering the tufts of white hair that curled out along the edges, popped into the opening of the window.

Talen tilted his hat to her.

"You, young sir"—the woman pointed at Talen, her white glove wagging into the air just outside the carriage— "take off your hat."

Blunt and bordering on rude, but the woman didn't seem to take note, her tone almost frantic.

Talen glanced at Ness, then removed his top hat from his head. "Ma'am?"

The elderly woman poked her head fully out of the window, her eyes squinting as she studied Talen's face. Then her cheeks went pale. Paler. Paler.

Her lower jaw dropped, a whisper on her tongue. "No, no, it couldn't be."

Talen stiffened on his horse. "Did you have something you needed to say to us, ma'am? We were just about to make it up to the main house to inquire as to who is in residence. We have some inquiries to make on the history of the place."

"Inquiries, what sort of inquiries?" Her look went sharp on him.

"I am told I have history here that I am attempting to uncover. Might you know who currently resides here?"

The older woman bristled, her gloved hand gripping onto the lower edge of the window. "I reside here—I'm the Dowager Countess of Washburn, and you are, sir?"

"I am Talen Blackstone." Talen turned to motion to Ness. "And this is Mrs. Docherty."

"Mrs. Docherty." The woman rolled the name over her tongue several times, but couldn't tear her stare off of Talen. "Mrs. Docherty. I should know that name. Where should I know that name from?"

Her eyes squinted harder at Talen. "But you. You I know. Your eyes."

Talen stilled. "You do?"

"I do. I do. Why do I know your eyes, young man?"

The dowager gasped a breath, shuddered, and then retreated for a moment back into the carriage before poking her head in front of the window again, her look searching Talen's face. "Conner? Little Conner? No. Impossible. It cannot be." Her dark brown eyes looked haunted.

Talen stared at her, his jaw solidly in place. Silent.

Everything in Ness clenched, and she couldn't look away from Talen, trying to discern what he was thinking.

The silence stretched onward, the dowager and Ness staring at Talen. Talen sitting stoically atop his horse, not moving, not acknowledging the dowager's words.

Ness gave a tiny cough. "It is him. Conner. I recognized him and brought him here. It is him, but he doesn't remember that time."

"Doesn't remember that time?" The dowager finally swung her look to Ness and her nose flipped up as she scrutinized Ness from head to toe. A vacant smile pasted the edges of her lips to her cheeks. "You, Mrs. Docherty, you are…forgive me, but my memory fades me…you've been here before?" Her head shook with a long blink, her turban hitting the upper part of the window. "Are you Baron Gundall's girl? I thought she married into the Whetland family?"

"I did. I am Nessia. But I am a widow now."

"Nessia—ahh—you are? Did you marry the eldest or the youngest grandson of Lord Whetland?"

"The youngest. Gilroy."

"I am sorry to hear that, dear." Her finger flicked out to point at Ness's left arm resting in her lap. "Your arm looks to be in pain."

Ness looked down with a shrug. "It is mostly healed now, it doesn't pain at all."

"Good, good, good," the dowager whispered slowly, mostly to herself in what looked like an attempt to purchase a modicum of time to gain her equilibrium.

She exhaled a long breath, her look swiveling to Talen. "Forgive me for my bluntness on this matter, but you, lad… you don't remember? You don't remember who you are? How can that be?"

Talen lifted his shoulders. "I am attempting to piece together that answer for myself as well. Mrs. Docherty has been kind enough to show me this place in attempt to spur some memories forth."

The dowager nodded. "Of course, of course. Such a kindness. But you, you both must come up to the main house and sit with me. This isn't proper, a conversation like this out in the open in the drive."

Talen shook his head. "We didn't intend to interrupt your plans, as you were clearly on your way out."

She flicked her hand in the air. "Nonsense. I was about to do a round of calls, but that can wait. We weren't going to get far anyway, if the mud on your horses is any indication of the roads. This is far more important. You will follow me up to the house." Her head turned toward the front of the carriage. "Turn us around, Mr. Leopold. Straight to the house."

"Yes, mi'lady."

The driver nodded toward Talen and Ness before sending the horses down to the base of the drive where he could turn the carriage about in a wide swath of gravel. Within minutes, the carriage passed them on the way back up to the main house.

Ness glanced to Talen. "Are you ready for this?"

He looked at her, a steely glint in his pale blue eyes. "Why do I think my answer should be no?"

Her lips pulled back in a smile that didn't quite make it into a smile. The whirlwind whipping around in her belly reflected the exact thing in his eyes.

She wasn't sure either of them was ready for this. But there was no turning back now. "I am here with you, no matter what."

He gave her the slightest nod.

She inclined her head toward the manor house, nudging her horse into motion.

Onward.

{ CHAPTER 23 }

Talen stared at the teacup in Ness's hand.

She'd taken it to be polite, of course, but her hand had hung there, in the air, halfway to her mouth for the last ten minutes as the dowager countess bustled about the drawing room doing what, he couldn't quite place.

Closing doors. Rifling through drawers. Pulling out papers. Disappearing into an adjacent room for a moment, then returning with what looked to be a frame under a white cloth that she leaned against the wall beside the side door of the room. Scurrying out into the main hallway, her steps echoing down the corridor only to return minutes later, a flush spotting her wrinkled neck.

For the wear of time on the dowager countess's face, she moved about the room swiftly, her robust form spry from one task to the next.

Ness's hand had eventually failed, setting the teacup back down onto the saucer without taking a sip.

Finally, the dowager sat across from him and Ness at the round card table where she'd had tea brought in and settled them.

The dowager's hands were empty now and she poured a cup of tea for herself. For long moments that stretched the silence, her bare fingers skittered to and from the edge of the saucer under the cup, about to pick it up, then thinking the better of it. Again and again.

Just drink the damn tea.

Maddening, the whole of it, for how little she'd said once they'd arrived at the house. A house that manifested no memories for him upon entering.

He cleared his throat. "May we come straight to it, my lady? You believe you know me. Correct?" Direct, but they could waste the whole day watching this woman fiddle about. He could be back at the coaching inn right now with Ness in his bed, enjoying her naked body on top of his. The preferable option, since they were going to be stuck in the area for another day waiting for the roads to become passable.

The whole of this was a mistake.

The dowager finally committed to the tea and picked up her cup and saucer, taking an elongated sip, her look bouncing between him and Ness. "I do know you. I cannot deny it. What have you remembered?"

"I can be blunt?"

"Please, it would make the whole of this easier."

His lips pulled back tightly, not sure his flavor of bluntness was appropriate for the woman, but then he forged forth, discarding the thought of delicacy. What happened to his parents, to him, was brutal and he wouldn't sweep over the truth of it.

"I remember my father being shot and my mother murdered in front of me after hours of watching her be tortured. I remember being beaten to near unconsciousness and then choked until I left this world. That is what I remember."

The dowager winced, her teacup clattering on her saucer as she dropped it onto the table, brown liquid bouncing and sloshing to splatter onto the inlaid wood. Her hand went onto her chest and she took several long breaths, appearing to get her composure only slightly back. "I feared that. What else?"

"Nothing. Nothing before that. Nothing after."

Her brow wrinkled, half of it disappearing under the turquoise turban. "Nothing after? But you are here, before me. Where have you been?"

"I woke up on a Royal Navy warship thirteen years ago. I lived at sea for seven years. London for the last six years. A sailor named me, for I had no name I could recall. Talen Blackstone. That is my name. All of that, I remember."

Her head bobbed up and down, her turban slipping slightly forward as her fingers pressed into her chest. "But… you don't remember me, sweet lad?"

The nerves along the back of his neck spiked at the term of endearment. He was the farthest thing from a sweet lad. "No."

"I saved you."

His head angled down, his glare slicing into her. "You what?"

"I saved you." She puffed an exhale, her weathered brown eyes darkening with memories. "They were choking you, those awful, awful men and you—you look so much like my Clayborne and I had to stop them. I was too late for your mother, for your father, but you…you I had to save."

"Who in the hell did you save me from?" The words barked out, harsh and loud, and Ness reached out and set her hand on his thigh, squeezing his leg.

Calm.

She wanted him calm when there was no margin for calm after what the woman had just told him.

The dowager knew. Knew exactly who had killed his parents. Who he now had to hunt down and slit from throat to gut.

The dowager blanched, cowering across the table from him and it took her a moment to speak, her stare on the table between them, her finger tracing a line beside the spilled tea.

"I must first start with who I am. I am your aunt, married to your Uncle Fredrick, the younger brother of your father. There were three boys, and the eldest, Walter, was dying of consumption during the summer that your parents died. Your father was the second son. And your grandfather, the earl, had just died the spring before."

Her eyes darted up to him, then slid back down to the table. "My husband was convinced…well, he believed your father, Thomas, was insane, that the loss of his leg in the war had made his mind mad. Fredrick believed that Thomas wasn't fit to hold the title should Walter die. They argued about it endlessly that summer, the three brothers."

"My father lost his leg in Boney's war?"

"He did. He was highly decorated—a hero—but he saw a lot of death. That death—what he endured— your mother always said it changed him. Changed him drastically."

"You're saying my father had gone mad?"

Her shoulders lifted. "I don't know. Whenever your mother said anything to me, it was short and whispered, behind closed doors. And my husband had his own opinions of the fitness of your father's mind that were much…stronger."

Talen had to look away from her. Had to take a steeling breath.

He didn't want to hear any of this. None of it. This was a story about another family. Another life. Not his life. Not his parents.

He stared out the window at the view along the east side of the estate. A wide, open-air pavilion sat along a rectangular pond, stretching the entire length of it. Bloody opulent.

"What did your husband do?" He couldn't look back to the dowager.

"Something I didn't think him capable of. But he had become obsessed with saving the earldom, saving it from madness, saving it from anything that would taint the gild of it. But beyond that, I think it went deeper with him. Your mother and father and you—you three were happy in each other's company. A happiness that had always eluded him…us. I know he envied it. It festered within him and only added fuel onto his obsession to save the estate from ruin."

"He was third son, it wasn't his concern." Talen's words were wooden, the rasp in his voice more pronounced than usual.

"No, but that didn't deter my husband. I tried to stop him—to talk reason to him, but I could not sway him from his obsession. He was determined that he was the only one that could save the earldom." The dowager's lips pursed, a deep frown setting on her face as she paused. "He hated

being under his brothers' thumbs—Walter, Thomas. He'd had a lifetime of it. He tried to hide how it ate away at his soul. But then one day…he just broke…his mind broke so fully and I found out too late what he had set into motion."

"You're saying my uncle did this? To my parents? To me?" Talen's words came out slow, measured, regaining all the indifference he'd mastered at the Alabaster when dealing with the scummiest vermin.

She gave an exhausted nod. "He lured the three of you to that cottage where men he had hired were waiting." Her fingers went up to her mouth, tapping her lips against her own horrified words. "I am so sorry that I found out too late—too late to stop him. Too late to save your father. Too late to save your mother. But you. You were determined to live, so I got you out of the cottage."

His glare skewered her. "He murdered my parents?"

Her face whitened to ash as her hand dropped to her throat. She nodded.

"And you saved me?"

"Except I was a failure. I was too late. Too late to stop any of it. Fredrick had come in with blood on his waistcoat and by the time I found you—them—one of those vile, vile men was choking you. You. A boy. A mere child. I threw myself at him, shoving him off you, threatening them— they knew I was Fredrick's wife. And I got you out of there. Out of that cottage. But I was afraid my husband wouldn't stop at your parents' deaths. He wanted your life as well. My fear for you was so great that I whisked you to the port in Whitehaven and paid a doctor aboard a departing ship to take care of you. It was all I could think to do."

"Why would you send me away? Why not keep me safe?"

Her head tilted to the side, the turban slipping along her left ear. "I didn't have that power, Talen. Your own father couldn't keep you safe, so what could I have done? I couldn't risk your life by keeping you near and within my husband's reach. The ship was the only option—I had to send you into exile."

Thundering rage beat in his chest, fighting to explode, but Talen tamped down on it, his words pinched. "What happened to your husband?"

"He died nine years ago."

Ness gasped next to him. A gasp not in surprise, but in pain.

His look shot to her, searching her face and then he glanced downward. Her hand was still on his thigh, but he'd grabbed it without even realizing it.

He'd been crushing it. Was crushing it still.

His hand instantly released her delicate bones, his knuckles cracking for the strain they'd been under. Bloody hell, he hadn't broken her hand, had he?

His stare jumped up to her face, panicked. The last thing he wanted to do was hurt her. Scare her.

She held his stare for a long second, hiding pain, he could see. But then she simply flipped her hand over on his thigh, her palm and fingers wrapping up around his knuckles, not letting his hand go. Weak, but holding on.

"Please, you must stay here at Washburn until my son arrives." The dowager drew his attention back to her. "He is due within the next two days and there is much that we must…consider and resolve."

Talen instantly shook his head. "No. We have to make it to Scotland. Stopping here at the estate wasn't even part of our plan. It was only the rain that held us in the area."

Her head jerked back. "Scotland? Whatever for?"

"Mrs. Docherty and I are to marry."

"An elopement?" Shock widened her eyes for a second, quickly being replaced with a smile. "How wonderful. Yet please, my son should only be a day, two at the most. But more importantly, this matter is most urgent for you. You do want to marry under your proper name, do you not?"

His right eyebrow cocked. "My proper name? Talen Blackstone."

"No, no. You must marry under your real name. Conner Burton—wait—Conner Josiah Bron...Bar...No, I don't recall the full of it. There are at least two more names in your full Christian name. It was so long ago. You will want all of those for the marriage to make it proper. I have all the names in the family bible, but it is not here. It is at the dower house a half day's ride away. I'll go to fetch it tomorrow." She jumped up from the table, going to the wall by the side door and picking up the large frame with a sheet over it that leaned against the wall.

Walking back to the table, she tugged the sheet off and dropped it to the floor, then turned the painting toward Talen. "Please, just look. I wanted you to see this, see them. See you."

The portrait held three figures. A brown-haired man in a red uniform standing behind a seated woman—a beautiful woman with blond hair, striking blue eyes, the slightest smile on her face and dressed in a resplendent peach gown that flowed down and to the width of the portrait. Poised just in front of her, a little boy with dark blond hair in a blue skeleton suit, maybe six or seven and staring stoically at the artist.

A boy with his very features. Nose and cheeks and jawline that matched his father's. Eyes that matched his mother's. Hair the color between the two.

The air disappeared from his lungs, leaving him weightless, groundless for several seconds.

"Please, just stay here at Washburn for a few days," the dowager said. "You do not belong in a coaching inn. You belong here. Stay and learn what you can, maybe remember who you are and then you can go into the marriage with the blessing of the family behind you. It is a miracle that you have returned to us." Her words paused, sudden tears in her eyes. "A true miracle."

With a deep breath she set the portrait down on the chair she had been occupying and her look shifted to Ness. "If I remember correctly, Mrs. Docherty—Nessia—you were such a sweet child. You were Harriet's favorite playmate as I recall. I'm sure you will make Conner a fine bride if you are as delightful as you once were. Please, can the elopement wait not but a few mere days?"

Her eyebrows lifted as her look went back and forth between Talen and Ness.

Ness squeezed his hand and he looked to her. She gave him a slight nod.

He hated the thought of it—of staying here.

Not when he could be headed north and making Ness his wife. Making certain she was protected. Though his

given name would be important to that end, he loathed to admit.

"It is just a few days, Talen," Ness said softly. Not imploring or demanding, just letting him know it was right by her.

His head heavy, he nodded. "We can stay. Two days is all we can afford."

{ CHAPTER 24 }

"This is the spot?" At the water's edge, Talen looked to Ness as he stopped his horse next to hers.

She glanced at him, at the rigid hold his body still held. The cords along his neck so taut they could snap with the slightest provocation.

Talen had insisted to the dowager that they needed to travel back to the coaching inn to gather a few items and let their driver know of the plans to stay at Washburn Manor for a few days, but Ness knew he'd just needed to get out of that drawing room, out of that house. He'd been near to jumping out of his skin, he'd been so tense.

No wonder, for the monstrosities that his aunt had described.

She could see full well he needed to injure someone— kill someone if he could. But there wasn't anyone to attack, to make suffer for what had happened to his parents. Not anymore, and that was the cruelest blow of all.

Ness nodded to Talen's question. Their trip to the coaching inn could wait an hour. He needed to breathe. Breathe air that wasn't tainted with death and the past and this was the most secluded spot she knew on the Washburn estate.

"This is it. This is what I wanted to show you." She looked out across the crystal-clear pond, the water always so peculiarly pure without the usual muck of ponds this size.

Tucked into a glade of the forest surrounding the main estate, the pond was lined with tall reeds on the left of the waterside, a raft of ducks floating in and out of the spikes of green.

"I spent countless hours out here with Harriet when we were young, mainly because bunnies were always nesting in the thick of the grasses at the far side of the pond where the trees skirt up from the water." She pointed across the way. "And we loved to uncover the bunnies and play with them, holding them tight in our skirts before tucking them back into their little burrows."

A crooked smile came to Talen's face and he dismounted, then tied the reins of his horse to a nearby low-hanging branch. He came to her side, grabbing her by the waist and lifting her down from her mare.

So easy for him, as though she was a little scrap of tulle he barely had to extend a muscle for.

He set her down, his hands not moving from her waist as he held her stare for a long, silent moment. A twinge of uncertainty made the edges of his light blue eyes crinkle and he leaned slightly away as his left hand went to her right arm, pulling it up between them until both of his hands could clasp around her palm.

He looked down at her hand, his fingers gently tracing bones and ligaments from wrist to fingertip. "Your hand. I hurt it in there."

"It is fine."

His head shook, his gaze downward as the tips of his fingers ran across her knuckles and then her palm, tickling the skin. "Your hand—"

"Is fine."

"I saw your face and I didn't mean to hurt you. I'm sorry. I didn't even know I had grabbed it, much less crushed it." His head bent downward and he kissed her palm.

She reached up and set the fingers of her left hand along his jawline. "I know you would never hurt me."

His eyes lifted to her, his look wary. "You seem so certain of it."

"I am."

"How?"

She shrugged. "The same reason you knew you had to protect me in London. Whatever this is between us, it's innate. Without logical reason. All I've been doing during the last month is looking for logic on why I trust you so much, when maybe I just needed to accept what is between us instead of questioning it."

He didn't agree with her, neither did he argue. He kissed her hand again and then lowered it between them. "I don't want you sleeping outside of my bed."

Her look flickered off of him toward the direction of the manor house. "We promised the dowager we would stay at the house. Sharing a room isn't proper—even if I am a widow and you are obviously a rake."

"Then we have separate rooms, but you'll be sleeping in mine or I'll be sleeping in yours."

"Talen, your aunt—"

"Can judge all she wants. I don't give a boar's ass about it." His hand went along her neck, his thumb trailing down along the slope of her breasts. "And not just because I

want your body under my hands. I still need you safe. Just because we're closed in behind grand stone walls doesn't mean I'm about to let my guard down."

She nodded, utterly at a loss to argue the point for she didn't want to be anywhere but in his bed.

"Good. We are here for a few days, no more. We'll tell the coachman to come round when the roads are passable. Then we'll leave. We'll leave no matter what. Whether or not her son arrives by that time."

"Agreed." Ness exhaled relief. She too, would rather be traveling north. Staying here a few days wasn't ideal, but she would be safe enough. And Talen needed this, needed to find some memory of happiness that he could hold onto. *She* needed it. Needed him not to be left with only the terror of what had happened to his parents. "We can always return on our way back south."

He turned from her, his eyes on the water, not committing to any future visits to Washburn.

She followed his gaze, watching the ducks sending ripples across the sheen of water. "I never knew why this pond was always so clear. There must be a spring under it."

He inclined his head toward the water. "Why bring me here?"

"You needed to be still for a moment." She looked up at him, studying the strong lines of his profile that made her heart tighten in her chest. "You needed to not be in that house. Not riding. Not arranging the future. Not thinking of the border and marrying me. Still." Her hand flicked forward. "So I thought this place appropriate."

"I needed this?" He glanced at her, his eyes pondering her face for a long moment. "And?"

She expelled a breathless chuckle, her mouth quirking to the side. "And I have a memory of you here."

"Do tell."

"It is a sweet one. One where you weren't putting toads in my slippers."

"I hardly believe it."

She stepped toward the water's edge, the toes of her boots pressing into the ground where it started to sag with moisture and Talen followed, staying by her side. "Over there, where the ducks like to nest, the ground turns into mud, but one can't really see it until one's feet are locked deep into the muck."

"Which happened?"

"It did. One of the first times I was here. I was stuck for some time, but then I managed to get my feet out. But I lost one of my slippers in the process and I was crying about it and Harriet didn't know what to do with me. I knew I couldn't go back to the house with one missing shoe or my father would be mad at me and he was harsh, so I refused to go back."

"Why would your father even care if you lost a shoe?"

Her shoulders lifted. "I don't know that he would have even cared about the shoe. But he liked to be angry with me. Angry with my mama. Anything could spark it. The smallest thing like a lost shoe."

A spark flashed in the blue of his irises and his eyes went wide. "Did you have ribbons in your hair?"

She stilled, her look riveted on him. "I did."

His eyes closed, his head shaking slightly. "The vision is fuzzy, but they are there. Orange. They were orange. So strange. I'd never seen a girl with orange ribbons in her hair. Yellow, pink, white, red, but never orange. Orange against the dark chestnut curls. So stark. So odd. Orange."

Tears welled in her eyes as she stared at his face. She ached to reach out and grab him, shake him, shake every memory free from the web in his brain, but she held her hands at her sides, afraid to interfere with how close he was to finding the memory in his mind. "You remember?"

His eyes opened to her.

"Maybe." His voice was a whisper. "Maybe I do."

"That was the first time I met you."

He looked to the mud creeping along the edge of the pond. "Did I get the shoe out?"

"You did, but in the process, you fell in, getting muck up to your waist. You said your mother wouldn't care. You even struggled farther out into the lake, mostly on your belly, getting mud all over your white shirt so you could reach clear water and wash my shoe clean. You were my hero."

His look darted back to her. "I'm not your hero, Ness."

She smiled, unwilling to argue with him. "But you were that day. And you'll not take that away from me."

His gaze swung away from her, glossing over as he studied the edge of the pond for long seconds. Whether he remembered more or not, he wasn't admitting to.

His lips parted, his words coming slowly. "That image—that image of you with the orange ribbons and the fat chestnut curls. I want that. I want that memory. But I don't know if I want the rest."

She stepped closer to him, slipping her left arm under his, entwining the splint down along his forearm and curling the tips of her fingers into his palm. Her cheek went onto his upper arm, the wool of his tailcoat rubbing her skin as she looked up at him. "I don't blame you. I didn't know what had happened here, Talen. I never could have imagined. But if I had…if I had known all of it was as horrific as that, I never would have brought you here. Never would have insisted. You were right to avoid this place."

His chest lifted in a deep sigh. "But now we're here."

"We are." She shifted her look to the water, leaning into him, her temple resting on his arm. "And I don't know what is the right thing to do now. I wanted you here to remember the good, not the bad. That was all."

"I don't know either." The rasp in his voice hitched, his words a low rumble over the water, pain etched in the crevices.

They stood, silent minutes passing, watching the ducks dive and peck away at invisible delicacies under the water.

"She didn't say it." The words blurted from Ness's mouth, the thought that had been heavy in her mind since they'd left the manor house.

Talen looked down at her. "Didn't say what?"

Ness straightened next to him. "The dowager didn't say that her son is the earl and it's a title that is, by rights, not his. Not with you alive."

His eyebrows lifted, deep lines etching into his skin. "My aunt seemed overwhelmed by the whole of today, and understandably so. Our appearance. What she had to tell me of what had happened to my parents. Secrets like that are maggots on one's soul and she handled the whole of it

with more grace than I thought a woman like her capable of."

Ness's lips pursed and she nodded. True, the dowager had been under an incredible amount of stress with what she had to report.

"I hadn't given it a thought myself," he said. "But you found it odd?"

Her shoulders lifted. "I find this whole situation disastrous. What happened to your parents, what happened to you. You're right, I don't think anyone was thinking about the earldom today." She shook her head, dismissing the thought. "When did the dowager think she would be back with the bible tomorrow? I heard you ask before you mounted your horse, but I didn't hear her answer."

"She thought to fetch it and be back by early evening."

Ness smiled, leaning into his side once more. "I cannot wait to discover what your full name is."

"Talen. Talen Blackstone better be what she comes back with."

Ness laughed. "I will accept that as well. Prefer it, even."

{ CHAPTER 25 }

His feet bare, but with trousers and a lawn shirt on, Talen stepped into the library of Washburn Manor, holding the lamp from his chamber into the shadows at this side of the library. Just another one of the expansive rooms he'd wandered through that day with Ness, trying to spark memories of the past. Memories that remained elusive.

Stubbornly so.

The dowager had been gone the whole of the day and well into nightfall. He'd been convinced she'd fled and stayed at the dower house to avoid him, but the echoes of the front door opening and closing had reached into the bowels of the house and had pulled him from bed and Ness's warm naked body.

Not that he'd been sleeping. Not that he'd had any real sleep since arriving at this blasted place. Ness's body—burying himself in her—had been the only thing keeping him from tearing apart this place brick by bloody brick.

A heavy wool wrap still draped over her robust form, the dowager stood bent over a table by the fireplace, her back to him, her head cocked as she tilted a book toward the light of the flames.

"You returned."

She jumped upright with a squeak, her hand on her chest as she spun around. "Sweet lad, you frightened me. Do not sneak up upon a lady of my age or you'll find me duly expired at your feet."

"I believe you hardier than that, from what I have seen."

She smiled, taking his words as a compliment. Whether or not he meant them as one he wasn't sure himself.

He stopped a distance from her. "The travel to and from the dower house today wasn't as quick as you had hoped?"

"No, no, it was not." Her hand waved in the air. "My driver thought the road would be fine, but it was a slow slog, with far too many stops where the carriage had to be pushed through. Your driver was right to recommend against forging north at the moment."

She motioned for him to come closer. "Come, see. I have it—here it is, your proper name. Come see by the firelight."

Talen moved forward, setting his lamp on the table by the fireplace. She lifted up the book to him, holding it open to one of the first few pages. Long lines of names listed down the left and right sides of the pages. Names of people he should have known, should have heard of. People of his blood and bones.

She tilted the bible toward the fireplace and pointed to one line on the right side. "See, here you are. Right here. Conner Josiah Bartholomew Francis Burton. It was a handful, I remember that. Francis was your great-great-great-grandfather. I believe Josiah came from your mother's lineage, though I fear I don't recall the direct relation. And I was just studying the names of the past, as I'm not positive where Bartholomew came from. I don't recall one in the line, but I haven't looked at the bible in a long time."

Talen stared at his name, written in such a fine script. Beautiful, even, where the letters looped together with the flourish of an inspired quill. His mark on history when he'd never had one.

Yet he felt no ownership on it. Couldn't feel ownership on it. Not when this family that had created him had been the very same one that had destroyed him long ago, taking everything from him.

Taking his place in the world.

With a relieved sigh, a smile spread wide across the dowager's face, her thick skin crinkling with age. "I look at you in this light and you look so young again, Conner. You look just like my own boy, Clayborne. It makes my heart happy to see you again. Alive. Healthy. I have worried on you for so long."

His eyes flickered to her then back to the names scattered down the page. "My name is Talen and you see a past I don't remember."

She set the book onto the table and turned fully to him. "Being here hasn't sparked any other memories? Did you visit your room in the nursery wing? I know much of that has been covered and isn't in use now, but maybe there is something there that you would remember. A wooden horse or something akin to it?"

A caustic chuckle left his throat. "To my knowledge, I've never played with a wooden horse in my life."

"But you used to, I remember that. You didn't go anywhere without a horse in your hand."

"I didn't even learn to ride until I arrived in England six years ago. I have sea legs, nothing else."

Her hands nervously smoothed down the front folds of her wool wrapper as her lips drew inward, his tone cutting off her babblings of the past. Good. He didn't want to hear it. Hear what a happy life he had. Hear what was taken away from him.

He tapped his fingers on the corner of the bible. "This is helpful. Thank you for retrieving it."

"Of course. Of course, anything to make this easier on you. I am so sorry for the past. For all my husband wrought upon you."

His lips pulled back in a tight line. "You should know, aunt, that I don't want the earldom. I imagine that is why you have been insistent on us staying until your son arrives. Honestly, I want very little to do with this place and my connection to it. The name, I'll take that to the marriage vows only to protect Ness. Beyond that, I have my own wealth, my own life. I do not need a new one."

Her lips parted in a silent gasp. "But, you—you are certain? The earldom is yours by birthright."

He shook his head. "If I've learned anything in my life, it's that rights are earned, not given. And I don't want this right. Don't want anything to do with this place. With the past. Ness and I will leave on the morrow, whether or not your son arrives."

"But…but you are family. You must—"

"I must do nothing." His eyes narrowed at her, his fury from yesterday instantly igniting into flames and surging through his blood. "With due regard, Lady Washburn, you may have saved my life, but then you threw an eleven-year-old boy onto a ship, injured, with no memory of his past.

Everything of my life, of who I am now, is what I've built with my own two hands since then. Good and bad. I don't need to be delivered from it, don't need to be saved from it."

"Oh." Her hand flew up to her face, her fingers pressing against her lips. "I am so sorry, my sweet lad. So sorry for what path I sent you on. I don't know how you will forgive me."

"It is what it is." The statement made, not offering forgiveness or condolences against her distress. Noble emotions that he doubted he'd ever be able to extend to this woman and her family. He inclined his head to her. "You will excuse me."

Grabbing his lamp, Talen turned on his heel and strode out of the library, needing Ness. Her body, her arms around him. Needing him grounded to who and what he was. London. Harsh. Driven. Wary. Not to be trifled with.

Stepping into his room, he watched Ness sleeping on her side as he stripped down. The low light from the fireplace sent shadows across the top of her smooth breasts, her nipples just barely covered by the sheet he'd tugged over her when he'd left the bed. Her fingers moved on the empty mattress beside her, and her eyes fluttered open, drowsy.

Finding him standing next to the bed, she smiled and Talen crawled under the sheet, kissing her bare shoulder. At least the beds were comfortable here at Washburn. Thick mattresses that could cushion Ness from how hard he needed to drive into her.

Her hand lifted to land on his chest, her fingers curling into his skin. And just like that, the fury dissipated from his veins.

Ness looked up at him. "Is the dowager back?"

"She is."

"And who am I marrying?" She pushed herself to sitting, the sheet falling down about her waist and exposing her breasts.

Damned distracting.

"You're marrying Talen Blackstone."

"Yes. And?"

He held back a wince. "Conner Josiah Bartholomew Francis Burton."

The slightest smirk lifted the corners of her lips. "It is long."

"It is."

She nodded, her lips pursing. "But between us, it is Talen Blackstone I am marrying. Understood? You are Talen and no one else."

"Understood and appreciated." His head dipped, his lips moving down along her breast to her left nipple. Slipping it into his mouth, he swirled his tongue along it, marveling at how good she tasted. Always water to his thirst.

A mewl left her as she arched her back to angle herself better to his mouth and her fingers sank into his hair. "Did the dowager say anything else?"

"No." He lifted his lips from her body for a breath. "But I told her."

"Told her what?"

He moved onto her neck, finding the dipped burrow with his tongue where her collarbone, neck and shoulder triangulated, the exact spot that made the tiny hairs on her arms spike. "That I want no part of this family. No earldom. Nothing. That we are leaving on the morrow."

"You what?"

His head popped up, his look finding her stunned face. "That I want nothing to do with this life." He leaned forward, burying himself in her hair, his lips aching to be on her skin again.

She pushed against his chest, holding him away. "You just decided that?"

"I did." His eyebrows angled inward as he found her gaze. "I don't want this. This life."

"Why not?"

"Why not?" He jerked away from her hands on his chest, his arm swinging up into the air around them. "I don't want the monstrosity of this place. It only brings pain. It brought pain—death—to everyone that I cared about. Why would I want this? I don't. There's no reason for it. So I refused it."

"But you can't just refuse who you really are." She leaned forward, her fingers finding the center line of his chest. "It is your birthright, this place, the title. You must take it."

Her touch suddenly burning him, he jerked out of the bed, the full of his naked body pulsing in the flickering light of the fire, muscles twitching. "I don't want it. Don't want this. So stop pushing it, Ness."

She scampered to the side of the mattress, dragging the sheet with her. "Talen, no. I'm not pushing it—I'm just saying you don't remember everything yet. I only mean that you're making a decision that you might regret. A decision

not but two days after you found out what really happened to your parents. Of course you don't want that—what happened to them—in your life. But there was so much more. If you remember more about who your parents were, how they were, maybe that's your connection back to the good instead of the bad."

Her toes touched the floor and Talen took a step away from her, his fingers folding into fists.

She stood, clutching the sheet at her chest, advancing on him. "This family, this title. It wasn't all horrible, Talen. I remember that. I saw you happy here once. Happy like any child that had a carefree life. I envied you that life." She reached out, grabbing for his arm, but he snapped it away. Yet still she came at him.

"And your aunt even said so—she said you three, your mother, father and you, were happy. Happy. That was all I ever wanted you to remember by coming back here. That you were happy. Capable of it. Worthy of it."

Every word she said, a nail pounding into his brain. She kept talking about a happiness he'd never known, like it was a given.

But what happiness could have existed if it all ended like it did?

False happiness?

That was the only thing that could have existed. His mother took her last breath in front of his very eyes, reaching for him, and he'd been too cowardly to stretch out even a finger to her.

He wasn't fit to even sniff around happiness. Happiness had no place in his life. He'd always known that to his core and finally discovering what happened to his parents only solidified that fact.

"You were happy, Talen." Ness took a final step toward him, her amber eyes pleading, glowing gold in the firelight, and he had to thrust a long step backward, his heels touching the heat of the marble hearth.

"Yet instead of memories of happiness in my mind, you just set the reality of the nightmare that I've managed to avoid my whole life into my head." His words snapped, his voice shaking with a sudden rage he couldn't control, his yell filling the room. "That's what you gave me here, Ness. A nightmare that I have to live with every minute now. Horrors that cannot be avenged. That is what you gave me when you brought me here. Not happiness. The exact opposite of it. Hell. Demons I cannot escape. You did this."

Her head snapped back and she blanched white, her eyes wide.

Without a word, she dropped the sheet to the floor, grabbed her robe from the chair he'd flung it across earlier, wrapped it haphazardly about her body, and left the room.

He didn't stop her.

{ CHAPTER 26 }

He should have gone and found her.

Five minutes. Ten. Thirty. That was as far as he should have left it.

But he'd scared her half to death.

Scared himself for how much anger he'd spewed out onto her.

It wasn't her fault, none of this. She'd truly only brought him here to Washburn so that he would remember her from long ago. To prove to him she wasn't crazy. And she wasn't. But now he was starting to suffer madness in his own head he couldn't escape from.

For that, he'd screamed at her like she was the devil himself. She wasn't. He knew that, but fury had erupted out of him, uncontrolled, unplanned.

Fury that had caused for an agonizing moment, fear in her eyes. Fear of him.

Even a second of fear in her eyes was too much.

Setting fear into her was something he'd sworn to himself he would never do. Not with her past.

That alone kept him in his room, not going to Ness. Not wanting to admit to himself how he'd just failed her.

So instead, he'd left the last words he spoke to her to fester throughout the whole night. A whole night where he'd tossed and turned in an empty, cold bed.

And now he couldn't find Ness.

He'd been searching the estate for two hours with no sign of her. He should have gone to find her at daybreak before she could have disappeared on him.

Talen veered left at the main staircase, heading into the lower drawing room with the odd sense that he and Ness were just circling about each other in this giant house, not in the same spot at the same moment.

Time to start retracing his steps.

Walking into the lower drawing room, he was surprised to find the dowager sitting by the east window, her stare on a diamond-shape pattern of embroidery in her hands. He hadn't seen her all morning, nor when he'd checked in here a half hour prior.

"Lady Washburn, pardon my interruption, but do you know Ness's whereabouts?"

Her forefinger pushing needle through cloth, the dowager glanced up from her embroidery. "Good morning, sweet lad. She is not in her room?"

"No."

Her look went back down to her needle. "The solarium?"

"No."

"The portrait gallery?"

"No."

"The breakfast room or the library?"

"No and no." Was she going to name every blasted room in the place? He stifled a sigh. "She's not in the house."

"I see. Then she must not yet be back from the coaching inn."

Why in the hell hadn't the dowager started there?

He took a step toward the dowager, his voice incredulous. "The coaching inn?"

Ness wouldn't. Not without telling him. She wouldn't dare go alone to the coaching inn.

Would she?

"Yes." The dowager pulled free a long stretch of pink thread, her right hand going high into the air as she looked up at him. "She said she needed to go there early this morning, though she didn't say why. I thought she just forgot something she needed there that was with your coach. I thought she would be back by now." Her head angled toward the window. "You can check with the stable hand to see which horse she took."

"No. She wouldn't have."

The dowager smiled. "Wouldn't have what, sweet lad?"

"She wouldn't have gone there without telling me."

The dowager shrugged and looked back to her embroidery. "I can only report to you what she said when we crossed paths in the breakfast room."

"How long ago?"

"Two hours, maybe three. Possibly more. I did not note the time. What time did the sun arise this morning? It was soon after." Her gaze lifted to Talen, her grey eyebrows scrunching inward. "You seem worried, Conner."

"Talen."

"Talen. My apologies. But you seem worried." She set her embroidery on her lap. "Should I help you look for her?"

For a moment he thought to say yes, but then he shook his head, his foot lifting to leave. "No. No, I will find her."

"Forgive a prying question, but is something amiss between the two of you?"

His feet stopped and he looked to her. "We fought last night about me denying the title."

"You fought?" Her forehead wrinkled, the thought ruffling her sensibilities. "On that? Whatever for?"

"Ness thinks the title is my birthright."

"She is right, of course, it is your birthright." She leaned toward him, her voice dropping a notch. "But if I may ask, would she truly leave over something like that?"

"No."

Her lips pursed and she nodded. Though the nod didn't look definitive. It looked questioning.

For long seconds she looked to stay silent, but then her mouth opened. "How well do you know Mrs. Docherty? Would she leave you because you could be an earl but are choosing against it? Did she think that you becoming an earl was a given in traveling here? Why did she truly bring you to this place?"

Her lips pursed for a long moment. "I do not wish to speak ill of her. I only ask because if she hadn't recognized who you were and brought you here, you never would have known who you were, correct? You would still be in London moving about your life as you always were?"

"No." He stilled, the word drawling out from his lips. "No. Ness just wanted me to remember. Remember that I knew her once upon a time."

"As you say, sweet lad." She looked down to her lap, her fingers tapping along the edge of the tambour frame. "Though I hate to say it, it does not seem like you need someone like that, Talen."

"What?"

Her hand flew up to calm. "Forgive me, but I could hear part of the argument you two had last night as I was on my way to my chambers. Only a few words, of course, as I passed."

His eyes narrowed at her. "What did you hear?"

"Only that she wants you to take the title. That is what has me wary. If it was your choice, I would not question it. But the argument was about the very thing you told me you'd already decided." She drew in a deep breath, a frown settling on her face. "Believe me, I've seen plenty of fortune hunters going after my son during the years. Had to even scare some of them off. Ruthless it is, the marriage mart. I cannot even imagine how it will be for Mrs. Docherty being a widow."

Talen went deathly still, his words slow and punctuated. "Ness isn't marrying me because I'm in line for a title, Lady Washburn."

"No?" She picked up the embroidery from her lap. "If you say so, sweet lad. I am positive you are right. Again, I apologize for overhearing. I was walking up from the kitchens after tea as I couldn't sleep. Too much commotion in my mind with your arrival, bittersweet that it is. It has made me sad, remembering your parents. Your mother was a dear friend that I miss to this day."

Her fingers went busy with her needlepoint, her eyes squinting at the thread pushing into fabric. "Curious that Mrs. Docherty didn't just stay at Whetland Castle after her husband died. Or maybe she meant to move back with her father before she met you, though if I recall, I found him somewhat of an odious man back in the day."

"You aren't wrong on that score." Talen inclined his head to the dowager. "If you'll excuse me."

The dowager kept up her prattling, not even looking up as he started to leave the room. "I did send him word that his daughter was in residence, just in case he wishes to visit her. He is not too far away. I believe it has been many years since Lord Gundall came to Washburn."

Talen whipped around to his aunt. "You did what?"

She looked up, startled. "I sent him a message—why, what have I done? You are alarmed?"

He advanced on her. "You wrote that bastard that Ness was here?"

Her embroidery crumpled down to her lap. "Yes. I thought she would be grateful I sent the letter so she wouldn't have to. I mentioned it to her this morning before she left. She didn't seem upset."

"You did what?" The words so loud, his voice echoed out of the room and into the main hallway. "You told her you wrote her father?"

If he was ever going to strangle someone, it might very well be this old biddy.

Her hands shook, trying to pick up the needle that had dropped into the folds of her skirt. "I am sorry, what did I do? I didn't know it was a secret, that you and Mrs. Doch—"

"We're eloping for blasted sake."

Both of her palms flew upward, her words shaking. "But I—I thought that was just because you didn't want to wait for banns. It did not escape the maids that Ness's bed hasn't been slept in."

"Bloody meddling woman." Talen spun away from her, stalking toward the door.

He had to find Ness. Now.

He jerked to a stop, pacing back into the room, his hand running through his hair. "When will your son be here? I've changed my mind. We have details that need to be discussed."

"Details? What details?" She tossed her embroidery onto the table and started to stand, reflecting his sudden panic.

"Details about the title."

Her hand went onto her chest. "But I thought you didn't want the earldom. You—you said you wanted nothing to do with the title."

"Yes, well, I've changed my mind. I'll do anything to get Ness back. If that means becoming the earl—if that's what she needs to hear—I'll do it."

With a quick intake of breath, she shook her head. "You shouldn't bow to a woman like that, Conner. She will control you the rest of your life. If she's gone, she's gone. Let her be. You can go back to your life in London."

"Except I don't bloody well care about my life in London."

He paused.

Damn that it had taken him too long to realize the very truth of his own words, the realization and what that meant racing madcap in his head. "And I don't bloody well care about a life here. Ness is the only thing I care about and I mean to make it up to Scotland with her today. And if I have to claim the title to get her to come with me—to protect her—I sure as hell am going to do so."

Her eyes wide, the dowager looked struck for a long second before she blinked, nodding. "But of course, of course. I did not realize you held her in such high esteem. Do what you must for her, most certainly. Clayborne will be here today, I am sure of it. I expected him by this morning, if not earlier. He sometimes stays in Kirkby as that is only a fast three-hour ride away, so he should be here before you know it and you can speak to him."

"Good. I'm going to gather my belongings and set out in search for Ness. If she appears here, do not let her out of your sight. I can't keep chasing her all over Cumberland."

{ CHAPTER 27 }

She'd better be back at Washburn Manor.

Pushing the horse like a demon, Talen had made it to and from the coaching inn in Calthwaite in half the time it should have taken, but it still hadn't been fast enough.

Ness hadn't been at the coaching inn. The driver hadn't seen her and nothing had been touched in the luggage still strapped to the carriage. And there had been no sightings of her, though the landlady hadn't been present so his report had been limited.

She had to have been at Washburn and he just hadn't looked hard enough. There was nowhere else she could have escaped to.

Unless…unless the threat of her father coming to Washburn Manor had sent Ness off on a panicked, mad dash through the countryside.

He wouldn't put it past her. Not after her reaction the last time she believed her father was coming for her.

He needed help.

He never asked for help—never—not even from Declan. But he needed it now. Help from as many men—grooms, footmen, gamekeepers—any and everyone he could steal from the Washburn household to send out in all directions to find her.

Jumping from his horse and tossing his reins to a stableboy with instructions to ready a fresh horse for him, Talen could barely contain himself. He was at the stables

when he needed to be searching the house. He was at the house when he needed to be searching the countryside.

Where in the blasted hell had she gone?

He charged up the hillside toward the manor house, his stride long but not nearly fast enough for how every muscle in his body wanted to explode, the pathway through a narrow band of trees from the stables to the main house only slowing him down.

He looked up at the long, thick clouds across the grey sky. More rain hung in the air, though it hadn't begun to fall just yet.

Hell, if Ness was out in this. Out in the rain. The cold. No place to go.

He jerked his head from left to right, his eyes always searching, hoping to spy the tiniest swish of her blue skirt behind one of the perfectly manicured evergreens molded into tall cones that dotted this side of the estate. What if she was lying somewhere? Injured?

What if the real reason he couldn't find her was because he'd scared her so badly the previous night that she had fled? Fled him?

The sudden possibility sent a spear through his chest, slowing his steps. That she would ever be afraid of him—something he couldn't bear.

No. He swallowed back a growl. Ness was fine. His feet sped.

She was probably sitting in the drawing room at that very moment. Probably sipping tea with the dowager. Maybe she'd even picked up a tambour frame to do some embroidery. No matter that she'd told him weeks ago that she'd done more than a lifetime's worth of sewing at Whetland Castle and never intended to pick up a needle again if she could help it.

But maybe she was sitting there, docile and content and contritely waiting for him. And safe. Safe.

Almost there.

He yanked open the heavy oak north door into the manor house.

His body in full forward motion, he couldn't stop his momentum as a man barreled straight toward him on his way to the outdoors.

They rammed into each other hard, forearms hitting chests, one impenetrable body bouncing off the other.

Talen found slippery footing and jumped a step backward as the other man grabbed the doorframe to steady himself, then reached out to steady Talen. "By graces, you're a wall, man."

Talen shrugged off the man's hand pawing at him and took another step backward, then looked up.

The devil.

The man looked just like him. His cousin. Both products of their fathers. Their grandfather. Except for his eyes. His brown eyes looked just like the dowager's eyes.

Talen's eyes narrowed. "You—you're…"

"I'm Clayborne—your cousin. I saw you from the study charging up here and I thought to meet you before you made it inside."

The hairs on the back of Talen's neck spiked, his fingers instinctively curling into fists. "Meet me outdoors? Why? Where's Ness? What have you done with her?"

Clayborne's eyebrows drew together. "Ness? Who is Ness? What else do I not know? Blast me. I've only been back for fifteen minutes and my mother cornered me to tell me about your arrival. My cousin, back from the dead." He paused, his head shaking. "I saw you approaching and I wanted to catch you outside."

"Why?"

"Please, speak with me privately." Clayborne looked over his shoulder and then motioned toward the exterior and Talen took another step backward.

Clayborne closed the door behind him, looking to the left and right and only finding empty landscaping. "Out here so as to not have our first meeting in front of my mother. She can be a…handful. I thought this better to handle between the two of us."

"Your mother told you exactly who I am?"

"She did. But I have always known of you. I just thought you were dead. I gather you don't remember me?"

"I don't." Motion drew Talen's attention away from his cousin and he looked to the east side of the manor to see the dowager in a grey cloak walking down toward the pond and then shifting direction, disappearing into a long row of manicured hedges that led away from the house. Looking for her son, no doubt.

His impatient gaze shifted back to Clayborne. "There is very little that I do remember."

"I understand. She did say memories of those times were slowly coming back to you, but that you hadn't truly recalled your life here," Clayborne said. "I wouldn't expect you to remember me as it was. I was eight, almost nine, when you died. I would watch you playing from inside, wanting to join you, but I wasn't allowed. My mother always kept me away from my cousins."

Clayborne's mouth closed for a long moment and then he shook his head to himself. "Excuse me. This was a shock and I'm only just wrapping my mind around what my mother just told me. Forgive me, but I must verify the truth of it." His look pinned Talen. "When you disappeared, I thought you had died along with your parents. But my mother just informed me that was not the case? She told me you survived an attack on your family and that she found you and she sent you off on a ship for safety."

Talen gave him one nod.

He drew in a deep breath, his eyes going up to the sky as he exhaled it. His gaze dropped to Talen. "I am sorry for all that has happened to you. What happened to your parents. My mother said that you are still reeling from the new memories that have returned?"

"I am. It has only been a few days since I remembered…this place."

Clayborne nodded, his look fixed on Talen as his fingers ran along the backside of his neck. "I will come out and address head-on why I wanted to talk to you in private. The title. Mother claims you don't want it, but I think that is a mistake. It is yours. I can start the arrangements with the crown to transfer the title immediately. I can set it into motion today."

Talen didn't have time for this. More idiotic talk about a title he didn't care about. He needed to get on with

finding Ness. "I don't want it, but if it will get me what I want, I'll take it."

Clayborne's eyebrows lifted. "What you want?"

"Ness."

"Ness?" Realization crossed over his brown eyes. "Oh, is Ness Mrs. Docherty? Mother mentioned you had a lady companion with you."

"She is, and I'm more interested in finding her at the moment than talking to you." Talen pointed toward the door. "Is she inside?"

"Inside? No, mother said she left early today. Mother said something about a mistake she made? Where is Mrs. Docherty?"

"If I knew I would be with her and not talking to you."

Clayborne nodded. "Of course, what can I do to help find her?"

"Gather men of your employ and send them out in search for her. I don't know in which direction she's gone."

"Of course." Clayborne motioned toward the stables. "Come. Between the grooms and stable hands, we have six able-bodied men at the ready. And then I will gather footmen and my driver."

Clayborne started to walk as he talked, his long strides eating up the ground toward the stables. The man was rushing forth to help where he could and Talen had to give him credit for it. He was a man of action, something Talen was forced to admire.

Their walk through the woods quick, Clayborne kept talking. "The peculiar bit on the debacle of all this is that I never wanted the title. You don't know how many times in my life, growing up, that I wished you hadn't died. That I imagined you were alive. That you would show up and save me from my fate. Which is why I intercepted you at the door in hopes to talk to you in private."

Talen looked over at him. "So the dowager wouldn't interfere?"

"Exactly." He nodded. "She has always had much more…aspirational plans for me. She still does. Advancing in parliament. The expansion of the title. More wealth. It is never enough for her."

Talen looked ahead, his head cocking to the side as his feet crunched over fallen leaves. "She drives you?"

"That is putting it mildly." He shrugged the shrug of a weary, nagged-upon man. "Mother would have had me married off to an American heiress years ago if she'd had her way. The estate is now solvent, but it has taken me years to make that happen." He exhaled an obvious sigh of relief. "And now you are back."

Talen glanced sideways at him and instantly recognized the look now on his cousin's face. "And you suddenly look free."

A half smile lifted Clayborne's cheek. "If I help you find Mrs. Docherty, I have hope that I just may be. I never wanted the burden of the title, and it's been hanging over my head for the last thirteen years, ever since you and your father died, and then Uncle Walter died only months later."

"But I thought your father died nine years ago?"

"Yes, that is true, but he'd been incapacitated a month before I was born. Was so my entire life before he died."

"What do you mean incapacitated?"

"My father lost part of his skull—and brain in the war. He was never able to take over the earldom and died when I was thirteen. He never talked. Never walked. I never saw him out of bed. Rarely saw him awake. It's why my mother never let me play with you, she was always so fearful of something happening to me like it had to him. Never let me do anything, really." His hand ran along the side of his face. "And, to be truthful, my mother was disastrous at running the estate until I turned of age. I've been attempting to correct all she has wrought for years."

Talen's feet stopped. "What did she do?"

It took Clayborne a few steps to halt as well and he looked back to Talen. "To be blunt, my mother has expensive tastes and the uncanny ability to convince any and every vendor to take credit. Granted, marrying the American heiress would have been the smartest thing to do back in the day. But that was not to be."

Talen's eyes narrowed at Clayborne. "What did your mother tell you about my parents' deaths? Did she tell you how they died?"

His brow wrinkled. "Just that you three were together when you were attacked by cutthroats from London. She didn't expand beyond that. Was there something else I should know?"

Ice flooded Talen's veins.

She hadn't told him. Hadn't told him his own father had killed his parents.

Hadn't told him because it couldn't have happened.

Talen whipped around, frantically searching through the trees. "What is to the east of the manor house?"

"To the east?"

"Yes, man. To the east?"

Clayborne looked in that direction, his jaw shifting to the side as his confusion deepened. "Beyond the formal gardens and pond, there are several sheep fields, another pond, a hunting cottage, a small barn with the cows, the blacksmith's—"

Talen didn't hear another word.

He was running.

{ CHAPTER 28 }

Talen was poking her arm. No, shaking it.

Wait. He wouldn't be doing either. His lips would be on her neck, nuzzling her awake. This was shaking. Hard shaking. And she wasn't in bed—something hard was rubbing against her spine.

Where was she?

Wherever it was, the air was stale. Suffocating her like a gob of wet wool was shoved deep into her throat. No. That was her tongue. Her tongue too big for her mouth.

What the hell had happened to her?

Afraid to open her eyes, she scrunched her eyelids tighter closed, trying to remember what had happened last night.

She'd left Talen's room. Gone down to the kitchens for some tea—with a splash of brandy—to calm her nerves before returning to his room. For she needed to find her mettle before she stood in front of him again.

She'd run too quickly. Scampered off like a frightened little doe. Talen wouldn't hurt her, she knew that to her bones, but when his voice had raged at her, she'd fled in panic, the instinct uncontrollable as it drove her from the room. Avoid. Escape. Hide. It was all she knew to do.

She'd escaped down to the kitchens where she'd been warming a pot of tea when the dowager had appeared— appeared with a soft shoulder to cry upon for long minutes.

And Ness did. She cried for all of what she'd brought down onto Talen. All of the haunting memories that should have stayed in the forgotten wasteland where they belonged.

Lady Washburn had clucked and tucked Ness under her arm, pressing her head onto her chest. So like her mother had once done. The woman was a saint to listen to her, for all the dowager had endured herself over the years. Ness knew the guilt of the past weighed heavy on the dowager's suffering soul.

Lady Washburn had sat with Ness for an hour, probably more. And then what had happened?

Ness worked deeper into her mind, trying to remember. The dowager had encouraged her to go and speak with Talen, to set right whatever had set him off. She had poured Ness another cup of tea that Ness had splashed a dollop of brandy into. She'd sipped it.

And then…nothing.

Nothing until this very moment when her left arm was shaken, the harsh movement sending vicious pangs along the nerves still healing around her broken bone.

She opened her eyes.

The dowager hovered above her.

Had she fallen asleep in the kitchens? Or in a servant's room?

"Dear Ness. Do wake up."

Ness looked past the dowager's head bobbing above her. The ceiling was rough planks of wood. Dark. Not the kitchen ceiling. Not any ceiling she'd seen at Washburn. Where was she?

Her eyes shifted. A red brick fireplace, darkened with years of soot. Walls the same as the ceiling. Dark rough wood that had never been smoothed after the blade of an ax shaped it.

A bench. She was lying half on her right side on a bench pushed up against a wall of that rough wood, splinters digging into the back of her left shoulder.

"I am sorry for the uncomfortable conditions, dear. I thought to keep you here for just a few days until your father could come and collect you, as I imagine he knows how to take care of you properly, possibly to the same place your mother went to, if you are lucky. The man always was an ogre. But I underestimated Conner's feelings for you."

"What?" Ness's mouth opened, her tongue only able to form a whisper as the dowager's rapid words filtered through the fuzz in her brain. Her father? Collect her?

The dowager clucked her tongue, her head still bobbing above Ness. "I heard you last night, dear, pushing Conner to take the title. It won't do. He does not need you in his life. And I imagine your father will agree. Your father will surely have other plans for you. Did you know he once tried to sell you off when you were fifteen to our neighbor, Sir Hawlins? The old lecher was sixty-three at the time. But then the old goat died in his soup." Her head shook. "Your father has a very sick sense about how to use his property."

Her head stubbornly foggy, Ness frantically tried to clear it enough to follow the ramblings of the dowager.

Her look focused on the dowager's left eye, because it was too much work to shift her head enough to see both

of her eyes at the same time. "You brought me here to get away from Talen?"

Good. Her tongue worked. Now onto her body. Ness tried to shift, to sit up, and she understood for the first time that she couldn't. That her arms were bound together. She stretched her bent legs.

Hell, her ankles were strapped together.

She looked down to see rough rope twined about her wrists.

"I did." The dowager slipped her hands under Ness's left arm and pulled her upright with a grunt. "I thought with you gone, Conner would return to London and forget he ever came to Washburn. If you hadn't pushed him to take the title, I wouldn't have interfered and you two could have moved on from here and lived a nice life in London. But you pushed."

"I didn't push, I—"

"I heard you, dear." She clucked her tongue. "You pushed. So now you are here. But that is where I miscalculated and underestimated what Conner was willing to do for you. I thought it merely lust between you two. But now I don't think that merely removing you from his life is enough. I thought it would be. You would be out of sight, out of mind. He would go back to London, forgetting you, forgetting he ever stepped foot into Washburn. I thought your father could take you and that would be the end of it. You would be gone."

Her thin wrinkled lips pulled inward as she shook her head. "But now I fear that is not to be. Connor is now insistent on getting you back and taking the title to that end. I don't think he will let it be and he will overturn every stone to find you—including a visit to your father."

Upright, Ness could see the whole of her surroundings. A small cottage, dark. Only three windows that were skinny and high in the walls, letting in just enough light to see the interior. One small table with a black iron pot atop it. Two chairs. The bench she was sitting upon.

Mounting fear in her chest started to war with a panicked calm—both attempting to take over her emotions.

The dowager couldn't have possibly brought her here, could she?

She looked to Lady Washburn. "Where are we?"

The dowager patted her knee. "Nowhere important, dear."

Ness's lips parted so she could draw more air into her lungs as she stared at the woman in front of her. Such a kind face.

But a madwoman.

There wasn't any denying it. She'd been bound up. Set in this hovel. And the only one in front of her was Lady Washburn.

Reality was her only ally in this situation.

The sooner she accepted the fact the dowager was not her friend, not kindly—that the madwoman had intentionally dragged her here and tied her up—the better off she would be.

Ness glanced down at her bound wrists again. Fat rope. Talen had tied her up several times to teach her how to loosen the knots enough to free herself. With enough time, she could get out of the rope. She just needed time.

Hard won, the panicked calm took over. Talen would be proud of her.

Shifting her hands out of view under the table, her wrists started to work back and forth as her look lifted, her eyes narrowing at the dowager. "So, what do you propose to do with me?"

The dowager turned away from her and moved to the small square table by the hearth. She picked up the table, balancing a teapot and teacup atop it, and came back to Ness, setting the table down directly in front of her.

The dowager picked up the pot and poured what looked like tea into the delicate teacup. She set the pot down and nudged the cup closer to Ness, then stood straight, her hands folding in front of her grey cloak.

Ness looked to the table. The teacup sat in its bright white splendor, the prettiest painted blue bells lining the lower half of it.

Gorgeous destruction.

Ness's glare lifted, skewering the dowager.

She smiled at Ness. The same vacant smile that had been in her face when they had first met. A smile that somehow now managed to look both idiotic and sinister all at once. "Please, dear, just drink the tea."

"The last time I drank the tea, I faded into blackness and then woke up in here." Ness let every ounce of bitterness she was feeling lace her words. The damned woman was about to find out she wasn't going down without a fight.

The dowager's lips pulled tight, the hard glint in her eyes not shifting. She looked pointedly to the tea.

"What was in it last night? Laudanum?"

"Just drink the tea, dear Nessia. It will be easier for all parties involved. Cleaner. Less dramatic. Less fear. Less pain. Just quiet. Just slipping into darkness."

Ness scoffed a laugh as her hands started to work harder at the rope binding them. "You wish me to die quietly?"

The dowager took a heaving sigh and her hand dipped between the front folds of her cloak. She fished into an interior pocket for an extraordinary amount of time before pulling free something silver.

A pistol.

A bloody pistol, the elaborate etched scrolling motif along the silver barrel showing it was one of a fine dueling set.

She didn't actually know how to use it, did she?

The dowager pulled back the hammer of the pistol. *Damn.* The blasted thing was already loaded.

Lady Washburn aimed the tip of the barrel at Ness's head. "Please, dear. We both want this to be attended to with the tea. I fear for the pain you will be in if the bullet strays from my aim."

All of Ness's breath left her in that moment, the air seeping out of her until she was nothing.

No.

Fight.

What did Talen always say?

Stay alive.

Fairly simple instructions.

She tried to draw in breath past the dam of fear lodged in her throat and she looked up at the dowager, attempting to ignore the cavernous black hole of the pistol that was aimed at her forehead. "Why? Why do this?"

"Conner will not take the title from us. He won't. I worked too hard for it. It is mine. With you gone, his interest in it is moot."

Ness's eyebrows drew inward. "It's not your title. It's your son's."

Her lips drew into a vicious snarl. "It is ours. Mine. I did everything for it. Everything. Now drink the damn tea, Nessia. I do not have the patience for this."

Stay alive. Stay alive. Stay alive.

Her look fixed on the pistol, Ness reached out with her bound hands and wrapped her fingers around the teacup. She paused, staring at the brown water.

Death. So simple and easy.

Death she didn't want.

For how she'd wished for it once upon a time, that time was done. She'd been a fool. An utter idiot to have ever tried to escape this life.

"Do it."

Ness set the cup to her lips. How much could she hold in her mouth?

"Do it."

Raving desperation spiked the dowager's words and sent a shake into her hand holding the pistol. The last thing Ness needed was for the madwoman to accidentally discharge the pistol into her skull.

Her hands trembling, Ness parted her lips, letting the liquid breach her mouth. Bitter tasting, so bitter she could barely hold it against her tongue.

Don't swallow. Don't swallow. Don't swallow.

"Swallow it." The barrel of the pistol edged closer to her brow. "I said—"

The door of the cottage flew open, crashing into the adjoining wall.

Talen.

Talen standing in the doorway, raging.

The dowager spun around and Ness instantly spewed out all the contents in her mouth.

"Don't move." The dowager lifted the pistol high, aiming it directly at Talen's chest.

He stilled in place, his fists half raised as his look surveyed the cottage. Then Ness saw it plain as day in his eyes.

He knew this place.

Knew it well.

Terror. Pain. Death.

All of that had happened here.

And he froze.

CHAPTER 29

His father on the floor.

His mother dropping in front of him, her bloody head half on the brick hearth.

Their bodies in front of him. Cold. Lifeless. But so fresh into death, the smallest hope remained.

Until it didn't.

Their bodies shells. Their spirits gone to ghosts.

Ghosts.

Ness.

Ness.

Ness spitting out something brown all over the table.

Ness wasn't a ghost. She was gagging and tied up.

And Lady Washburn wasn't a ghost. A bastard demon—blood and skin the only thing making her fit to walk the earth. A demon holding a pistol.

Every muscle in his body burst alive. But he held still, not letting the evil woman see.

"What the hell are you doing, Dowager?" His words came cold, calculating, as he kept his focus on Lady Washburn. On the cocked pistol in her hand aimed at his chest. He only needed three steps forward. Three running steps and he could yank the gun from her hand.

An eerie chuckle bubbled up from the dowager's throat. "I am keeping Mrs. Docherty here for her father. He can collect the rubbish of this whore. She will do you no good, Conner."

"My name is not Conner."

"You're right. You're right." Another high-pitched chuckle escaped her, her words manic. "What was I thinking? To save lives? Mercy? What was I thinking? I need to just take care of you both. My boy doesn't have the stomach for it. Doesn't even know how much I've done for him."

Her right hand holding the pistol lifted, her forefinger twitching, then pulling the trigger at the exact moment a teacup flew through the air, hitting her hand.

An explosion of sound and instant pain sent Talen flying backward.

He slammed into the back of the door.

A full second—a lifetime—passed before he realized the pain was only in his upper arm. Not his chest.

Shit.

Ness was flying through the air—her hands and feet tied—diving head first at the dowager. She hit her at the waist, ramming the dowager into the brick side of the fireplace. And then Ness fell, her feet tangled and of no help.

Flat onto the floor.

The dowager's arms flew wide for balance against the fireplace and her right hand clanked onto the fire poker.

Before Talen could blink, the dowager grabbed the fire poker, swinging it high into the air.

He froze.

The same fire poker he'd watched swing down at his mother, sending her to screams.

To pain.

To death.

His mother's bloody temple. The life leaving her. He couldn't move. Couldn't save her.

The dowager swung down, the curved spike at the end of the poker aimed at Ness's temple. Just before iron met flesh, Ness rolled, dodging the spike. But it forced her body up against the bench, cornered.

A screech from the bowels of Hades ripped from the dowager's mouth and she pitched the poker upward, poised for another blow.

Ness on the floor. Just like his mother. Death looming above her. Death coming down swiftly at her head.

Frozen.

But no. His limbs were moving. Moving on their own. Not frozen. Lunging across the room, his arms flailing out, hitting iron in mid-swing, tackling the wretched woman.

Another scream pierced his ear and he had the dowager on the floor, holding her down by her neck as he grabbed her wrist and slammed it hard onto the floor, the bones in her wrist snapping as the iron poker flew from her grip.

Such a weak woman.

Yet such destruction she'd caused.

He grabbed the top of her scalp, his fingers curling into her tightly pulled back grey hair, and he lifted her head, then cracked it down onto the stone floor.

Not enough to kill her. More than enough to send her to tormented unconsciousness.

How he didn't kill her, he wasn't sure.

Scrambling off her inert body, he crawled to Ness, his fingers furious as he tried to calm them enough to untie the knots at her feet and then her wrists.

She was free. Free and looking up at him, wonder in her eyes.

His hands slid under her, crushing her body into his.

He needed to feel her breath. Feel her heartbeat. Feel her hands moving along his back, his torso, his arms.

"You didn't freeze." The choked words vibrated, muffled into his chest. She wedged her head free from his hold, looking up at him. "You didn't freeze. You saved me."

His right hand lifted, capturing the side of her face, needing her skin, her eyes on him. "No, Ness, you saved me. A thousand times over."

This. This one second in his life—a new defining moment.

He didn't freeze. Didn't fail. Not when his whole life, when his whole world, his whole future, needed him most.

He couldn't save his mother, but he saved Ness.

And Ness was everything.

Seconds count.

CHAPTER 30

"It is done?" Ness's look jerked up from the soap and washcloth in her hands as Talen walked into her room at Washburn. It had been dark for hours now, and she'd finally broken and pulled herself away from worrying at a window, her stare locked on the front drive to Washburn. She'd had the bath readied in a hopeless effort to calm her frayed nerves.

"It is." He closed the door behind him, dodging around the plump pink damasked chair that had been shifted away from the fireplace when the copper tub had been moved into the room. The deep circles under his eyes didn't escape her notice. He looked exhausted by what had happened that day.

"I wish I had come." She twisted the washcloth in her hands. "Seen that witch dragged into that place."

Talen pulled off his tailcoat and waistcoat, tossing them onto the chair, then wedged off his boots. Standing straight, he rolled up the sleeves of his lawn shirt as he walked across the rest of the room and bent down behind her, resting on his heels.

He leaned over the edge of the copper tub and set his lips to her wet neck as he reached around her and plucked the washcloth from her fingers. "One, I'm never letting you near another one of those monstrosities for as long as we live. And two, I did it myself, dragged her into the asylum,

so my mind and your mind can be assured it is truly done. Clayborne signed all the paperwork."

She involuntarily shuddered, the mere thought of a madhouse still striking innate fear deep in her gut.

But Talen knew what she needed, and the last thing she needed was to be delivering the dowager to the Devlon Asylum for the Insane. Though he'd always been like that. Always known, since the moment she showed up at his doorstep, what she needed.

"How is your arm?" she asked. The bullet from the dowager's pistol had gone clean through his upper arm. The wound had been cleaned and wrapped, but she knew it still must sting.

"It is nothing." His fingertips prodded her to lean forward in the tub and he dragged the washcloth against her back, sending ripples of pleasure up her spine.

As much as she wanted to revel in his hands moving over her wet skin, worry made her glance over her shoulder at him. "You are at peace with the fact that the dowager is in that place and not with a noose around her neck for all she has done?"

His knuckles that had been lazily tracing upward along the bumps of her spine stilled. "Her fate in that place will be torture for her mind, day in and out, so am I at peace with it?" He shrugged. "I am coming to that point."

He fell silent as he collected her hair, twisted it, and draped it forward over her shoulder. The only sounds in the room were droplets dripping from the cloth into the water as he washed the expanse of her back.

"I'm sorry."

Sorry? The worry balling in her gut intensified. Ness shifted in the water, half turning so she could fully see his face. "Sorry for what?"

"Sorry that I didn't see the dowager for what she was. Sorry I didn't remember her or my uncles or that time all together—if I had, I could have stopped her. If I had, you wouldn't have been in danger."

"Except I'm not in danger from her. You saved me. You protected me when I most needed it. I saw how you froze in that cottage. Saw the horror of the past reach out and take a hold of you." She reached up, pressing her palm along his cheek. "But you fought your way through it. You fought to me. You swore you would keep me safe, and you did. I think this proves you are not death, Talen. That I wasn't wrong when I trusted you with my life."

His light blue eyes seared into her, searching for salvation. "Was it enough?"

"I am here, naked in front of you. Unharmed." A soft smile lifted the corners of her lips as her left arm, unwrapped and whole, lifted up from the water. "Healed. I think it was more than enough."

His eyes closed for a long breath and she could see the demons still swirling in his head. See how lost and scattered he still was when all she wanted was for him to fight his way back to her. To *want* to fight his way back to her.

But maybe she wasn't enough. Maybe she'd ruined everything. Maybe the past and what he'd suffered would always haunt him, shadowing everything she could offer him.

Her hand on his cheek lifted, her thumb brushing along the edge of his eye. "I never got to tell you last night—and I should have turned around and come back into your room the moment that I left…"

Her head shook, fear taking a hold of her, and her hand slipped from his face. Maybe he'd reconsidered everything they were together. Everything she wanted with him. But if she didn't tell him everything now, she would be giving up without a fight.

And that's not who she was anymore.

Her look dipped down to the bathwater between them for a breath, then she lifted her face to him. "But I didn't. I didn't turn around because you're stubborn and it makes me want to strangle you, and yet I am just as stubborn. And I was scared. Scared by what I did to you—brought upon you. All those memories."

Her heart thundered in her chest. "So I cede. I thought I wanted something for you because it would help you, but I don't want it if you don't. I cede because I don't care if you're an earl or if you're a fishmonger. I never did. I don't care. I only want you. Talen Blackstone. I love you. Not who you could be. Not who you were. You. Do not doubt that."

His head dropped forward, hanging for a long moment and avoiding her gaze.

His silence, his avoidance, stole every last bit of her resolve, her hope.

His gaze lifted to her, his light blue eyes storming. "If I find a place with you, Ness, which is where I want to be, I have to give up what I am in London. Give up what I am at the Alabaster."

A flicker of relief shot through her chest. His hesitation wasn't that he thought her fickle. That he thought her love depended upon his station in life. "Which is what?"

"An arse. A man with little compassion. A man with loose integrity. A man not deserving of a woman like you."

Her throat clenched. She turned around fully in the tight tub, shifting to balance on her knees. "Talen, you don't need to give up anything for me."

"But I want to. That is the difference. I want my place in this world to be with you. With you where I can laugh and be free and not be constantly glancing over my shoulder, searching for the next man trying to take me down. I want simple. I want a life where seeing you puts a smile on my face and I don't have to fight it, don't have to hide it in order to keep you safe. I want to lie under the night sky with you in peace."

Her eyes went wide, the spark in her chest exploding. "You want to be my hero, don't you?"

The right half of his face lifted, close to pained. "Maybe I do."

She splashed forward in the tub, her hands clasping around his face. "Talen, you already are. I've just been waiting for you to admit to it."

He reached out, grabbing the full of her wet body and yanking her out of the tub, dragging her onto him as he stood, soaking his shirt, his trousers. His lips found hers as her slippery feet found traction on the wet floor.

His kiss hard, desperate, but giving way to the resignation that this was it. There were no excuses. No sense of searching for penance. He wanted what he wanted.

And he wanted her.

Her head went light with the realization, hope for a future with this man finally finding actual roots. Roots that would grow.

He pulled away slightly, his breath a caress against her face. "Then I admit it. I want—no—I need to be the hero you deserve."

She laughed. "Except you don't. You don't need to be a hero. You don't need to be an earl. You just need to be you. The man that made me fall in love with him despite my reservations—my mistrust. The man that held me and pointed out the stars. The man that thought I was worthy of being taught how to fight on my own. The man that knows me, my body, like no one else. The only man that I trust."

His lips found hers again as he crushed her body into his once more, but she was having none of it, her hands slipping between them, fast with the fall front of his trousers and yanking the lawn shirt off his torso.

A growl shook his chest that she'd dared to break their kiss for even a second. A growl that was soothed the moment she wrapped one leg around his waist, then the other, lifting herself onto him.

The bed had its place, but this wasn't it. This was carnal, the need for him to be inside of her crushing.

She ground her folds against him, his swollen cock already long and hard for her, just like she liked him. Her hands clasped around his neck and she pulled up as he lifted her by the waist, setting her directly on his member and thrusting upward.

The length of him to the hilt in one ragged thrust.

His mouth dropped to her neck, her chest, his tongue finding new spots to ravage as she arched backward against his hold on her back, her hips writhing.

She needed this fast and hard and he was always one to satisfy. His raspy chuckle into her skin told her he knew exactly what she wanted.

His hand slipped from the small of her back to her waist and he lifted her again, her thighs hitching onto his hip bones so she could balance herself.

Perfect.

She lifted and dropped, riding him at her own frantic pace until he slipped one hand between them, his thumb sliding into her folds to find her nubbin and increase the friction.

She yelped, her breath no longer her own, the pressure building harder than it ever had before, deep within her. Upward and another devastating plunge downward. For how hard she stretched backward, he held her stable on him, driving farther into her with each stoke. Until she was splintering, screaming, as she shattered into a thousand shards of light firing through her body.

Her contractions wrenched him along with her, his body shuddering as the wet heat of him exploded, burying into the depths of her.

Her body quaking, she fell forward onto him. Her arms draped over his shoulders and her ankles locked behind him as her face nestled into the crook of his neck and shoulder.

As she rode the ebbing waves, her fingers spread across his back, reveling in the fluttering of his muscles, the shivers that ran across his skin every time her sex contracted on his cock.

She wasn't moving.

He wasn't either.

Their bodies entwined, both of them refusing to let the other go. Neither would move for the chance of breaking the perfection of how their bodies fit together. Their souls.

Until finally, Talen broke and staggered three steps backward to land in the pink chair, though he refused to let her body leave his, his cock still firmly within her, her breasts still heaving against his chest. She curled her legs up on either side of him, straddling him, not willing to break away either as her left hand moved to splay upon his chest, her right locked firmly around his neck.

The only motion he made to ease the crushing hold he had on her was for his left hand to drag up her spine, his fingers entwining in her loose hair, dragging through wet strands over and over.

She let it go on for minutes before she broke the silence, her words into his neck. "You are still worried."

His hand stilled in her hair. "How do you know?"

"You have different silences." She turned her head slightly to see his profile. "This one, when your hands are playing in my hair, it means you're silently working a problem you're worried about."

"The men Gilroy hired. Your father." He said it simply, not hiding the truth of what was going on in his mind.

Her fingers involuntarily curled against his chest. "It is not resolved."

"No."

She pulled up, finding that unease had creased his brow. "It does not worry me."

"How?"

"One, you're worrying about both of those things, and if I've learned anything, it's to trust you when you say you're going to keep me safe."

Her forefinger and middle finger tapped on his chest as she locked her eyes with his. "Two, the only happiness I've had in the last four years has been when I am with you. It is the only place in the world that I trust. And I'm willing to gamble anything on that. Blindly, going into it with nothing but reckless trust that you won't hurt me. Always protect me. Maybe that's idiotic. Maybe that's the naivest thought in the word for me to have after the men that I have suffered under. Maybe I should be sailing off to a forlorn island to hide and live in a solitary cottage with nothing but a dog and a cat and cow for the rest of my life."

His bottom lip jutted up. "An island like that sounds somewhat idealistic."

"It's not. It's not, because you're not in it. I don't want that. I want you, Talen. Always. And I will fight for that."

"You don't have to fight, you don't have to gamble anything, Ness." His right hand slid along the side of her head, burying deep into her wet hair. "You have me. I love you. And I need you to want this with me. Want a future with me. Want children. Want a life we decide upon together."

She nodded, a smile cutting across her face so hard it hurt her cheeks. "That—that I can do."

He pointed north. "The last day's ride to the border? If your arm is up for it, we will take horses and forget about the damned carriage and the damned muddy roads. Hell—even if you're not up for it I'll drag you onto my lap and change out the horse every hour to get you up there."

Her right hand tightened around his neck, her eyebrows lifting. "We leave at first light and you can be mine by nightfall?"

"As long as there is a willing blacksmith, or farmer, or clergyman, aye. And you can be mine." His face suddenly went serious. "But I jest—we only go if you have the energy."

"For you? Nothing could hold me back."

He smiled at her, one of his rare smiles that made heat pool in her chest, spreading out to every limb.

The rasp in his voice vibrated with pride, with intention. "I always knew you had a warrior's spirit."

She chuckled. "Thank you for showing it to me."

"Thank you for letting me find it."

She nuzzled her face into his chest, utterly content that he was her true place in the world. Finally found, finally secure.

Finally hers.

{ EPILOGUE }

It had to be neutral territory.

Neutral, where someone could hold him back from killing the bastard.

Thank the devil Juliet married a hulking man.

Evan Docherty clamped his hand on Talen's shoulder, stilling him from charging at the wretched old goat.

Standing next to the wooden bench where Talen sat in the front drawing room of Whetland Castle, Evan, the future Earl of Whetland, was a massive, imposing force with a brutal grip. A grip that held Talen in place, reminding him of what was at stake.

How Juliet had ever fallen in love with the man, he couldn't guess.

Yet he could.

In the week that they'd been at Whetland Castle, it was quite clear why Juliet fell in love with Evan. The man's every thought was directed at his wife. From the constant hand he had on the small of her back, to the look in his eyes when she was talking to him, to the way he'd snarled at Talen when Juliet had first introduced them.

Evan didn't want any other man even looking at his wife and he was more than willing to crush anyone that glanced at her a little too long.

It was a good thing that Talen and Juliet had only ever been friends, nothing more. It was his saving grace and

helpful, for Talen needed Juliet and her husband to help set this last piece of the puzzle right.

Talen hadn't come to Whetland thinking he'd like Evan—the man had let his brother, Gilroy, torture Ness for years without interference. But somehow, Talen had found himself warming to the man.

It helped tremendously that the very first thing Evan had done when they had arrived was to pick up Ness in a bear hug and apologize profusely—grovel, even. Over and over. It was clear the torture he'd put upon himself for not knowing what Gilroy was doing to Ness. To being blind to it.

Despite himself, Talen had to appreciate the code of honor Evan lived by. Loyalty was everything to the man. And that his loyalty lie unequivocally with Juliet had to be respected.

Juliet got what she always deserved. A man that would love her wholly and fully.

For that alone, Talen had to like Evan.

But in these seconds, Evan was infuriating him. Talen should be strangling Baron Gundall at the moment, his fingers crushing into Ness's father's throat, sending him to the floor, eking the life out of him slowly, so he could recall all of the horrid transgressions played against Ness and her mother. So he could beg for forgiveness. Pray for heaven.

When everyone already knew that only hell awaited the monster.

Talen expunged the murder scene from his mind with a long, silent exhale. He'd sworn to Evan that he would do Ness's father no harm. Not in front of the ladies, at least.

Evan knew well enough that Talen's promise would expire in due time. Possibly days. Or hours. Or minutes if Talen was lucky and Lord Gundall set one foot out of line or gave Ness even a glance of hostility.

He could be done with the bastard here and now.

Silence.

Silence permeated the cold room—a sparsely furnished space with cold stone walls. Only the worst rotters were brought in here to this drawing room. Most of the rooms in the rest of the castle had plush furniture, wall hangings, anything to make the castle warm and comfortable with bright fires always burning in the common rooms.

Not so this drawing room. It was colder in here than outside. No fire. Only hard chairs and the bench. A sure message to Ness's father that he wouldn't be staying long.

The silence intensified.

Talen also made the mistake of swearing he would be silent. He made that promise to his wife.

Another promise he didn't think he could keep for any length of time.

But that was the thing about promises—they could be measured in seconds and be fulfilled.

His wife pulled tighter on the shawl about her shoulders and Talen's look flickered to her. Ness had purposely sat on the chair closest to where her father was seated. Talen had wanted her by his side on the bench, but she had insisted on sitting apart. She wanted to face her father on her own terms, not skulking and cowering under Talen's arm.

Begrudgingly, he'd agreed.

Begrudgingly, he'd been proud of her. He knew how sitting there, staring at her father terrorized her, even if she didn't show it.

But she was strong now. Strong enough to not let him bully her. Not let him chisel away even a speck of the courage she now possessed.

He'd let it be, but that had left Talen alone on the bench with Evan hulking over the side of him, as Juliet's husband hadn't bothered to sit. He knew the baron wasn't going to be here long.

Talen's hawk eyes studied Lord Gundall. One little motion. That was all he needed from the bastard. One pinky raised toward Ness and Talen could spring, be damned Evan's iron clamp on his shoulder.

"But, but…" Lord Gundall's face twisted, red splotching his pasty skin from his balding head to his jowly neck. He'd just been told of his daughter's marriage.

"But nothing," Ness stated plainly with no emotion. "I have made a fine match without your interference. I am happy. My husband is happy. You are owed nothing from us." Her eyes narrowed at her father. "Nothing. We offer you exactly what you gave me in life. Nothing."

The red splotches expanded, spittle gathering at the corners of the baron's mouth, his top lip snarling as his forefinger jabbed about the room. "I will tear this marriage apart one way or another for this betrayal. You'll see. You'll all see and rot in the consequences."

Ness very simply shook her head. "You will do no such thing. Talen and I are married and you can no longer touch me, Father. In fact, you will never see me again, nor will you attempt to intervene in our lives in any way."

"We'll see about that, you ungrateful little wench." His clammy hands folded into fists. "You're just like your mother—you were worthless from the first and you belong in the same wretched hole I flung her into."

Too far.

Sensing him coiling, Evan's hold on Talen tightened, pushing him down. That's why the bugger had stood. He needed leverage.

Juliet smoothly jumped to her feet and moved to the tea on the low table in front of Talen. Her eyes not lifting to Talen, she poured a cup of tea and turned back to Lord Gundall, handing him the cup as she sat on the chair directly to the man's right side. Her eyes were locked solely on Ness's father.

Talen hid a smirk to himself. It always was a pleasure watching Juliet work her magic. The baron had no idea what was about to hit him.

"Truly, Lord Gundall, I do not imagine you would want to make an enemy of not only your son-in-law, but my husband as well?" Her voice soft as a kitten, Juliet's eyebrows arched slightly, as though she was asking a small child if he stole an extra sweet from the kitchens. "It is my understanding that the Whetland family and the past men in your line have been allies in certain business ventures for decades, almost a century. No?"

The fire petered out from Lord Gundall's eyes and he nodded, though his look remained wary as he stared at Juliet. "That is so."

She nodded, the sweetest smile on her face. "I would hate to see any future opportunities be jeopardized by a sour response at this juncture."

"Juncture?" Lord Gundall's voice lifted in ire, his forefinger flinging out to Talen. "That man stole my daughter from me—my property."

"Come now." Juliet drew his attention back to her, her voice even softer. "I think that after the death of Gilroy, if Ness was anyone's property, she wasn't yours. She would have become the Earl of Whetland's property—his responsibility. Do you not think that would have been the order of things? I thought it was, but maybe you know something I do not?" She batted her eyelashes a little too long.

Lord Gundall's head snapped back. "I guess…"

"And the earl, my husband's grandfather"—she motioned to Evan—"whole-heartedly approves of Ness's union with Mr. Blackstone, especially since he's been restored to his rightful place as the Earl of Washburn. In fact, Lord Whetland was just telling me during tea this morning how much he enjoys Mr. Blackstone's company."

The baron heaved a sigh. "But I—I get nothing from the union."

"Nor will you." Talen spat out, his words venom. He'd stayed quiet long enough. "Ever. Never. If one hair on Ness's head is put out of place, if the slightest scratch appears on her arm, if she so much as flinches because someone breathes the wrong way upon her, I will destroy whoever caused those mishaps without a second thought."

Evan's hold disappeared from his shoulder and Talen stood, moving around the table and leaning over his father-in-law, his glare slicing him in two. "I will destroy them with a healthy dose of torture along the way. And I do not blink twice at blood or screams for mercy. Are we clear?"

The baron's mouth slackened, agape for a long moment, and then he nodded.

Juliet slipped the teacup from his hand.

"It is good that we are all in accordance on this." Talen stood straight, motioning to the open doorway. "You may leave now."

"But I—I just arrived."

"And now you are leaving. Your horses and carriage have been waiting since the moment you alighted."

With a huff, Lord Gundall scrambled to his feet, his attempt to avoid bumping into Talen not successful. Talen's lips twisted into a snarl at him and the man scurried out of the drawing room and to the front door of Whetland.

Talen and Evan stalked him out.

Evan slammed the front door closed before the baron even cleared the doorway.

Talen exhaled a long breath, satisfied at his own restraint at not killing the miserable rat. "Good riddance to the bastard. Though I don't know that I won't be seeing him again. There will always be another chance to kill him, I guess."

Evan's left eyebrow lifted. "You think he'll come back begging?"

"Most likely, from what Ness has said. No morals, no pride that man. Only aware of his own needs. But if I have

to buy him off with some pitted, rock-strewn swath of land to be rid of him, I'll do it."

Evan turned away from the door. "Why give him the satisfaction?"

"Because I don't care about him." Talen glanced at Evan as they started a slow stroll back to the drawing room. "I don't care about the land. If it keeps the wretch content and out of our lives until he withers away and dies, it's but a small price to pay for what I gain."

A half smile lifted Evan's cheek. "Ness?"

"Aye. She is worth it."

Evan nodded, but then his feet stopped before they reached the drawing room. "I received other news."

"And?" Talen paused, turning to him.

"The men Gilroy had sent after Ness. They've been found. Your man in London—Declan—confirmed it and I verified they were the same men that Gilroy had used in the past to do his dirty work."

Talen's hand slammed against the stone wall of the castle. "Why didn't you mention that right away? Are they still a threat?"

Evan shook his head. "They've been taken care of."

"Do you know of anything else Gilroy may have set into motion?"

"No. And it's been three months." Evan's voice dipped low. "But let me know if any threats still exist and I'll take care of them. I do not care for how I failed Ness so completely. That I let what happened to her happen under my roof and I did not know—did not think to see. That is a regret I will carry with me to my dying day."

Talen lifted his hand and clamped it on Evan's shoulder with a slight nod. They both understood words could not take the guilt away, especially words said to placate the moment, so Talen said none.

Arms linked, Juliet and Ness walked out of the drawing room.

Ness's gaze found him immediately, and he saw it clear in her amber eyes without her uttering a word.

Thank you for not killing him in front of me.

Thank you helping me find the strength to face him.

And then a wicked smile curved the right side of her lips.

You will be rewarded handsomely for this when we make it up to our chamber.

Talen's chest swelled almost as much as his cock at her look.

All he'd ever wanted to see in her. She'd forged herself a spine of steel and the pride he felt was ridiculous and only shadowed by his love for her.

Ness's gaze shifted to Evan and she stepped from Juliet to thread her arm along Evan's elbow. "Thank you for arranging this meeting with him. It has been months in coming and I'm beyond relieved it's over."

They started walking deeper into the castle ahead of Talen and Juliet.

"It was the least we could do." Evan patted her forearm linked with his. "You know I'll never forgive myself for all that you suffered here. If I had known—"

Ness shook her head. "You didn't. I've told you, you mustn't flog yourself for it."

"I can flog myself if I wish and you can't do a thing about it." He leaned down to half whisper to her, "I can even supply some cat-o-nine-tails for you if you're in the mood, as long as you don't let your husband near them."

Ness laughed, the glorious chiming bells of it lifting into the castle, creating cheer against the heavy ancient grey stones. The sound of it so light, Talen's feet stopped, his head tilting as he listened to the echoes of it.

There was no better sound in the world, even if he hadn't been the one to just make her laugh like that.

Juliet clamped her fingers along the crook of Talen's arm. "I am proud of you."

"How is that?"

"You didn't kill that old cur. I don't know that would have been the case if we were in London at the Den or at the Alabaster."

A frown crossed Talen's mouth. "Probably not. Though I'd never wanted my fists in someone's face more."

Juliet flashed him the smile that had sunk thousands of hearts in London. "You are a better man now, Talen. I like that."

He took her smile and the compliment as gracefully as he could as they walked. In front of them, he watched with amusement the difference in height between Evan and Ness, though it did little to hinder their conversation. He angled his right ear forward, then shook his head as he realized they were talking about, of all things, the lambing of sheep.

He glanced at Juliet, then nodded forward. "Why did you send Ness to me, of all people?"

She shrugged, a grin playing about her lips. "I had my reasons."

"Which were?"

Her eyes lifted to the ceiling. "I don't know if I can tell you without you becoming insufferable for knowing what I actually think of you."

His mouth pulled back in a chuckle. "Try me."

"Well, I couldn't think of anyone more equipped to be a hero for Ness than you." She leaned into the side him. "You take care of yours, Talen. You always have. I only hoped Ness would become yours." She looked up at him, her dark blue eyes serious. "You are a hero, even when you don't think you are. Anyone with two eyes can see that."

His throat closed up.

Juliet truly did see people. Saw them for what they themselves never knew they could become.

"Thank you, Juliet. You have my undying gratitude for that, for sending her to me."

"As I should, and I do feel like you owe me a new favor for this one." The grin on her face was entirely too self-satisfied. "But seriously, this was never the place for her. I am only happy that she has finally found her place in the world with you."

Talen chuckled to himself. For how many times Ness had proclaimed again and again since they'd married three months ago that he was her place in the world, he knew better. Much better.

She was his place in the world.

With a nod, he stepped away from Juliet, his eyes locked on Ness.

He had a wife to take upstairs.

{Extended Epilogue}

A kick.

That was it. There was no more denying it.

That was the seventeenth kick Ness had felt deep in her belly. She'd been keeping track, counting them one by one during the past three days.

It wasn't something she ate. Wasn't a weird strain on her muscles.

It was a kick.

True, she'd been gaining weight for the last four months. But it seemed like she always needed to gain another layer of insulation against the chilly Cumberland weather at Washburn Manor. The weight had added onto her frame, not a lot at first, but in the last two months, her breasts and her middle had gathered a thick layer of flesh.

She hadn't wanted to admit it to herself, much less Talen.

Maybe he had already noticed. Or maybe his mouth was so quick to latch onto any part of her skin that he didn't really note if there was any extra padding. His hunger for her, remarkably, had only grown during the last year, not waning in the slightest.

Her hand flattened onto her abdomen. She hadn't dared to think it, to hope it. But it was time.

She had to tell Talen.

She found him in the open-air pavilion that stretched along the rectangular pond on the east side of the Washburn

estate. He sat at his desk that he'd moved out here, books piled atop the surface, some open, as he chatted with Clayborne.

He liked to work outside as often as possible. After he'd been stuck in the stifling air of a ship or London most of his life, he'd found he could breathe easiest out in the pavilion. So he worked outside, rain or shine, until the weather got too cold.

Talen hadn't seen her approaching yet and she paused her stride on the far side of the pond, watching him. Clayborne said something with a smirk on his face and Talen's head threw back with laughter, the hearty sound of it—even with his rasp—echoing across the pond to her.

Her heart fluttered as the sound wrapped around her chest. This. This was everything. His laughter here at Washburn again. The ease with which he had come back home and integrated his life into the bones of Washburn.

He had remembered so much of his childhood—not all of it—but enough to set his body at ease in the place.

Clayborne had disappeared for six months to travel on the continent after the title was transferred. Something he'd never been allowed time or margin for before Talen had appeared. Since then, Clayborne had settled in London to Talen's convenience.

Talen depended on him, and Clayborne rather liked handling Talen's London affairs without all the pressure of the title bearing down upon him. A gentleman set free to pursue whatever he saw fit—and by all counts, he was partial to pursuing young London widows if the rumors were to be believed.

Talen's look caught her across the pond and if it was possible, his smile grew wider.

She continued around the side of the pond and approached the open pavilion with its wide arches just as Clayborne started to leave.

"See you in a few months, Clay," Talen said as she stepped under one of the arches, her slippers soft on the wide marble stones of the pavilion floor.

Clayborne inclined his head to her as he exited the pavilion. "Ness, I trust you will take good care of my cousin as I am off again?"

She smiled. "You are? Where to now?"

"Morocco. There may be a new trading partner available to us."

Her hand landed on his arm. "I promise I will take good care of him as long as you take good care of yourself so I don't need to worry on your ill-advised adventures."

"Adventures?" His dark blond eyebrows lifted innocently.

She pointed with her thumb to her husband. "Talen has told me stories—and I imagine he's left out the most salacious bits."

Clayborne laughed. "I hope he did."

She rocked up onto her toes to kiss his cheek. "But truly, take care, watch your back."

"Aye." He kissed her cheek in return. "I already got the reminders from my cousin. Be well."

He walked away from the pavilion, his gait easy, unhurried.

How she liked the man. For who he had grown up under, Clayborne was a good soul, through and through.

"That was all well and good, your pandering to my cousin, but I've been waiting patiently for you to come crawl onto my lap since I saw you across the pond."

Ness stepped farther into the pavilion, her eyes on her husband leaning back in his chair. He was already full in his trousers, his member iron hard and waiting for her. She chuckled. "Jealous?"

"Hungry." He patted his lap, licking his lips as his light blue eyes ate away her skin.

Ness pondered for a moment whether or not Talen would be as irresistible to other women as he was to her. Devilishly handsome. Yes. A little arrogant. No—a lot arrogant, especially when it came to how much she loved his body doing wicked things to her in broad daylight. But she wouldn't have it any other way.

Pulling up her skirts, she crawled onto his lap, straddling him, telling herself that the only thing the servants could see from the main house were the top half of their bodies above the desk. She just had to keep her bodice in place. Something that was hard to do when it came to her husband.

His hands settled around her waist as his lips sank directly onto her neck. "You look like you have an extra glow about you today, my wife."

She leaned back slightly, pulling her neck from his kiss. "There may be a reason for that."

His brows drew together. "A reason?"

She nodded, her stomach doing flips. She had to tell him, it was only right. But the closer it came to saying the actual words out loud, the more fear collected and balled in her gut.

Her hands settled around his neck and she looked down at her own cleavage, the mounds of her now-hefty breasts piling higher above her dress than ever before. "Have you not noticed how much more"—she squeezed her upper arms together on the outside of her breasts, making them plump up even higher—"juicy I am?"

A low groan rolled from his chest. "The devil take it, don't do that to me, Ness." His head dropped, his tongue licking her flesh. "I'd rather like to get out of my trousers before I explode."

As much as she loved his tongue flickering over her skin, she clasped her fingers into the back of his hair, pulling him up slightly. "There's a reason for it."

It took several long breaths before his head whipped up, his eyes impossibly wide. "A reason? Are you saying…"

Her bottom lip dragged under her teeth and she nodded.

"Wait." His left hand moved to flatten on her belly in between them, his words breathless. "Just so we're absolutely talking about the same thing, are you telling me there is a babe in here?"

Slowly, she nodded, studying his face.

Shock. Alarm. And then a beautiful, genuine smile filled his face. Happiness.

He shook his head. "But I…I didn't think…"

She gulped back a sob. "I didn't either. Not with my past."

His hands lifted to her face, capturing her between his palms. "A child. You are with child." He repeated the words, whispering them, saying them out loud so he could believe them. "You are with child. You...this is...the best. That is what this is. Best."

She tried to force a smile, but could barely hold the sob in her throat without letting it escape.

"But no—you are not happy?" His hands tightened along her cheeks. "Wait—no—you're terrified."

She couldn't answer him, only nod.

"Ness?"

"I was afraid to tell you."

He laughed, pure joy. "But I am happy, Ness. Ecstatic. How could you think I would be anything but?"

She looked away from him, tears she couldn't control filling her eyes.

"Hell, Ness. You aren't terrified of my reaction." His hands gently shifted her face toward him. "You're terrified of what will happen."

She opened her mouth, grasping at breathless words. "What if...what if the babe doesn't sur—"

His hands left her face, cutting her words as he dragged her onto his chest, his mouth next to her ear, his words rough. "Then I will hold you. We will both lose a part of us, but I will hold you. And you will hold me."

She nodded into his chest, inhaling the scent of him, letting it give her strength. She didn't know if she could go through this again. Not with Talen's babe.

His words were a low rumble in her ear. "I know you're scared. I know it. I can feel it in you. But we live in fear, Ness, and we're not living."

She pulled away, finding his eyes, nodding. "I know. I know. You're right. But I don't know if I can stop the worry."

He kissed her forehead. "Worry if you need to. I will pick up the optimism on this score."

The smallest chuckle escaped from her throat. "You will?"

"I will."

"It's not in your nature."

His eyes searched her face as his thumb swiped up along her cheek. "No. But I will make it my nature for the next four—five?" His eyebrows lifted at her.

"Five."

"Five months." He smiled—forced—but it was there. "Nothing but sunshine and rainbows."

She laughed, her forehead dropping to land on his chest.

His hands slipped up her neck, his thumbs tilting her chin upward. "I'm with you, Ness. Through it all. Always. No matter what comes."

And he was.

Five months passed and not a day went by when his hands didn't set onto her belly, telling their babe that the world was patiently waiting for her, but that she should keep growing and getting strong right where she was.

Until she was actually ready.

On a beautiful spring day, she decided to join the world.

Except the she turned out to be a he.

Thomas Blackstone Burton. Only one middle name.

Six years and two more babes—Valance Blackstone Burton and Headon Blackstone Burton—were born before Talen finally got it right.

Fiona Mariana Burton finally came into the world. Named for her grandmothers. Dark hair with amber eyes that opened wide that first day, looking like molten gold straight from Mount Olympus.

And they were complete, their place in the world ever expanding, but always true.

~ About the Author ~

K.J. Jackson is the *USA Today* bestselling author of the
*Hold Your Breath, Lords of Fate, Lords of Action,
Revelry's Tempest, Valor of Vinehill, Box of Draupnir,
Exile,* and *Flame Moon* series.

She specializes in historical and paranormal romance,
loves to travel (road trips are the best!), and is a sucker for a
good story in any genre. She lives in Minnesota with
her husband, two children, and a dog who
has taken the sport of bed-hogging
to new heights.

Visit her at www.kjjackson.com

~ Author's Note ~

Thank you for allowing my stories into your life and time—
it is an honor!

Be sure to check out all my historical romances
(each is a stand-alone story):
Stone Devil Duke, *Hold Your Breath*
Unmasking the Marquess, *Hold Your Breath*
My Captain, My Earl, *Hold Your Breath*
Worth of a Duke, *Lords of Fate*
Earl of Destiny, *Lords of Fate*
Marquess of Fortune, *Lords of Fate*
Vow, *Lords of Action*
Promise, *Lords of Action*
Oath, *Lords of Action*
Of Valor & Vice, *Revelry's Tempest*
Of Sin & Sanctuary, *Revelry's Tempest*
Of Risk & Redemption, *Revelry's Tempest*
To Capture a Rogue, *Logan's Legends, Revelry's Tempest*
To Capture a Warrior, *Logan's Legends, Revelry's Tempest*
The Devil in the Duke, *Revelry's Tempest*
The Iron Earl, *Valor of Vinehill*
The Wolf Duke, *Valor of Vinehill*
The Steel Rogue, *Valor of Vinehill*
The Heart of an Earl, *Box of Draupnir*
The Blood of a Baron, *Box of Draupnir*
The Soul of a Rogue, *Box of Draupnir*
Exiled Duke, *Exile*
Wicked Exile, *Exile*
Dangerous Exile, *Exile*

Never miss a new release or sale!
Be sure to sign up for my VIP Email List at
www.KJJackson.com

Connect with me!
www.KJJackson.com ~or~ kjk19jackson@gmail.com

Printed in Great Britain
by Amazon

18048765R00181